A Fair Prospect

A Tale of Elizabeth and Darcy: Volume II

Darcy's Dilemma

A Fair Prospect:
A Tale of Elizabeth and Darcy
In Three Volumes

Volume I: Disappointed Hopes
Volume II: Darcy's Dilemma
Volume III: Desperate Measures

ISBN: 978-1482356649

ISBN-10: 1482356643

This book is dedicated to

Rachel and Tom

My lovely, lucky Thirteens!

Author's Note

A Fair Prospect is a story inspired by Jane Austen's *Pride & Prejudice*. It begins at the point in that story where Mr Darcy makes his first, ill-fated proposal of marriage to Miss Elizabeth Bennet.

For the purpose of this particular story, the Gardiners have no children of their own and the Militia left Meryton before Elizabeth travelled to Hunsford to visit her friend, Charlotte Collins.

Acknowledgements

A full list of acknowledgements appeared in Volume I of *A Fair Prospect*. However, such is my gratitude to those concerned that I believe they bear some repetition in Volume II!

Therefore, I would like to repeat my heart-felt thanks to the Pinkers (you know who you are!), the readers at *Pen & Ink* and *The Derbyshire Writers' Guild*, especially those who took the time to give feedback or comment as each chapter of this story was posted.

For their encouragement, support, suggestions and/or invaluable advice, I also thank again Mel, Jan, Renée, Abigail, Sybil and specifically for this Volume, for her support and insights, Roxey

Special thanks also go to Adrea and Diane, for the beautiful cover artwork of this volume, and to Rebecca for the gorgeous cover design (and her endless and patient support with formatting!)

Last, but never least, to Julian – for everything.

Thank you!

Chapter One

"DASH IT!"

Charles Bingley's exclamation caused Fitzwilliam Darcy to start and, roused from his introspection, he turned from his position at the drawing room window of his London townhouse to look at his friend, seated at a nearby writing table. From the evidence before him, Bingley's pen had just snapped in two.

"Forgive me." Bingley swept the broken pieces into his hand and dropped them into the nearby wastepaper basket, and Darcy frowned.

"It will hardly hamper your progress. You have yet to set ink upon the page."

Raising his hands in a gesture of acceptance, Bingley leaned back precariously on his chair. "You know me, old friend. I am more of a mind to play with the instrument than use it! Why does letter-writing always assume such devilish proportions?"

Darcy shrugged. "Perhaps your practice of it is too infrequent."

With a grunt, Bingley righted his seat and got to his feet. "Well, that is about to change, my friend. I have been reflecting much upon my estate of late – and my neglect of it." He joined Darcy at the window and stared out into the street for a moment.

"And this is connected to your attempt to pen a letter?"

Bingley turned to face Darcy. "Absolutely! I know that we have previously discussed my surrendering the lease on Netherfield, but on reflection I believe I should return to Hertfordshire and take up the mantle, get to know my steward and see if I can master being a man of property. Surely Netherfield is as good a manor as any to test my mettle?"

Darcy studied his friend for a moment. "Good decision. I wish you well with it." He hesitated, then added: "Will you ask your sister to accompany you?"

With a grimace, Bingley shook his head. "No, and I doubt very much she could be persuaded even should I wish it. But what about you, Darcy? Would you care to join me? The city is best escaped as summer approaches, and I have seen but little of you of late."

For a moment, Darcy reflected upon Elizabeth Bennet's reaction should she return from her stay in Town only to find that he was but three miles distant across the parkland. A small sliver of temptation struggled to rise, urged on by the desire to be near her, but he squashed it ruthlessly.

"I thank you for the invitation, but on this occasion I must decline. Having just been away for several weeks, I cannot leave Georgiana so soon."

"Understood," Bingley nodded. "Though it will test my writing skills in earnest, for no doubt I shall need your constant counsel as I attempt to find my footing!"

Darcy refrained from repeating his avowal of the previous day, to be circumspect in what advice he might offer his friend going forward. "I am sorry that your stay with us is to be curtailed. When do you intend to leave for Hertfordshire?"

Bingley turned back towards the window, pulling restlessly at the rope holding the drapes to one side. "Miss Bennet has been away from home these several weeks, and no doubt she will be returning soon." He glanced back at Darcy. "I do not wish to be perceived as in pursuit, and thus I believe I should be there ahead of her. A matter of days should be sufficient for the servants to set to rights sufficient rooms to accommodate me."

Darcy turned from the window and Bingley did likewise.

"That is a sound notion. Well, perhaps you had best send your instructions by *Express*. There are spare pens in the left-hand drawer. I shall leave you to your duty."

Leaving the room as his friend resumed his seat at the writing desk, Darcy headed along the hallway to his study at the rear of the house intent upon reviewing the morning's news in the as yet unread paper, a potential distraction for his wayward thoughts – or so he hoped – with no other company about to serve that purpose.

On their return to the house following their recent stroll around Berkeley Square Gardens, Georgiana had elected to spend some time with her companion, Mrs Annesley. Having endured his sister's curious gaze as they walked home, but conscious that she would say little of the chance encounter with Elizabeth Bennet and her companions in Bingley's presence, he felt some relief from the plethora of questions that she no doubt wished to ask.

Closing the study door with a snap, Darcy settled into a fireside chair with the papers, yet he found himself unable to immerse himself in the day's news. Much against his will, his mind would return to what had occurred that morning, and in frustration, he tossed the paper aside and pushed himself out of his seat, walking over to the bookcase that lined the far wall. His gaze moved restlessly over the spines, seeking a title that might grasp his attention, but to no avail. There was little that could alter the pattern of his thoughts and, realising he was in danger of succumbing to the temptation of going over every moment of his meeting with Elizabeth and her companions, he turned his back on the bookcase and walked over to the full length windows and stared out into the walled garden. A quick glance at the sky confirmed their suspicions from earlier: the cloud had darkened considerably and a rainstorm looked imminent.

Unbidden, his mind returned swiftly to Elizabeth: had she and her party reached home yet and were the lady's thoughts as engrossed with him as he was with her? Darcy blew out an impatient breath; what foolhardiness this was! He knew full well her opinion of him, and improved though it may be since she had read his letter, she was hardly likely to dwell upon him in his absence.

To further augment this notion, he then recalled Nicholas Harington – the gentleman considered a fair prospect for her hand. Was he even now enjoying her company, furthering his cause? Had he, Darcy, achieved anything by requesting the introduction earlier, other than finally putting a face to the man he so envied?

The ladies of Gracechurch Street were enjoying a refreshing cup of tea when the drawing room door opened to reveal Nicholas. The surprise of his appearance, having seen him off to his hotel not an hour since, was soon explained: a message from Sutton Coker had awaited him – he was summoned home without delay and had come to make his farewells.

Taking a cup from his aunt, Nicholas turned to face the anxious expressions of Jane and Elizabeth and was quick to reassure them.

"There is no need for alarm. The command is not unexpected. It seems one cannot take ownership of an estate without signing all manner of documents, and there are some that require my signature as a matter of urgency. My father will not be gainsaid – he had not anticipated my trip to Town at this time of year and made it a condition of my journey that I return the minute I was required."

"There, Aunt," Elizabeth smiled ruefully. "I shall be able to wear my new gown for walks in the park after all. It would be a shame not to make use of it!"

Nicholas turned to her at once. "Oh, I am quite determined to return for the ball, have no fear! Papa knows of it and says that if I can be in Sutton Coker directly, I may be freed up to return for eight and forty hours to attend and complete my farewells in a more fitting manner. Thus, the sooner I depart, the earlier I return. It does mean I must forego this evening's recital and Saturday's opera, though."

Mrs Gardiner smiled at him.

"It is your company we shall miss, my dear, not the entertainments that you planned for us."

"You are welcome to attend should you still wish. The reservations are in place – I will leave it to Uncle to make the decision."

Nicholas glanced over at the clock and sighed. "I must away – time is pressing on, and I will need to reach Basingstoke by nightfall."

Mrs Gardiner threw an anxious look out of the window and stood up. "Let me fetch that parcel of silk for your mother. You may as well take it today as next week."

Nicholas drained his cup and likewise got to his feet, an action echoed by both Jane and Elizabeth, but as the other ladies moved out into the hallway he turned towards the latter as she reached his side and said urgently, "We have had no time to talk, Lizzy. I would hope that on my return we can find a way or my purpose in coming to Town will have been entirely thwarted." They had reached the open door and Nicholas met Elizabeth's eye with a serious air. "I know that we must exercise caution, but I would wish to speak in private."

Elizabeth frowned. "Is it not something you can speak of now? I would not have you troubled and unable to share it."

"Dearest Lizzy," Nicholas took both her hands in his. "It is not something that can be discussed near company. I fear I will take you by surprise with what I have to say, would that you might have time to consider... to give some thought to your response. I am determined to secure us a moment when I return."

Elizabeth was struck once more with the uncharacteristic seriousness of his demeanour. "It is a pity, then, that we had to give up our correspondence." His eye brightened momentarily, and she let out a splutter of laughter. "Nicholas! I was in jest! Pray do not take such a chance!"

"I would dare anything in this matter." He paused, then shook his head. "But do not fear. It is something that I could not – *would* not – elicit your response from by letter; you are wise to caution me so." With a final squeeze of her fingers, he dropped her hands. "Excuse me one moment."

Elizabeth watched him walk across the hallway to her aunt's sitting room, recalling the letter she had received but days ago from a certain gentleman. A sudden and inexplicable urge to read it again seized her, and as Nicholas reappeared in the hall, she determined to do just that.

"Come, you must be on your way." Aunt Gardiner emerged from her husband's study and ushered him along the hallway, handing him a neatly wrapped package and kissing him warmly on the cheek as he took his great coat up from the chair. With a flurry of good wishes for a safe journey and a speedy return to Town, he was down the steps and into his waiting carriage and they waved until it turned the corner.

Unable to shake the sense of unease that had gripped her as Nicholas' intent gaze met hers from the carriage, Elizabeth turned to follow her aunt and sister back into the house and, under the distraction of the door being closed and the others returning to the drawing room, Elizabeth hesitated as she turned her steps to follow. With a frown, she recalled Nicholas' manner and words from the previous evening and, coupled with this latest request for a private audience with her, a worrying thought crossed her mind, to be instantly dismissed as nonsensical. Surely he was not intending to ask for her hand?

Fanciful though such a notion seemed, it could not help but remind her of her earlier intent with regard to Mr Darcy's letter, and poking her head into the drawing room she quickly excused herself. Thus it was that she was soon settled upon the bed in quiet solitude, her writing case beside her.

Yet she had only gone so far as to remove the first packet, that which contained Serena's latest letter, and she took it out to read once more, finding the closing paragraph as confusing as ever.

The pattering of raindrops drew Elizabeth from her thoughts, and she glanced over at the window, wondering whether Mr Darcy had arrived home before the storm broke and then chided herself for the thought. It did, though, remind her of her real purpose in coming upstairs, and she put Serena's letter aside, picked up a second bundle and loosened the ribbon that tied it in place.

Chapter Two

THE RAIN THAT HAD threatened all morning had long arrived in Mount Street. As the clock on the mantel sounded the hour of three, Darcy rose from his chair by the fire and walked over to one of the windows and studied the scene. The rainwater fell steadily, gathering in muddy pools in the road, and as he glanced upwards he could discern the ominous dark grey that indicated no immediate cessation of the downpour.

Wondering if heavy skies and rain would forever be synonymous with the events of the previous Sunday, he blew out a breath of dissatisfaction. Thus it was that he welcomed the interruption as a knock on the door heralded the arrival of a footman with a note on a silver salver.

The servant bowed deferentially in his master's direction before crossing the room to present his offering to Bingley, who dragged his gaze away from the fire and took the note with a smile, quickly scanning its contents.

"Darcy?"

Bingley rose to his feet, the note still held in one hand, and Georgiana looked up briefly before returning her gaze to her book.

"You have news?"

"Of a fashion."

Darcy frowned as he watched his friend glance at the note in his hand before crossing the room to join him at the window.

"This is from Harington – he has been summoned home on business that cannot be delayed and thus has departed directly for the West Country." Bingley paused and threw a glance out at the poor conditions. "Even in this weather. It has presented me with a dilemma."

"How so?"

"He was to host a small party attending a recital in Hanover Square this evening. He had invited me to join them, but I felt it poor manners on my part to desert you on my first evening's stay. I had left a note for him at the Pulteney to that effect this morning."

Conscious immediately who might constitute members of this party, Darcy tried to keep a rein on his interest in the matter. "And your dilemma is?"

"Harington begs that I reconsider and host the party on his behalf. I am unable to respond, for he says that he will be on the road by the time I receive this, and he is trusting to my good nature to step into the breach."

"Then why not do as he requests? I can assure you that, had you mentioned the invitation in the first instance, I would have had no hesitation in encouraging you to attend."

"It would have been ungracious."

Darcy shook his head. "Our friendship is too old for standing on such ceremony!"

Bingley glanced once more at the note in his hand and then turned to stare out of the window. For a moment, the two friends remained there in silent contemplation of the scene, the only sound in the room being the crackling of the logs in the fireplace and the occasional sigh from Georgiana, who continued in apparent enjoyment of her book.

After a few minutes, however, Bingley became restless; Darcy was conscious that his friend had looked at him several times before returning his gaze once more to the rain-swept street and was thus unsurprised when eventually he broke into speech.

"I say, Darcy, I weary of the ticking of the clock competing with the pattering of raindrops on glass."

Darcy turned to face him. "Would you care for a game of cards? Do you wish to talk? I apologise for my introspection; I am a poor host."

"Not at all, my friend. I am merely restless, being confined to the house by the weather. You know I much prefer to be out of doors."

Darcy understood, for his own persuasion would have him in the open air as opposed to a drawing room, inclement weather or not.

"We could take the carriage to the Club, if you so wish? A game of billiards might cure your restlessness."

Bingley looked rather sheepishly at him before glancing about the room, fidgeting with his cuffs. Darcy frowned, but his puzzlement did not have long to take purchase, for his friend soon burst into rapid speech.

"I would very much like to go and call upon Miss Bennet. I am certain they are at home from what they said this morning." He paused as Darcy absorbed his words, conscious that his sister's attention was no longer held by her page.

"Bingley – making a call at this late hour is not entirely-"

"Appropriate? Have no fear, I have not lost all sense of etiquette."

"Then?"

"The party in Gracechurch Street will be unaware of my hosting them this evening." He waved the note in the air. "Harington says that he did not intend offering my services to them in case I could not oblige. My aim was merely to attend the Gardiners' home briefly so that I may offer my carriage to them. Harington said last night that he intended to make use of his own to save Mr Gardiner the trouble and the crush of too many people within – theirs is a smaller conveyance, as I understand it."

Darcy could not help but smile at Bingley's design, not only of spending as much time as possible in Miss Bennet's company now they had become re-acquainted, but also to find a reason to go out.

Casting a glance over his shoulder at the window, through which it was now difficult to detect much owing to the water coursing down it, he turned back to his friend with a raised brow. "And you do not think sending a note with a servant might suffice?"

Bingley gave a self-deprecating smile. "I am certain that it would! But they would be less likely to decline my offer if I am there in person."

"Well, they will surely admire you for your persistence."

Bingley laughed and studied the note in his hand once more before raising his gaze to his friend.

"Will you not join us this evening?"

A sudden movement over by the fireplace caught Darcy's eye, and he met his sister's wide-eyed stare as she nodded emphatically at him.

He shook his head. "No. No, I thank you for the invitation, but I have only just returned to Town and will not leave Georgiana alone. With my cousin away, it would be most unkind."

Bingley had the grace to look a little ashamed, turning towards Georgiana who had quickly dipped her head and appeared to be engrossed in her book once more.

"Miss Darcy, will you forgive my poor manners? I did not mean to deprive you of your brother's company – I selfishly hoped to keep it for myself without considering the effect."

Darcy struggled to suppress a snort at this, knowing that his own company was hardly the focus of Bingley's upcoming evening, but he managed to silence the reaction as his sister, with an air of innocence, raised her head once more to enquire, "Forgive me, Mr Bingley. To what is it that you refer? I am certain that you could not be selfish if you tried."

"You are too generous, dear girl! I am attempting to persuade your brother to join me – I have been invited to a recital in Hanover Square."

Now that she was given leave to contribute, Georgiana fixed Darcy with her eye.

"Brother, you must go."

"No, I must not."

"I am more than content now that you are come home to me; I can easily spare you for some evenings of entertainment and varied company. To be certain, you cannot think me incapable of amusing myself? Besides, I am endeavouring to complete this novel for I am eager to discuss it with Mrs Annesley – she has long finished her copy."

"There, Darcy, if your sister has no objection, you must come."

"I repeat, I must not."

Bingley frowned and muttered, "I do not understand you at all, sometimes. Well – if you will not attend, then I shall not go either."

A feeling of disquiet began to assail Darcy, and he said quietly, that his sister, whose attention was once more with her book, might not overhear, "But you will disappoint Miss Bennet!"

Bingley let out a short laugh at this, and responded equally low-voiced. "No, Darcy. *You* will – for you will be the cause of my absence."

"But I…" Darcy broke off. Bingley, who had raised his chin, would have looked positively stern had not his fringe been flopping restlessly on his forehead as usual.

"I am quite determined, Darcy. You will not persuade me otherwise. We both attend the recital, or neither."

Darcy knew that he was caught, and he ran a hand through his hair before clasping his hands together as the tell-tale flexing of his fingers began to take hold.

"Then you leave me no option, Bingley. If you insist, I shall accompany you."

A soft knock on the door some time later drew Elizabeth from further exploration of her writing case, and she turned from the task to discover that one of the maids had entered.

"Excuse me, Miss, but the Mistress is requesting you attend her in the drawing room."

Surprised by the formality of the application, Elizabeth eyed the maid thoughtfully. It was not like her aunt to summon her presence; indeed, she would like as not have come herself or sent Jane.

"Is something amiss?"

The maid's blank expression was of little help, but then it cleared. "Oh, no Miss. But there is a caller – a gentleman."

Realising that her depth of introspection must have precluded her from hearing the doorbell, Elizabeth gave the maid a smile of dismissal and followed her out of the door, pushing aside the immediate thought that it might be Mr Darcy. She laughed softly at her foolishness as she set off down the stairs – firstly, for entertaining such a ridiculous notion as that gentleman placing himself in a neighbourhood as beneath his notice as Cheapside; secondly, for imagining that he might wish for any further contact with her. After all, had she not been speculating how his demeanour that morning had been indicative of a desire to escape her presence, not court it?

Dissatisfied with her thoughts, Elizabeth hurried along the hallway, only to be distracted as she espied a letter lying upon the silver salver on the side table. A quick glance at the direction confirmed herself as the recipient and Charlotte as the sender, and taking it up as she passed, she pushed open the drawing room door to see Mr Bingley rise hurriedly from his seat to greet her.

"Miss Elizabeth. How delightful to see you again."

"Indeed, Sir. And so soon!" Elizabeth could not help but smile at his eager expression, but catching the warning shake of her aunt's head out of the corner of her eye, she suppressed her humour at the situation. "You do us great honour in paying us a call this afternoon."

"Mr Bingley came with a purpose, Lizzy." Mrs Gardiner got to her feet as she spoke and headed for the door. "Now that you are come, I shall order some tea, and our guest can enlighten you. Please excuse me." She left the room, and Elizabeth turned to take a seat next to her sister before the gentleman resumed his own.

Fingering the thickness of the parchment in her hand, Elizabeth silenced her curiosity as to what Charlotte could have to relate so soon after her departure and smiled over at Bingley. "A purpose? How intriguing!"

He shook his head. "I am merely come to offer my services to your family, Miss Elizabeth, as I have explained to your aunt and Miss Bennet."

"Mr Bingley has accepted an invitation from Nicholas to host this evening in his absence," Jane intervened gently, and was rewarded for the effort by a widening of Bingley's smile. "He has called to offer his carriage to us, that we may all travel in company."

Elizabeth looked from her sister to their guest. "That is most kind of you, Sir."

"It will be my pleasure."

"And are you familiar with the musicians who will be performing or any of the proposed pieces?"

Bingley looked a little shame-faced for a moment, then laughed. "I must own that I know nothing of it! Harington failed to enlighten me when he invited me, and having only just this past hour determined to go, I have yet to seek out the information!"

Jane got to her feet as he spoke these words and walked over to the desk. "Nicholas brought us a programme the other day," she said over her shoulder, before returning her gaze to the desk top and starting to shuffle through a pile of papers.

Conscious that Bingley's gaze was fixed upon her sister, Elizabeth dropped her eyes to the letter resting in her lap and frowned. The paper had been folded in such a way that the envelope appeared somewhat bigger than was customary, and the thickness of it implied several sheets were contained within. What could possibly have happened to warrant Charlotte writing in such detail? Elizabeth looked up and realised that

Jane had returned with the pamphlet that outlined the programme for the recital and had handed it to Bingley, who invited her to take the seat beside him whilst he perused it. Hesitating only briefly, and casting her sister a quick glance, she took the seat indicated.

Seeing them become engrossed in discussing the order of performance, Elizabeth said quickly, "Would you excuse my attention for a moment?" And when they both glanced up in her direction, added, "I have received a letter from Charlotte that I would dearly like to read." She waved the envelope in the air at them, and was not surprised when advised to enjoy her letter, as they were well entertained with anticipating their evening of music.

Soothed by the murmur of their voices, Elizabeth quickly broke the seal on the letter and sat back in her chair to enjoy its contents, but as she unfolded the pages, something fell from inside, bounced off her knee and skimmed across the floor until it came to rest against Jane's skirts.

With amusement, she observed both Bingley and her sister instinctively reach down for it, bang heads, apologise, retrieve what appeared to be some closely folded pages and a small tug of war ensue as each held onto them, before Jane conceded and Bingley raised his prize triumphantly aloft, both of their faces washed with a most becoming shade of pink.

"Yours, I believe, Madam," Bingley declared grandly, and getting to his feet he stepped across the rug to present it to her, resting it on his palm as if it were a salver. With a smile, Elizabeth leaned forward to receive Charlotte's enclosure, but Bingley's raised brow as he glanced down upon the contents of his hand caused her eyes to follow his, and suddenly she felt all colour drain from her face.

In the precious seconds that realisation dawned upon her, she got quickly to her feet and stepped forward to grab the letter, staring wide-eyed at the familiar direction.

"Lizzy, whatever is the matter?" Jane joined them in the middle of the room, her eye moving quickly from the letter in her sister's hand to the paleness of her face.

"I... I... nothing. Please, I beg you would excuse me," and grabbing Charlotte's letter from the seat where it had been discarded Elizabeth hurried from the room.

Chapter Three

OBLIVIOUS TO THE FADING LIGHT, Elizabeth sat motionless on the end of the bed, her eyes fixed unseeingly on the wall opposite, which hosted the fireplace and a painting above it – a watercolour landscape that had hung there for as long as she could remember. Yet though her eye was steady, her mind remained conflicted, for the potential enormity of her error had struck her a heavy blow. What carelessness to have left Mr Darcy's letter behind; he had placed his trust in her, yet she had been so thoughtless, failing to recall that she had not placed it safely in her writing case. If his letter had fallen into the wrong hands…

Elizabeth's head drooped upon her slender neck and her gaze returned, as it had done repeatedly these past thirty minutes, to Charlotte's letter. That she bristled with curiosity was much apparent, and in itself very reassuring, for it indicated that, whatever the temptation, her friend had not succumbed and read the letter. There was, to be fair, an air of smugness about the missive – having long suspected Elizabeth to be an object of interest to either the Colonel, Mr Darcy or both, it was clear that Charlotte believed it to be a token of affection. That she could not approve such a deed she had felt it her duty, as the wife of a clergyman, to express, but there was such an underlying dryness to her turn of phrase that Elizabeth could well detect the lack of seriousness in the alleged censure. Charlotte hoped for a reply that would satisfy the questions her discretion warranted and was adequate reward for the protection of her friend's privacy.

Elizabeth got to her feet and walked over to the window. The rain showed some sign of abating, yet the street remained awash with rainwater and mud, the carriage wheels spraying dirty splashes upon the pavements as they crashed through the puddles. She leaned against the sill and sighed. How could she have forgotten placing the letter under her pillow?

Before her thoughts could resume the same repetitive cycle, a sound alerted her to the fact that someone was out on the landing, and turning her back on the window she was unsurprised to see her sister peer cautiously round the door.

"Lizzy? Are you quite well?"

With a self-deprecating smile, Elizabeth walked across the room as her sister entered and took the hands that she offered to her, giving them a reassuring squeeze.

"Forgive me, dear Jane. My behaviour was intolerable. I do not know what Mr Bingley must think of me."

"Pray do not concern yourself. I longed to come to you sooner, but he stayed this past half hour and drank tea with aunt and myself. He expressed the hope that you would be well enough to attend the recital." Jane hesitated. "I must own that our aunt is somewhat confused, and indeed was rather surprised to find me alone with him – but it was merely for a couple of minutes, and I did explain that you were suddenly indisposed." Jane blushed, and Elizabeth gave her sister's hands a final squeeze before relinquishing them.

"She would have come to you herself as soon as our guest departed, but I begged that she allow me to check upon you. Tell me, Lizzy. What was that letter, that it should discompose you so?"

Elizabeth shook her head before walking away from her sister to stare once more out of the window. There was so much that she had not shared with Jane. Now that she had seen Mr Darcy, and had made the acquaintance of his sister, she felt all the likelihood of their meeting again. Would it be better to inform Jane of what had happened in Kent, that she might have her counsel and support?

"Lizzy?" Jane's prompt forced her to turn to face the room again, and she met her sister's concerned eye warily before releasing a soft sigh and gesturing towards the bed, where both Charlotte and Mr Darcy's letters lay.

"I think you had best be seated, Jane. I feel obliged to recount something that will astound you."

Georgiana had persuaded Darcy to play a round of Piquet in what he perceived was an attempt to distract him from dwelling on the forthcoming evening. Yet his attention was hard bought, anticipating as he was Bingley's return from Gracechurch Street, and it was with a rush of relief that he saw his friend's head appear around the drawing room door.

"Was your venture successful? You do not appear too dampened from the exercise."

Bingley's smile widened as he joined them at the small rosewood card table, pulling out a chair and dropping into it with easy grace.

"Most indubitably! My services have been accepted; I am to call at Gracechurch Street at six for drinks."

Darcy raised a brow. "That leaves you little time for dining."

His friend shook his head and then grinned as he patted his midriff. "I am well fed on cake. Mrs Gardiner does keep a particularly fine cook. I am sure I shall manage until supper time."

Darcy grunted. "Well, I shall not."

"Then let me call for some tea." Georgiana rose to her feet, smiling at both gentlemen, "and then I shall leave you to talk. I must seek Mrs Annesley out to arrange our plans for this evening." She crossed to the fireplace and pulled the bell, and once the servant had been given instructions, she left them alone.

For a moment, silence reigned. Darcy cast Bingley a quick glance, but he seemed to be miles away, his eyes smiling almost as much as his mouth. Unable to bear the suspense longer, he cleared his throat, aware that his friend had started, and said as casually as he could muster, "And how was Miss Bennet this afternoon, Bingley? I trust that she and her party had taken shelter before the rains came?"

"She is well, Darcy. Indeed, she looked *extremely* well." Bingley leaned his arms on the table with complete disregard for the cards that lay there. "I must own, my friend, that I am gratified that Harington's absence presented such an opportunity as this. She was much more at ease in my company today, even when we…" Bingley broke off suddenly, a deep blush rising into his cheeks, and he quickly cast his eyes down.

Darcy blinked, somewhat astonished, conscious that his companion had lapsed into the silent meditation of his hands which were now clasped in front of him on the table. "When you what?"

Bingley raised his eyes to meet his friend's curious gaze and let out a huff of embarrassed laughter.

"Ah, well – through no fault of our own, I confess we were left alone in each other's company for a full five minutes." He laughed openly as Darcy frowned. "And no, my friend, I did not grasp the opportunity. Much as I am keen to secure her, I am not foolish enough to think I have redeemed myself in her eyes yet – or in those of her family."

This mention of family caused Darcy's frown to deepen. He had been much impressed with Mrs Gardiner. She was most definitely not what he had anticipated, for though a sister by marriage, he really had not held out any hope that the brother of Mrs Bennet would have wed a woman much different to his siblings. Yet this contrivance to leave his friend alone with Miss Bennet, so soon after their tentative re-acquaintance, seemed out of sorts with the lady he had met that morning. And what of Elizabeth?

"I can see you are puzzling over how such a circumstance could arise!" Bingley grinned. "It was purely accidental, I assure you, and indeed I do believe it adds weight to my suspicions with regard to Miss Elizabeth Bennet and Harington."

A wave of envy swept through Darcy, but his inability to say anything further was disguised by the arrival of Mrs Wainwright and a serving girl bearing trays containing a pot of freshly brewed tea, along with platters of thinly sliced bread and butter and freshly baked biscuits.

Darcy would have felt some amusement in watching his friend as he piled a plate with several items, but all he could think about was what might cause Bingley to say such a thing and how it had led to him spending time alone with Miss Bennet. The awful thought crossed his mind that somehow Harington had not yet left for the country and had called to take his leave of Elizabeth and that somehow… somehow, he, Harington, had managed to remove her from the room for a few moments of privacy, leaving her sister with his friend. As the feelings of discomfort increased, Darcy stirred restlessly in his chair.

"These really are the most delicious biscuits."

Darcy rolled his eyes. "Unable to last until supper after all then?"

"I would never risk hurting your cook's feelings by abstaining."

"You remind me of my cousin."

"The Colonel? Have you received word of when he returns?"

Darcy shook his head and reached for his teacup. "His expectation was that he would be away no more than four and twenty hours. I suspect he will be with us some time on the morrow."

Bingley nodded and took a slice of bread and butter, and Darcy observed him impatiently as he munched contentedly, keen for him to continue his explanation. Yet as nothing further seemed to be forthcoming, Bingley's attention now on dropping sugar cubes into his tea, Darcy essayed, "Er – you were saying?" and when his friend looked up from the stirring of his tea, a spoon held aloft, prompted, "Your visit earlier?"

Bingley grinned and dropped the teaspoon carelessly onto the tray. "Ah yes! Miss Elizabeth's sudden departure – she quite fled the room, you know, and I believe she gave little thought to the situation she left in her wake."

"She is not unwell?" Darcy struggled to restrain the anxiety in his voice.

"I am certain she is quite well. She merely received a letter which seemed to cause her some disturbance of mind. "

"I fail to see how you could be privy to such an incident."

"Oh, it was quite natural, I assure you. Miss Bennet and I were perusing the programme for tonight's recital; Mrs Gardiner had excused herself to arrange for our tea to be brought, and Miss Elizabeth began to open a letter she had received – she said that it was from her friend, Mrs Collins."

The reminder of Elizabeth's recent stay in Kent caused Darcy's throat to tighten, and he cautiously took a sip of his tea in an attempt to ease the constriction.

"But another letter fell from its pages and skimmed across the floor to where I sat with Miss Bennet. We both reached to retrieve it at the same time," Bingley paused and his cheeks began to take on the pinkness of earlier. " She – I – we bumped heads – only lightly, I assure you. No injury was sustained, but we both had grasp of the letter by then, and I was highly gratified for the incident, because before letting go, she –" he hesitated. "She – er – she squeezed my finger."

Darcy blinked, unsure if he had heard correctly. "Squeezed your finger?"

"Yes. We were both grasping the letter, you see. Our hands were very close. I believe it was a sign." Bingley beamed at his friend.

"Of what?"

"Why, of a return of her affection, of course!" For which Darcy found he had no answer. "But I digress; I walked over to offer the second letter to Miss Elizabeth, but here is the thing: I suspect it was from Harington. I happened a glance at the direction – it was only for a mere second, and upside down, but the hand was most definitely a gentleman's. She and Harington – well, you were not there, you did not hear the tale – they used to correspond in their youth, up until they were discovered. It was all innocence, you understand, but Harington hinted that their illicit correspondence might still be taking place. I suspect Miss Elizabeth is welcoming of his attentions, for that letter must have meant a great deal to her. It is no surprise that her friend sending it on to her was somewhat unanticipated – one must suppose she had left it behind by mistake!"

Darcy got up and walked over to the window, leaving Bingley to continue his indulgence of the tea tray. He leaned against the sill and stared out into the rain-soaked street. Just when he thought his feelings were becoming more manageable, something further would discompose him. That Elizabeth held someone in tender regard he had suspected; gratified though he was that Wickham did not seem to be the man, he was no happier to hear Bingley's news, but before he could wallow in this, a more powerful and disturbing thought struck him as a memory from his stay in Kent returned to haunt him: he had once interrupted Elizabeth at the parsonage writing a letter – had she been writing to Harington?

How could he have been so foolish, contemplating a proposal to a woman whom he understood so little that whilst he had been assured of their future together, she thought only of another? He shifted his position restlessly. It was indeed a fair prospect: a lifelong friend from an old and wealthy family, someone she clearly, in his friend's eyes, had an affinity with, and now this. A couple in correspondence must surely have come to an understanding?

With a suppressed groan, Darcy passed a hand across his eyes. He had thought that Elizabeth's rejection of him was the most anguish he could feel; the thought of her committed to – enamoured of – another, was a further sore trial and one he struggled to contend with.

Chapter Four

HAVING COMPLETED A rather rambling account of the events of Sunday to Jane, including those parts of Mr Darcy's letter which she felt she could reveal, Elizabeth awaited her sister's reaction. Having recounted what she could of their confrontation, she had not felt able to confess to Jane their close embrace when she fell from the curricle.

Though clearly surprised by some of her sister's revelations, Jane had remained silent throughout but her first words were not what Elizabeth had anticipated.

"Dear Lizzy, he must be very deeply in love with you, to approach you with so little encouragement!"

Elizabeth got to her feet and crossed to the dresser, pouring herself a glass of water from the pitcher. Every thought of Mr Darcy's apparent affection for her caused a multitude of sensations the like of which she little understood, and she swallowed a cool draught of water before turning to face her sister.

"I cannot deny that there must have been some depth to his feelings. Indeed, he made it perfectly clear when detailing all that he had to overcome. Yet," she paused as she walked slowly back towards where Jane sat in a chair near the fireplace. "I was, at the time, more distracted by the manner of his making the offer." She gave her sister a look of regret. "But though the delivery left much to be desired, I cannot deny the reasoning of much of what he said."

"It must have been very difficult for him to see you at Rosings the next day."

Elizabeth sat in the chair opposite her sister, casting her mind back to that awkward dinner. "Taxing in the extreme – no less so than for being a complete surprise to him. Yet his manner towards me once he had overcome his initial shock was both polite and courteous – more so than I perhaps warranted, having been so abusive towards him the day before."

"But he would have understood that you were under a misapprehension."

"Indeed. One can add graciousness, understanding and compassion to Mr Darcy's growing list of attributes!"

"Lizzy! You cannot always be so flippant."

"Dearest Jane." Elizabeth shook her head sadly. "I assure you I was serious at the time. It sobered me, to see how much I had erred, how seriously misled my judgement had been. You must excuse me if I seem to make light of it. You know it is merely my way."

"But Lizzy – to have received two offers of marriage!"

"Aye – and refused them both, as you are no doubt thinking."

"No! No, your refusals were understandable. Mr Collins – well, you and he were not suited at all; and Mr Darcy, he – well, it is not as if – you did not ever – oh dear, poor Mr Darcy."

Getting quickly to her feet, Elizabeth began to walk to and fro before the fireplace, trying not to think of Mr Darcy and his suffering.

"You are too sympathetic, Jane. Mr Collins was a man of little sense, and Mr Darcy – well, there is an element of folly in offering his hand to someone who held him in such low esteem!"

"I believe you do him an injustice. He values you. What further proof of good sense is required?"

Elizabeth laughed and turned about on the rug. "Very well. You make an excellent point. Admiring me shows the utmost good sense! But though I see the error of my misjudgement of his character, I cannot deny that his manner of address – his whole demeanour towards our friends and family in Hertfordshire – does not make me regret my decision…"

She broke off as the voiced these words. Did she really mean that? Elizabeth shook the thought aside; of course she did not regret it.

With a self-deprecating laugh, she shrugged her shoulders at Jane. "Well, I must hope that at least one more proposal comes my way – for it would be a sad day to have to regret Mr Collins!"

"I am sure you will meet someone."

"Well, I fear if he is a man I can tolerate and has the good sense to make his offer without fawning or offence, I may just have to accept – or else end an old maid!"

"You are not serious?" Jane got to her feet looking somewhat discomfited. "You know it is not what you wish."

Elizabeth shook her head. "No, it is not what I wish – though I do begin to comprehend a little better those that do settle for companionship. Liking someone seems to bring far less distress than when love is a factor!"

She stopped abruptly, reminded forcibly of her earlier speculation over Nicholas' purpose in desiring a private audience with her. If he did intend to ask for her hand, would she accept him for this very reason? Conscious that this thought did not comfort her at all, Elizabeth gave her sister her full attention, determined to turn the conversation away from such pointless conjecture.

"Do you forgive me for leaving you so precipitously now? I know I should not have done so, but hopefully you understand my discomposure."

Jane walked over and perched herself upon the bed, clasping her hands in her lap.

"Of course I understand, and I think you are worrying too much. Our aunt returned within moments of your leaving the room, and though surprised at your absence, nothing was amiss. Once I had explained to her that you felt a little unwell and needed privacy, she was appeased, though of course concerned for your welfare."

"And you, Jane?" Elizabeth walked over to stand in front of her sister, but Jane dropped her gaze to her hands. "Did you feel more comfortable with Mr Bingley this time?"

A sigh emanated from the bowed head in front of her, and Elizabeth dropped to sit on the floor, crossing her legs and peering up at her sister, drawing a reluctant smile from her.

"Come now. Tell me; you appear to be more at ease in his presence, and that can only be to the good."

Jane was silent for a moment, but Elizabeth's patience was rewarded when her sister raised her head and said softly, "I pinched him."

Elizabeth let out a huff of laughter. "You *pinched* him? Dear Jane! Were you taking your revenge for his having left Hertfordshire so abruptly?"

The colour had flown into Jane's cheeks, and she looked very embarrassed. "Oh Lizzy. I *did* feel more comfortable. He is so amiable, with such pleasing manners. Yet as soon as I become more myself, I nip him sharply on his finger!"

"Oh dear," Elizabeth tried to sympathise, but in reality she could not help her smile from widening. "How did it come about that you were touching Mr Bingley's finger?"

Jane got to her feet quickly, and Elizabeth watched as she walked two paces towards the window, stopped, turned about and hurried to the dresser containing the pitcher. As she poured some water into the basin, she glanced over her shoulder at Elizabeth where she remained on the floor.

"It was when we reached for the letter. We banged heads – I am sure you saw. Somehow, our fingers met as we both held on to the letter and instead of parchment I found myself... I found myself gripping his finger very tightly. I let go as soon as I realised, but there was quite clearly a mark!"

Turning her back, Jane dipped her fingers into the water and then patted her cheeks. Elizabeth struggled to maintain her composure, but sensing her sister was sufficiently disturbed about the incident to not appreciate her humour, she schooled her expression into one of sympathy.

"I think we can be certain that Mr Bingley will not take it personally. If it will comfort you, I promise to observe him this evening to see if can detect any unease in his manner."

Jane paled. "Oh dear. In the light of what you have just shared with me, I feel I must tell you – Mr Darcy, he is to attend this evening. We had it from Mr Bingley himself before he left."

A wave of disbelief swept through Elizabeth; was the gentleman seriously prepared to put himself in her way? Having convinced herself of his desire to distance himself, something she felt every sympathy for, she could not account for such contradictory behaviour.

"I confess I am surprised."

Jane bit her lip. "How will you bear it?"

Ruminating upon that very thought, Elizabeth gave a weak smile. "I believe that I can bear it very well. I had been considering how I might explain what has happened. This may be the perfect opportunity."

"But you surely cannot converse privately at a recital?"

"Well, I shall endeavour to secure a moment all the same. If that does not arise, then I shall have to trust to fate bringing our paths together once more."

"But Lizzy – do you feel there is a need to tell him, now that the letter is safely returned to your care?"

"I believe so. It is not merely a selfish attempt to clear my conscience, I assure you, and though I once courted Mr Darcy's ill opinion willingly, I no longer have any desire to provoke his wrath." Elizabeth hesitated as she reflected upon his words during his proposal. "He claimed to abhor disguise. His offer – offensive though it was to me – was founded in honesty." She grimaced at her sister. "And honesty can be cruel and unpalatable, can it not, but it does not make it any less of a truth!" She sighed. "But nonetheless, truthfulness is what he appreciates, and I feel it incumbent upon me to let him know that there is one other who knows of his addressing me in such a manner, even if the content remains confidential."

Jane walked over and resumed her place on the bed, and Elizabeth, who had got to her feet and picked up Mr Darcy's letter once more, came to sit beside her.

"I seem to forever be in need of apologising to the man – it is a difficult pill to swallow." She shook her head as she stared at the lettering of her name. "Though I deserve little better; I have let him down."

"You are too hard upon yourself, Lizzy."

"I assure you I am not. Can you imagine if our Cousin Collins had retrieved it rather than his wife? Do you think he would have read it, Jane? Despite his position within the church, I am not confident that he would have avoided the temptation – perhaps if he did not perceive the signature – but if Charlotte, even in her endeavour to seal it quickly, saw that, one can only surmise that Mr Collins would have seen it also. I do not think he would have let it rest."

"But what reason might he have for reading someone else's correspondence? And had he done so, what was to be done with the knowledge?"

"He may have felt obliged to pass it to his patroness. I do not know that all that pertains to Miss Darcy is known by that branch of the family." Elizabeth's gaze dropped to the letter in her lap and she unfolded it almost without thinking, reading the opening lines again. Then, her eyes widened, and she glanced at Jane. "Oh dear."

"What is it?"

Smothering a desire to laugh out loud, Elizabeth smiled.

"I cannot help but wonder at what might well have passed through Mr Collins' mind had he been in a position to read the letter's opening, that it did not contain any *'renewal of those offers which were so disgusting to you'*. Our cousin would never imagine that someone as superior as Mr Darcy would offer marriage to me." Elizabeth could tell from Jane's horrified expression and the colour that invaded her cheeks that she understood her sister's meaning.

"Lizzy!"

"Dear Jane," with difficulty, Elizabeth brought her amusement under control, "do not be alarmed. I am certain Mr Collins would never have read it – and let us conjecture no more. The letter is here safe and sound, and Charlotte's curiosity I can soon quieten."

"But how can you treat it so lightly?"

"Oh I am sufficiently uncomfortable, I assure you. I think it may be relief that the outcome was so favourable."

There was silence for a while, the soft ticking of the clock and the steady patter of raindrops against the window panes the only sound. Then, Jane said quietly, "Knowing what I do now of the happenings in Kent – Lizzy, how did you feel when you encountered Mr Darcy this morning?"

Unable to formulate an immediate response, Elizabeth lifted her gaze from the letter in her lap and found herself staring at the painting over the fireplace once more. She studied the landscape for a moment, a wild expanse of countryside with craggy outcrops exuding an almost untamed quality; then, she sighed.

"I do not know. Even now, I am not sure what my feelings are. I cannot even account for accosting him."

Jane gasped. "You accosted him!"

Elizabeth nodded. "How fortunate I am that Aunt is unaware. Bless Nicholas for keeping his counsel!"

"But what possessed you?"

Elizabeth shrugged. "I confess I do not know. An instinct? I must own that I gave it no thought whatsoever, I merely acted." She started to fold the letter slowly, smoothing her thumb across the pages as she did so. "I am both foolish and fickle, Jane. I – I just wanted to speak to him."

"That is surprising, given your history – even prior to his offer."

Elizabeth completed her attentions to the parchment on her lap before responding. "I know. I do not pretend to understand it. I must be the last person he wishes to encounter, harbouring feelings of rejection, not least resentment, as he must be; so why did I do it? I hardly achieved my object, for he kept his distance well after our initial discourse, and even worse, he was obliged to introduce his sister to our acquaintance."

"To be fair, though, it did not seem as if he minded. I mean, he was clearly not entirely at ease, but then I have always believed him diffident in the company of those with whom he is not familiar. There were striking similarities between him and Miss Darcy this morning – do you not think so?"

Elizabeth smiled ruefully. "I confess, I do." She got to her feet and placed Mr Darcy's letter safely inside her writing case with the others and locked it. Turning to face her sister, she studied Jane for a moment, then held out her hand to her.

"Come. Let us be done with this and repair to the drawing room, or Aunt will wonder what has become of us. No doubt I am due a reprimand for my behaviour earlier, and I would not delay giving her the satisfaction any longer!"

With a smile, Jane got to her feet and taking her sister's hand they both quitted the room.

Chapter Five

LONGBOURN WAS UNCHARACTERISTICALLY quiet, Mr Bennet being out with his steward to inspect some new fencing and his wife on her daily visit, weather permitting, to her sister, Mrs Philips.

Though dry at first, a fine rain had been falling steadily since late morning, probably the cause of Mrs Bennet's extended visit in Meryton, but by afternoon the heavy clouds had moved southwards towards London, leaving behind a misty drizzle. The three daughters who remained at home were thus still confined to the house, and they had sought solitary occupations to amuse themselves, Mary diligently working on an alter cloth at the dining room table, Kitty perusing a picture book in the drawing room and Lydia in the kitchen dyeing some ribbons.

Peering out of the drawing room window, Kitty narrowed her gaze. Her eyesight was not at its best when attempting to decipher a distant object, but something – some movement – had caught her eye as she sat next to her puppy in the window seat and now she strived to perceive what it might be.

A few moments later, she leapt to her feet, the puppy yelping and scrambling up likewise. There was most certainly a figure approaching. Now and then it faded from sight into the shadow of an overhanging tree, but then it would be revealed once more, and despite the discrepancies of her vision, she was almost certain she recognised the stature and gait of the visitor.

Turning away, she hurried from the room, her puppy gambolling in her wake, calling as she went, "Lydia! Lydia! You will never guess who is coming along the drive!"

Having finally been ushered out of his own front door by a sister who seemed more like his guardian every hour, Darcy sank back against the leather of the carriage seat and closed his eyes.

What was he doing? He had been in Town but eight and forty hours, yet here he was, attending a recital that in ordinary circumstances he would have avoided like the devil *and* throwing himself once more in the way of a woman who had made her displeasure in his society all too plain – a woman he professed to love so deeply, yet still he could not put her wishes before his own. What she would be thinking, knowing as she must that he was to be in attendance that night, he knew not, but one thing was certain: he had no intention of forcing his company on her. He was not there to cause her discomfort or unease. Agitatedly, Darcy rubbed his fist across the back of his closed eyes and then blinked before opening them fully to stare out of the window at the passing streets.

In all reality, he could have walked the distance from Mount Street to Hanover Square, so why had he not? True, the rain that had ceased earlier still threatened to return at any moment – yet when had the elements ever concerned him? Was he falling victim to the whiles of the society he scorned, whereby to arrive in anything but one's finest conveyance would be derisible? He doubted it. Was it not more that it gave him the chance – even now – to rap on the hood and tell his coachman to turn about? And even should he arrive at his destination, he could observe the arrivals in anonymity before taking that final step to enter the building; and should he wish to leave quickly…

With a rueful shake of his head, Darcy recalled an earlier exchange with Bingley over his plans for the evening, when attempting to persuade him to accompany him in his carriage.

"I would prefer to travel under my own direction…"

"… that you may leave under it also?"

Darcy straightened his shoulders. No – he would not turn tail or hide. He had come for his friend, to whom he owed much. He would do his best to keep out of Elizabeth's way, would ensure that she was not obliged to enter into needless conversation with him other than what civility demanded, and at least with Harington gone into the country, there would be no need to envy another for being the recipient of her attentions.

The recollection of that gentleman brought little solace, absent though he was. Bingley's assertions over the potential intimacy that existed between Elizabeth and Harington had plagued Darcy as he had prepared for the evening, the ache in his breast intensifying every time his mind recalled his friend's words. He was tormented by what he did not know for certain, yet conscious of some respite by it all being mere supposition.

The jolt of the carriage as it rolled to a halt roused him from his interminable speculations, and he reluctantly pulled on his gloves, hating their restrictive feel. Conscious that a porter had moved forward to open the door, he shook aside any further notion of retreat and stepped down onto the rain-soaked pavement, accepting his hat from his footman and walking rapidly up the steps and into the building.

Having arrived at the concert hall in Hanover Square in good time, Bingley's party had taken up a place at the rear of the vestibule to await the call into the main auditorium, along with Mr Darcy's arrival.

Though she had been forewarned of his attendance, Elizabeth found her mind in conflict, torn between wanting to speak to him regarding his letter and not troubling him further with her presence, and still struggling to comprehend his own purpose in attending. Thus it was that an air of complete composure remained elusive, but conscious that her aunt had given her more than one glance of question, she forced herself to join in the conversation.

"Are there many of your acquaintance here this evening, Uncle?"

Mr Gardiner patted the hand of his wife where it rested on his arm, and smiled at his niece.

"I suspect not. As you know, your aunt and I tend more towards Holborn for concerts, the neighbourhood being more convenient. But when Nicholas is in charge, one goes where one must!"

Elizabeth smiled. "And yet he has had the temerity to desert us, leaving us adrift in a sea of strangers!"

"Then we are fortunate that Darcy is to join us, are we not?" chimed in Bingley.

Mr Gardiner inclined his head. "I look forward to making his acquaintance. Is your friend as fond of music as you are, Sir?"

"Indeed, he is. His sister is a true proficient on more than one instrument, though I must own that Darcy is happier by his own hearth listening to her play than joining the masses at a public performance!"

The conversation soon moved into a discussion of the evening's programme, and as the voices drifted around her, Elizabeth turned to look casually about the room, attempting a nonchalance she did not feel. This was the second occasion in a matter of days that she had approached an evening knowing she owed Mr Darcy the courtesy of an apology. Not lacking in courage, Elizabeth could nonetheless feel her heart falter at the notion of having to admit to him that his faith in her had almost been misplaced. Then, she took herself to task. Considering the events of last Sunday, what further damage could her confession do to their beleaguered acquaintance?

Meeting Jane's concerned look, she smiled at her, the reciprocal smile reassuring though it faded rather quickly, and detecting that her sister's eye had been caught by something behind her, Elizabeth spun around in time to see Mr Darcy enter the vestibule.

Blinking in the glare of several hundred candles, Darcy handed his hat and great coat to a porter and walked purposefully across the foyer, his eyes fixed straight ahead in order to avoid having to acknowledge anyone. It was a pointless exercise, and well he knew it. Even if he affected ignorance of those around him, they sought his company, courted his society.

A sudden memory of Elizabeth's words, *'your selfish disdain for the feelings of others'*, seared through his mind, and his step faltered. Had he not recently owned his tendency to remain aloof from London society in equal measure? He came to a complete standstill, oblivious of the concertgoers milling around him, yet his hesitation cost him dear, for no sooner had he halted his progress than he was approached from both sides.

"Mr Darcy! How delightful!"

"Oh Sir! Mr Darcy — what a pleasure to have the opportunity to further our acquaintance…"

Casting a slightly panicked look to his left, where a heavily bejewelled woman wearing far too much rouge had borne down upon him, the members of her party in her wake, and then his right, where a concoction of feathers waved before his eyes atop a very short woman, he released a slow, controlled breath. His expression settled out of habit into one of disinterest, and he straightened his shoulders in preparation for enduring their unsolicited attentions.

Despite her apprehension, Elizabeth observed Darcy's ambush with a resurgence of spirit and, biting her lip to contain her smile, she turned her back on him. Both his air and countenance were reminiscent of when she and her family had been introduced to the Netherfield party some months ago. He seemed to hold the society of London in as much contempt as that of the country, and she found it highly amusing, albeit somewhat gratifying, and might well have indulged herself at the gentleman's expense had she not seen Bingley's eye caught by what was happening.

"Oh Lord. Darcy looks in need of rescue."

Glad for an opportunity to release a light laugh, Elizabeth turned to look where the rest of their party were now gazing.

"Rescue, Mr Bingley? Does he often have need of such service from you?"

Bingley grinned at her as they watched the feathers of one of Darcy's disciples catch him on the nose, causing him to flinch and take a step backwards.

"Almost never, in truth, for by the time I reach him, he has usually managed to shun everyone to his satisfaction." He frowned. "This is most singular. I do not understand why he is tolerating their interest tonight." With a shrug, he smiled around at his small party. "Shall we join him? It may help to dilute the attention?"

Meanwhile, having made as much of an attempt at civility as he could muster, Darcy slowly extricated himself, making the need to join his party his excuse. He drew in a much-needed breath as he emerged on the other side of the people pressing around him and allowed his glance to move over the many faces that now filled the vestibule, not surprised to observe Bingley and his party who had made their way through the crowd towards him. He quickly determined Elizabeth, who stood beside her sister, but ignoring the urge to stare at her or engage her in a conversation she would doubtless wish to avoid, he turned to greet her aunt and accept the introduction to Mr Gardiner.

Conscious of a sense of guilt that having met Mrs Gardiner earlier, he held less trepidation at being introduced to Mrs Bennet's brother in a public setting as he might have, he tried to force the thought aside, and was pleased at his success, for – the necessary introductions having been performed – he found Mr Gardiner to be a gentleman by manner and, it must be acknowledged, as like his sisters as day was akin to night.

He could delay the inevitable no longer, though, and excusing himself from the Gardiners, he turned to exchange greetings with his friend and Jane Bennet, whom Bingley had secured at his side, her hand upon his arm, before finally acknowledging Elizabeth.

"Mr Darcy."

He returned her greeting with a bow, permitting him time to gather his wits. For a moment, they stared at each other in silence, and he was certain that once again his own cheeks bore a colour not dissimilar to that upon Elizabeth's, yet he could not countenance that it would sit quite so well on him as it did on her.

Conscious that Bingley and his partner had become engaged in a conversation with the Gardiners, he sought urgently for some inane comment before he could excuse himself and leave her in peace.

"I trust that you reached shelter before the storm broke earlier?"

"We did, I thank you." There was a pause. She looked almost as awkward as he felt, and there was an air of diffidence about her, but before he could determine if her manner was down to displeasure at his behaviour – doubtless she had seen his struggle to find anything commonplace to say to the people who had accosted him – or simply dissatisfaction over his presence at the recital, they were joined by the rest of their party, and he stood aside to make way for them.

"I am given to understand that you hail from Derbyshire, Sir." Mr Gardiner smiled at his wife before returning his attention to Darcy. "My wife is particularly attached to that county."

"I was born there and retain very fond memories of the country thereabouts. It is exceptional, is it not?" Mrs Gardiner gave him a warm smile that he could not help but respond to.

"Indeed, it is, most pleasing. And you, Sir? From your implication, am I to understand that you do not share the attachment?"

"Oh, I find it a very fine place, do not mistake me; but it is not whence I hail and thus holds no nostalgic sway over me."

Mrs Gardiner laughed. "My husband is from a southern county, Mr Darcy, and is used to less wild and untamed country. Indeed, I believe there are many that find it too rugged for their liking, but I find the unpredictability of the scenery both striking and original."

"I am a Bristolian, and proud of it!" declared Mr Gardiner. "The West Country will always have a special place in my heart, not least because it was where I first met you, my dear." He placed a gallant kiss upon his wife's hand, and that lady, with a shake of her head at her husband, turned to Bingley with a smile.

"And you, Sir? I know you have recently considered Hertfordshire as home, but where does your family hail from?"

"Yorkshire, Ma'am: a very rugged northern county, as you may know, and thus the scenery of Derbyshire is nothing new to me. Though I have not lived there these many years, I have family yet in Scarborough. 'Tis a long journey from Town, but one is well rewarded for its arduousness, for the coastal views are breath-taking."

Chapter Six

AS THE DISCUSSION EVOLVED into a comparison of their various travels around the country, Darcy glanced at Elizabeth who had stood in silence throughout the exchange. She met his gaze and a hint of a smile graced her lips; then, she returned her attention to the conversation and before long she entered into the fray, defending her uncle's claim of Somerset being the fairest county of all.

The word could not help but conjure up its association with the name Harington, and unwilling to allow his thoughts any purchase in that direction, Darcy forced his attention to remain fixed on the dialogue taking place before him, thankful that he had not had to seek a topic of conversation.

However, conscious that the last thing he wished for this evening was for his inherent reticence to be construed as arrogance or pride, or that he considered himself above his company, he determined to think of something that might be of interest to his new acquaintance, and on discerning that Bingley had engaged both Bennet sisters in an exchange over their own county of Hertfordshire, he turned slightly away from them to address her aunt and uncle, and was soon in an enjoyable conversation with the latter about the East India Company, in which they both had common interests.

Elizabeth soon found her concentration somewhat distanced from the discussion around her, and left Jane and Mr Bingley to themselves. Watching her aunt and uncle's interactions with Mr Darcy, she was comforted to have reinforced that which she had long known: she did have some relatives for whom she had no need to blush. Turning her attention to the gentleman presently engaging them in conversation, she sighed. Her perception of him had undergone a significant upheaval in recent days; now here he was, confounding her anew on more than one count. It was blatant from what she had just witnessed that his distaste for society was all encompassing and not, as she had originally believed, born purely of a dislike for small-town country neighbourhoods. Furthermore, here he was, being civil, and – if the expression upon her aunt and uncle's faces was to be believed – charming, to her relations.

Elizabeth shook her head. The man was an enigma, and she must not allow herself to be distracted by his contrary behaviour. Tonight she had a purpose, and she was determined to grasp any chance to make her confession.

"Lizzy?" A hand upon her arm drew Elizabeth from her introspection, and turning towards her sister, she smiled.

"Forgive me, my mind was adrift. Did you speak to me?"

Jane gestured towards their companion. "No, it was Mr Bingley. He asked when we are anticipating Nicholas' return."

"Harington's note, Miss Elizabeth," Bingley added with a smile, "indicated his being called home on an urgent matter of business, but he made no mention of how long he was to be in the West Country."

"I believe his intention is to return by Monday latest, but of the exact day we are uncertain. We are due to attend a ball that evening, and he assured us that he would return to accompany us."

"Do you know if his elder brother plans to attend?"

"James? No, I do not. He is but rarely in Town, being groomed as he is to take over the estate. Is it some time since you met?"

Bingley frowned lightly. "It is sadly a while ago. Our paths crossed unexpectedly in Town, but we barely had time to exchange more than pleasantries. I understand he was just beginning his Grand Tour." Bingley sighed. "I am a poor correspondent, I will own. Harington – James, that is – writes me now and then, but my responses are sporadic to say the least!"

Elizabeth smiled but her attention was soon drawn back towards the other members of their party. Her uncle appeared to be recounting some tale or other, his wife watching him affectionately and Mr Darcy listening with apparent interest. She studied the latter thoughtfully, wondering how she might manage to engage him in conversation at sufficient distance from others to avoid being overhead, but before she could once more become embroiled in such thoughts, there was a commotion near the entrance to the concert hall and she heard Bingley say, "Ah, here we are. I believe we are ready to go in."

The party turned as one to follow the wake of concertgoers now surging towards the auditorium, but as she saw Mr Gardiner lead her aunt forward, followed by Bingley with Jane upon his arm, Elizabeth realised that Mr Darcy might feel he had a duty to offer to escort her. Had the distance they needed to traverse been sufficient to generate both the time and discretion to allow her to say her piece, she would have found it hard not to present herself promptly to him. As it was, she suddenly found herself dreading the possibility of having to partner him, knowing as she did that it would mean taking his arm, and without thinking she began to move forward, following the rest of their party who were all but out of sight.

"Miss Bennet." Darcy's voice caused her to still, but she did not turn around, and he cursed himself for his hesitation. "Forgive me, would you allow me to escort you to your seat?" He waited for a painful few seconds before she turned to face him, unsettled by her unreadable expression, but offering his arm to her, he felt the utmost relief as she made to take it, only to find himself gripped by the deepest sense of regret as he saw her reluctance.

He was determined, though, that their progress into the concert hall should not be conducted in silence.

"It is unfortunate that Harington was unable to attend. I understand from your aunt that he made the arrangements some time ago – that the composer is a particular favourite of his."

Conscious that she had thrown a quick glance up at him as they merged with the throng of people making their way towards the auditorium, he met her eye for a moment.

"I believe it was beyond his control; an urgent matter at home."

"I did not mean to infer…"

"Mr Darcy." She looked up at him again, and then away. "I know you meant no censure – I am merely explaining such a precipitous absence."

Darcy frowned. Her manner was constrained in a way that he had not encountered throughout all their acquaintance, and she was resting her hand so lightly upon his arm that if he had not the visible evidence before him, he would think it was not happening. Did she detest him so very much that to even touch him caused her such consternation? Her colour was extremely high, and her manner... it was as if she could not wait to get into the concert hall, that she might be free of him. Even as he realised the galling truth of this, she spoke, and amidst the crush around them, he leaned nearer to hear her words as they walked through the doorway.

"As I mentioned at the time, Sir, it was a pleasure to make Miss Darcy's acquaintance this morning."

Darcy could not help but feel gratified by the sentiment, and trusted to her honesty that she meant it.

"It is kind of you to say so. I can assure you that the feeling is mutual." An awkward silence fell, but before either of them had need of finding further words, they had fetched up near the row of seats where their party awaited them.

Mrs Gardiner and her husband had taken their places, and conscious that the last thing Elizabeth would seek from him was a prolonged period in his direct company, Darcy handed her to Bingley, who was waiting at the end of the row to lead her to the next seat, and her sister was soon settled on her other side. Taking his place next to Bingley at the end of the row, Darcy leaned back in his chair and closed his eyes briefly before releasing a long, steady breath. If he survived this recital intact it would be a miracle, and he thanked providence for placing him so far from Elizabeth. To have been seated at her side and perhaps obliged to share a programme with her was more than his stretched nerves could handle at present.

As everyone settled into their seats around her, Elizabeth leaned back against the brocade cushion, affecting an interest in the programme that she now held, when in reality her gaze saw nothing of the words upon the page.

Deeply unsettled, she hoped that the high colour that had doubtless invaded her cheeks had receded somewhat, and was thankful for the lower lighting afforded in the concert hall, that she might have some respite from feeling so conspicuously out of sorts. What was it about that man's touch? Ever since Sunday... *no*. No, if she were to be completely truthful, ever since the first time they had made contact she had experienced a reaction to him. But now – since the events of Sunday, it had become more of an awareness of the man himself combined with an actual physical response somewhere within that she had little control over. *Can there be so much awareness in a man's touch?*

Swallowing with difficulty, Elizabeth attempted to clear her throat quietly. This would not do. Such thoughts were of no assistance, and indeed clouded her clear thinking. Conscious of a movement at her side, Elizabeth glanced at her sister, and Jane gave her a sympathetic look, knowing full well what her sister intended to try and achieve. Yet how was she to speak to the man? It was most obvious that he had no desire for her company, distancing himself where possible within their small party, and clearly reluctant to escort her into the auditorium.

As the musicians finished tuning their instruments, ready for the first piece to begin, Elizabeth roused herself and glanced to her right. Her aunt peered around her uncle, a look of concern upon her features, and Elizabeth smiled reassuringly at her before glancing to her left. Jane was now engrossed in whatever it was that Bingley indicated in the programme, and beyond them all she could see was Mr Darcy's hand resting upon his knee, his fingers drumming restlessly on the programme that lay there.

Feeling the tell-tale warmth rising in her cheeks once more, Elizabeth turned to face the front, focusing her gaze upon the soloist as she took up her place, and with grim determination she applied herself to attending the concert, shutting out all thoughts of the company around her.

At the intermission, Bingley led his party out into the vestibule and along a corridor to the antechamber set aside for refreshments.

There was such a crush of people that it took some time to find a table, and when they did it had space only to seat two. After a few moments of discussion, Mrs Gardiner and Jane Bennet took the chairs on offer, Elizabeth choosing to remain standing at her aunt's side. The gentlemen ranged themselves against the wall behind them, and as soon as a servant had been despatched to fetch their order the conversation turned to the performance they had recently enjoyed.

From his position, Darcy had an admirable view of the back of Elizabeth's head – one which he was happy to contemplate. Without having to worry about her catching him staring at her, he enjoyed the stolen pleasure of having her within his range of vision even as he maintained a conversation with Bingley and Mr Gardiner.

However, with the arrival of the refreshments the gentlemen were obliged to return to the table and as Darcy collected his glass of wine, he found Elizabeth had stood aside from her aunt's chair and was facing him, clasping her own glass with both hands.

"I trust you enjoyed the performance, Mr Darcy?"

"I did, though I am no concert-goer in general. But I am charged by my sister to relate every detail to her, so I am paying more attention than is my habit."

He was pleased to see Elizabeth smile at this. "It is heart-warming to know that you place her interests above your own, Sir."

"And how did you find the soloist? Was she to your liking?"

"I found her voice most pleasing, but will own that I was quite distracted by the feathers of her headdress! Every time she reached a high note, they positively quivered. I feared at one point they might even take flight."

Darcy smiled, stepping aside as Bingley eased his way past him to place his own glass upon the table as he leaned down to speak to Miss Bennet, conscious that Elizabeth's gaze had followed his.

"It is good to see Mr Bingley in such good spirits. I trust his sister is well?"

"I believe she is." Darcy hesitated. "I have not had the pleasure of Miss Bingley's company since my return to Town. She resides with the Hursts in Grosvenor Street..." his voice petered out as recognition flashed in Elizabeth's eyes; no doubt her sister had related the coldness of her reception there.

She said nothing to this, however, merely taking a sip from her glass. "I understand from Mr Bingley that he is residing with you during his stay in Town. I trust he is more appreciative of your library than you were of his at Netherfield."

Darcy gave a rueful laugh. "Bingley and libraries are two elements that would feign fit together. I do admit to keeping an ample selection of reading matter here; however, whether Bingley has noticed is entirely another matter." He glanced over at his friend where he was in earnest conversation with Miss Bennet. "I trust you are not suffering from a surfeit of his company; this does, after all, make it three occasions in one day." Darcy bit his lip suddenly, conscious that Bingley's lack of attendance prior to this was all down to his interference, but to his relief, Elizabeth laughed.

"It has been a pleasure to see him once more, Sir."

There was silence for a moment, and he saw Elizabeth glance over her shoulder and look around at the press of people. As she turned back to him, Darcy seized upon something that he had longed to ask her on Monday evening.

"Will you be staying long in Town?"

"I am at my aunt's disposal, but as I am certain I am little missed, other than by my father, I am in no hurry to return home. The purpose of my coming so precipitously was to see Nicholas – forgive me, Mr Harington. As you will comprehend, I have scarce seen him before he was summoned home. I will await his return and, indeed, I am also anticipating the arrival of a dear friend from the north."

Uncomfortable at the ease with which Elizabeth referred to Harington by his given name, even though it likely stemmed from the length and familiarity of the acquaintance more than anything personal, Darcy resented the reminder of how intimate they might be. With piercing clarity he recalled Bingley's thoughts over the letter Elizabeth had received earlier, and conscious that to discuss Harington with her was quite beyond him at present, he grasped at something she had said by way of distraction.

"You have connections in that part of the country?"

"My aunt's half-sister."

Only half attending, he said, "And what part of the north does she hail from?"

The conscious look that spread over Elizabeth's face immediately drew his interest. "Derbyshire. More precisely, from a small town called Lambton, Sir."

His attention was suddenly riveted on her face. "But that is not five miles from Pemberley! Did you – have you never visited with your friend?"

Elizabeth's eyes had widened momentarily, but then she shook her head. "My aunt's family home was there until she was about ten years old, but her father put the manor up for lease following her mother's death, and they moved southwards."

Darcy frowned. "Yet you say her sister has been staying there?"

"Oh – yes. Mr Seavington remarried some years back, and upon the expiration of the lease recently, he and his wife returned to the family home. Serena travelled there to spend time with her father, as he had experienced a bout of ill health."

"Not too severe, I trust?"

Elizabeth shook her head. "No. My aunt felt there was no need to travel northwards." She frowned. "I am surprised at Serena making such an arduous journey in the circumstances." Then, she smiled. "But I look forward to seeing her very much."

Chapter Seven

IT WAS AT THAT MOMENT that the bell sounded, and Darcy relieved Elizabeth of her glass, placing them both upon the table. He threw her a quick glance, convinced he heard a heavy sigh emanate from her, then dismissed the notion as fanciful; she had even now stepped away to join her sister. The crowd began to swarm out of the antechamber, and Bingley's party made their way around the table to join the masses. Before they could move further, though, delayed as they were by the crush of people, Darcy was hailed from nearby by a gentleman.

Glancing over, he narrowed his gaze. The man was but a slight acquaintance, but it was clear that he intended to make use of that introduction now and as Darcy instinctively went to withdraw, he recalled his intention to attempt to improve his manner in such a situation, and conscious that Elizabeth had probably seen his reticence when he arrived, he made an effort to receive the gentleman and his party with civility as they made their way towards him.

Elizabeth's step had faltered upon hearing Mr Darcy's name called, and she looked back over her shoulder as her aunt and uncle moved forward in time to see him greet an elegantly dressed couple accompanied by a very striking young lady attired in what she could only presume was the latest of fashions.

"It is not like Darcy to tarry with people who are barely known to him, but let us not delay. He will find his way back to us." Bingley smiled widely as he joined her; Mr and Mrs Gardiner had made their way out into the throng of concert goers in the hall and were out of sight, and Bingley, who had Jane upon his arm, offered his free one to Elizabeth, who roused herself from her speculation on the identity of Mr Darcy's acquaintances to smile at him and accept his offer.

They left the ante-chamber and made their way back towards the auditorium, Elizabeth regretting that her opportunity to converse with Mr Darcy had not offered enough privacy for her to raise the matter which most concerned her. She frowned briefly; though there was no doubt that he had entered into conversation with her more easily than on the previous few occasions they had met that week, there had still been moments when his manner had betrayed his discomfort or indeed reluctance to be in her company. Displeased with this notion, conscious though she was of its contrariness, Elizabeth attempted to put it aside. They were now nearing their row of seats and there was a little delay as the people in front of them assorted themselves into the correct order before easing themselves along their own row.

Bingley, Jane and Elizabeth stood patiently, chatting amiably about the earlier performance for a few minutes, and then Bingley glanced behind him before turning back to the ladies.

"Poor Darcy! He is always so beleaguered when he attends these functions. He will be cursing me for my persuasion!"

He beamed at Jane and Elizabeth, as if being cursed by Darcy was really the best thing a man could hope for, and Elizabeth could not help but smile widely at him in return. "Your persuasion, Mr Bingley? How so?"

He laughed. "You will probably not be surprised to know that Darcy is no frequenter of public gatherings! He takes much cajoling and influence to succumb, and I feel flattered that I am one of few who can occasionally succeed – the Meryton assembly was one such occasion that you both may recall! Indeed, his attendance at my own ball at Netherfield was even in question for a while!"

Jane looked somewhat shocked at this revelation and exchanged a worried glance with her sister, but Elizabeth merely laughed. "You do not surprise me, Sir!"

"But I will own," here Bingley paused, looking slightly embarrassed, as if he would recall the words and threw a hasty glance in Jane's direction. He cleared his throat, and then gave a rueful laugh. "Yes, I must own that he is here this evening against his will."

For some reason, this gave Elizabeth a feeling of disquiet, but not pausing to consider why, she pushed the sensation aside. Mr Darcy's reasons for attending or not this evening could have no relevance for her, though she could not deny that his disinclination may well be down to an understandable reluctance to be in her company. The fact that he had come along at his friend's request actually showed him in good favour.

Soon they were settled once more in their places, only this time Mrs Gardiner had taken the seat next to Elizabeth. As soon as she settled in her seat, Elizabeth took up the programme she had earlier discarded and tried to attend to the order of play for the second movement.

"Lizzy?" She looked up and smiled questioningly at her aunt. "Are you feeling unwell, my dear? You do not seem yourself."

Elizabeth summoned a smile. "I am perfectly well. My mind is wandering a little, but that is all." She lifted the programme in her hand and waved it. "I was about to read up on what the second performance might entail."

Mrs Gardiner looked over towards the musicians as they returned to their seats. "Well, it looks as though the players are preparing..." She stopped and peered along the line of seats. "Pray, where is Mr Darcy? Has he become lost in the confusion?" Elizabeth shook her head before looking over her shoulder to see if he was in sight.

There were few people left standing now, and it was therefore with little difficulty that she saw Mr Darcy enter the room; only he was not alone. Upon his arm was the very beautiful young lady who had been in the antechamber, and he was escorting her to her seat with what appeared to be great willingness.

Observing him deep in conversation with the lady caused a strange sensation to take hold of Elizabeth, and before she could prevent it, her mind ventured down the path she had so recently been travelling: did this lady feel the same sensations Elizabeth did when her arm rested upon Mr Darcy's? Did it make her heart race, her skin feel warm, her insides twist unaccountably... quickly brushing aside these thoughts, she cleared her throat and turned back to face her aunt. "He is just coming now. It seems he was delayed by an acquaintance."

Mrs Gardiner had clearly seen the information for herself. "Ah, yes." She gave Elizabeth a knowing smile. "One can see there might have been some inducement to tarry a while longer! The gentleman certainly displays good taste!"

Elizabeth said nothing to this and was hard put to give any due to the remaining performances. Her spirits were somewhat dampened, though she knew not why. She was conscious that her earlier awareness of Mr Darcy's presence further along the row had intensified. No matter how hard she tried to focus upon the music or the vocalists, any movement caught by the corner of her eye in his direction distracted her. She could only put it down to her frustration at not being able to address him as she wished, and she determined that she would not let the evening end without making one final attempt to secure a few moments of conversation with him.

Unfortunately, circumstance conspired to thwart her aspirations. Once the concert had drawn to an end, Bingley's party began to make its way towards the foyer, and Elizabeth found that by the time she had extricated herself from the row of seats, there was some distance between herself and Mr Darcy, who walked by Mr Gardiner's side, both gentleman engaged in conversation.

Attempting to keep his back within her vision, she was further frustrated in her endeavour to catch up with him for, having forgotten her shawl, she had to return to their seats to claim it. When she emerged out of the auditorium some minutes later, the crowd had thinned considerably and of their own party only her aunt and sister awaited her.

"Mr Darcy has taken his leave," Mrs Gardiner waved a hand in the direction of the departing gentleman, "and Mr Bingley has ordered his carriage and is waiting outside with your uncle. We decided to remain indoors as the air is quite cool this evening."

Conscious that Mr Darcy was even now some distance away, heading towards the porter's lodge on the other side of the vestibule, Elizabeth hesitated. Though she suspected their paths might cross further, she knew not when or whether it would allow for a moment of relatively private discourse, and seizing the opportunity, she turned to her aunt and Jane with a bright smile.

"Would you excuse me for one moment, Aunt? I would just speak with Mr Darcy quickly - something regarding his sister, but which I had no opportunity to raise earlier."

"Of course, my dear. We will accompany you."

Struggling to conceal her dismay at this pronouncement, though to be certain she should not have been surprised by it, Elizabeth's mind raced over how to extract herself from company and still manage to reach Mr Darcy before he was gone.

"Aunt, I think perhaps if Lizzy hurries she will just catch Mr Darcy. I am feeling a little the worse for the heat – would you mind accompanying me to the open door? I could well use some fresh air but as there are only gentlemen outside…" Jane left the sentence unfinished, but as Mrs Gardiner turned to her in concern Elizabeth mouthed a heartfelt 'thank you' at her sister before turning on her heel and setting off in pursuance of Mr Darcy.

After wending her way around a group of chattering women, she eventually caught up with him as he neared the porter's window, and reluctant to once again demand his attention by calling his name, she made sure to step within his side vision before speaking.

"Mr Darcy," she gave a hasty curtsey as he turned towards her, conscious that she had taken him unawares. "Forgive me for detaining you."

"Not at all," he responded quickly, his expression guarded.

Glancing quickly over her shoulder to confirm her supposition that they were indeed at a safe distance from being overheard, Elizabeth took a step closer to him, but to her dismay he immediately stepped backwards, his back now against the wall.

"Mr Darcy," Elizabeth hissed, her gaze fixed intently on his. "Be not alarmed, Sir. I merely wish to speak with you on a matter of the utmost delicacy. I appreciate that our current situation is not ideal, but as I have no notion of when another opportunity might arise, I must take whatever chance presents."

His attention was now fully fixed upon her, and he left the security of the wall behind, sweeping his gaze quickly over their immediate neighbours before returning his eyes to hers.

"I fear that once more I must refer to your letter." Elizabeth looked down briefly, knowing she must take advantage of these few minutes, yet almost reluctant to begin; then her glance met that of the gentleman, and conscious of the sudden frown upon his face, she found herself rushing into speech.

"Please do not concern yourself, Sir. It is not the content so much as the document itself that I wish to speak of…"

"Lizzy, dear! There you are." Mrs Gardiner's call from several feet away caused her to break off. "Forgive the interruption, Sir, but my niece must come directly. The carriage is here, and her uncle is waiting."

Closing her eyes for a second, Elizabeth opened them to meet Mr Darcy's intent stare. For a second they both looked at each other; then, Elizabeth released a quick breath and forced a smile.

"Coming, Aunt," she said over her shoulder before turning back to the gentleman. "It would seem our aunts conspire against us."

Seeing the momentary confusion upon his face, Elizabeth elucidated. "On the last occasion I attempted to speak to you of your letter, it was Lady Catherine who prevented it."

He inclined his head. "I believe your aunt carried her point with more finesse."

Elizabeth smiled, conscious of a glow of warmth from his acknowledgement that her own relation displayed a little more grace than his.

"Well, good evening, Mr Darcy. It was an enjoyable concert, was it not?"

"It was – has been – unexpected. I did not-" he stopped, then gave a self-deprecating smile. "Yes, Miss Bennet. It was most pleasant."

"Please send my regards to your sister."

"It will be my pleasure."

Giving a quick curtsey in response to his formal bow, Elizabeth turned and followed her aunt across the room, but unable to resist the temptation of glancing in his direction as she passed through the doorway. Expecting him to have resumed his quest for his coat and hat, she was startled to find him exactly where she had left him, and she met his eye across the distance with a jolt that shook her. Turning quickly away, she hurried from the room and down the steps to where their party waited, thankful to gain some distance from the unsettling man. He took up far too much of her thoughts, and the sooner Nicholas returned and Serena arrived to distract her, the better.

Chapter Eight

WAKING EARLY THE following morning, Elizabeth stretched languorously, turning her head towards the light. A slow smile graced her lips as she realised the day looked set to be fair, and easing herself gently from the bed so as not to disturb her sister, she wrapped a shawl about her shoulders and padded over to the window.

Pulling one of the drapes aside, she peered out into the new day. The sky was the pale watery blue of early morning, hung with soft wisps of cloud that would disperse before long, and so reminiscent of the sky in Hertfordshire that she felt a sudden pang of homesickness.

"What is the hour?"

Elizabeth turned around to see her sister sitting up sleepily, her hair a tousled curtain on her shoulders.

"Forgive me. Did I disturb you?"

Jane smothered a delicate yawn with the back of her hand and shook her head.

"It is early yet." Elizabeth walked over and clambered back onto the bed, pummelling her pillows into shape before leaning back against them. "The rain has gone; it will be pleasant to be able to go out."

Speaking of the previous day's inclement weather, which had rendered them housebound for the afternoon, reminded her of its events: Mr Bingley's visit and the realisation that she had left Mr Darcy's letter behind. The instant that gentleman returned to her consciousness, she was aware of a return of her uneasiness, and Jane leaned forward and placed a hand on her sister's.

"What is it? You look troubled."

Elizabeth attempted a smile as she pushed her hair back over her shoulder. "Not troubled, precisely." She paused. "My mind is disagreeably engaged on a subject that has rarely left it of late."

"Mr Darcy?"

Reluctantly Elizabeth nodded. "You have no idea how relieved I am to have shared the events of last Sunday with you, Jane, for it is easier to bear for being able to talk of it. But in doing so, I had hoped to escape some of the repetitious thoughts that will persist in haunting me so."

"And is it Sunday and what happened then that preys upon your mind? 'Tis understandable, Lizzy, for it was so unexpected – and unpleasant for you both. Or is it something else about the gentleman?"

A sudden image of Mr Darcy's rain-soaked visage as he held her securely in his embrace flashed through Elizabeth's mind, and she shivered. Then, conscious of her sister's eyes upon her, she drew in a deep breath and then let it out on a huff of laughter at the ridiculousness of her foolish thoughts. Shaking her head, she squeezed Jane's hand before once more swinging her legs off the bed and standing up.

"I know not – it is perhaps a little of both."

The memory of last Sunday had unsettled her further, and dropping her shawl onto a chair, she walked over to the window and opened the drapes, fastening them securely, before turning to face her sister again, who sat patiently waiting on the bed.

"I will own that Mr Darcy's proposal does intrude on occasion; but it is not what disturbs me most." She paused. "Would that it had not happened, of course, but wishing for an event undone is futile."

"Then what is it that unsettles you so? That you left his letter behind?"

Elizabeth leaned back against the window sill and folded her arms across her body, hugging herself as if she would give herself some comfort.

"No – it is not entirely that either, though I was disappointed not to have occasion to carry my point last night. Dear Aunt – little did she know what she interrupted."

"I did try my utmost to detain her, but I am not practised in such matters."

"Indeed you are not, but I do appreciate the effort you made initially to distract her!"

Jane looked a little guilty. "I was not entirely prevaricating, Lizzy. I did truly feel in need of some air."

"Of course you did. And I am absolutely certain it had nothing to do with a particular gentleman being outside, either!"

Jane's culpable expression increased, as did the colour in her cheeks, but it was obvious that she not averse to discussing said gentleman.

"Mr Bingley is all that is charming, is he not? He took such solicitous good care of us."

Elizabeth refrained from pointing out that Mr Bingley's attention was almost entirely taken up with Jane and very little, beyond the common courtesies, had been extended to anyone else. The situation was all too pleasing to indulge in such flippancy. Pushing herself away from the sill, she walked over to the dresser and picked up a comb before seating herself in front of the mirror. Conscious that Jane had clambered off the bed and had come to stand behind her, she met her sister's gaze in the mirror.

"Then pray what is it, Lizzy. Tell me."

Elizabeth stared at her reflection for a moment, then sighed. "I struggle to comprehend how Mr Darcy can occupy my mind to such an extent, when prior to Sunday he was a man for whom I had little interest and less time. I admit I do have a desire to let him know about what happened with regard to his letter, and should an opportunity present itself, I will endeavour to do so. But my preoccupation would seem to stem from more than that – it is certain that it predates my awareness of my error yesterday."

Elizabeth began to apply the comb to her tangled locks, but Jane took it from her and undertook herself the restoring of her sister's hair to order as she talked.

"At first, I believe I was engrossed with trying to understand the man. His letter revealed things about him that caused me to rethink my own assessment of him and indeed my own belief in my judgement of character." Elizabeth smiled ruefully and let Jane tug at her hair with the comb for a moment. Then, she added, "You know all this, from our conversation yesterday, and I shall not bore you with it further."

Jane stroked the comb through her sister's hair once more, then placed it on the dresser before walking around to her side so that she could better observe her face.

"And now? What else is it about him that preys upon you?"

Elizabeth turned in her seat and grasped both her sister's hands, squeezing them lightly before dropping them and getting to her feet, conscious of the need to conceal some of her memories and the feelings they engendered from her sister.

"I feel as though Mr Darcy wishes to avoid my society – understandable, of course. I am the woman who misjudged his character and threw the offer of his hand back at him in no uncertain terms." Elizabeth walked over to the bell pull and tugged it, knowing it would soon result in a maid appearing bearing hot water. "Yet here is what I cannot comprehend, which makes me so... confused. I have this sense of almost – disappointment. I feel... I wish it were not so." Elizabeth clutched her midriff as once again her insides gave an unaccountable lurch. "How can this be? Why is it that I would wish him to seek my company, not shun it? It is nonsensical."

Jane shook her head.

"I do not think it is how you see it." Picking up her own comb, Jane started to drag it through her tresses methodically. "I believe that Mr Darcy harbours strong feelings for you yet."

Conscious that her recalcitrant insides had swivelled once more and that colour filled her cheeks, Elizabeth crossed swiftly over to the closets that ranged the far wall, swinging the doors wide and rifling through the dresses that hung there.

"I assure you, Jane, it is the contrary. Mr Darcy is quite over me." Her voice became muffled as she reached further into the cupboard. "His attempts to distance himself from me, both in the gardens and at the recital, are proof of this, should any be required other than the reason of a rejected man wishing to avoid the source of his humiliation."

Emerging finally with what she sought, Elizabeth turned to face her sister, confident that any colour in her cheeks could at least now be credited to the exertion she had just displayed scrabbling about in the closet. She was disconcerted, however, to find her amenable sister quite adamant in her opinion for once. Having finished removing the tangles from her own hair, Jane placed the comb on the dresser and walked over to where Elizabeth stood clutching a gown to her chest.

"Have you not considered that perhaps he does not aim to please himself? I believe he seeks to avoid you for your sake, not his own – to ease your discomfort at being in his presence. After all, you have made it very plain to him that you desire nothing from him and that surely includes his company."

Forced to acknowledge that there may be some sense in this, having previously conceded that Mr Darcy's disposition was far nobler than she had earlier given him credit for, Elizabeth met her sister's eye with grudging acceptance before walking over to lay her gown upon the bed.

"There may be some truth in that – and once again I am culpable. I am judging the man against his character." Elizabeth knew her expression must be somewhat forlorn, as had her words been, for Jane walked over and wrapped her arms about her, giving her a hug before releasing her.

"I do not believe I err in this. Everything implies that his love is deep – just consider what he said to you of the arguments he overcame to declare himself. Though his offer was ill-conceived and ill-rendered, the truth of the matter stands: his love for you outweighed all his reservations. He will not have been able to conquer such a depth of feeling in so few days, no matter the manner of your refusal."

Elizabeth sighed; Jane's words provided little comfort, did she but know it. The confusion over her feelings merely added to her discomfort, and hearing her sister reinforce the depth of Mr Darcy's affection for her stirred something within her that she could not explain.

Turning away, Jane walked over to the closet to select her own gown for the day ahead, but she said over her shoulder almost tremulously, "One does not stop loving just because the object is unattainable – one cannot," and she turned her attention to the garments in front of her.

Feeling all the implication of Jane's words, Elizabeth shivered. Whatever the cause, these sensations and the disturbance of mind they were inflicting must be overcome, and with the utmost haste.

A knock on the door heralded the arrival of a maid bearing a vessel of hot water which she poured into the two bowls on the washstand, and making her way over to one of them, Elizabeth picked up a towel and eyed herself warily in the mirror. There was, of course, that one other thing she could not speak of with Jane, something for her secret thoughts alone and one that haunted her more than any other – her growing consciousness of the man himself and how it felt to be held close against him.

Darcy had been pleased to awaken to a morning that heralded blue skies, and though he had passed a disturbed night, he found himself feeling less weary, and he knew with certainty that it was due to the solace he found in spending time – however brief or interrupted – with Elizabeth. Somehow, she had lessened some of his pain; though he could not account for the how or the why, some of the intensity of his despair was gone.

Futile though he knew it was to indulge in it, there was no denying that he had derived some comfort these four and twenty hours from seeing her again and conversing with her in a way that tempered the awful memories of

Sunday's confrontation. He resolutely refused to think beyond that; there was too wide a gulf between them to ever hope for his former wishes to come to fruition, and her affections being engaged elsewhere was a reinforcement of the futility of any further speculation. He prayed that this would be sufficient to aid his attempts to put the disaster of Kent behind him.

Bingley accosted him the moment he emerged from his rooms, dressed for the outdoors and admitting that he would forego the morning repast. As Darcy accompanied him along the landing and down the stairs, his friend advised him that he was destined for his attorney's office once more. He had matters that needed settling before his return to Hertfordshire and the last thing he wished was to have to return to Town due to unresolved business too soon after taking up the mantle of his estate once more.

Throughout breakfast Darcy focused his attention on his sister, making more effort than was his wont or indeed his habit to make small talk. He could tell from Georgiana's expression that she was not taken in. She clearly understood his intent to discuss no further the events of the previous day, but with her newfound growth of confidence and her avid interest of late in his affairs, he was not convinced of her obeying his silent wishes. It was thus no surprise to him when, their meal completed and only a last cup of tea to be consumed before them on the table, she turned a seemingly innocent eye upon him.

"Well, Brother? Was it – how was it?"

Chapter Nine

DARCY EYED GEORGIANA in silence for a moment. There was little point in prevarication, yet he knew he would make the attempt all the same. He dropped his napkin onto the fine linen tablecloth and picked up his teacup.

"What would you wish to know, Georgie? There is a programme hereabouts – I made sure to bring one home for you."

As expected, a small frown marred her brow, and she shook her head, carefully folding her napkin up. "No, Brother! I refer to the evening – how was the *evening*?"

"Well, much as one would expect: the musicians played their instruments, the soloist sang, the audience listened…"

"Fitz!" She narrowed her gaze at him. "You are deploying the game that Richard is so fond of!"

Darcy could not help but smile at his sister's expression and took a welcome drink from his cup, watching her carefully.

"Please, tell me about it, Brother. I have been awake half the night wondering if you were able to gain some enjoyment from attending, for you seemed so tense when you left the house."

Darcy studied his sister's earnest expression for a moment, then sighed. "The evening was… not how I expected it to be."

"Is that a good thing?"

"I am not certain."

"Well – was it better, or worse, than anticipated?"

"The music was certainly much better."

"Fitz!"

He shook his head. "Forgive me. I know that you seek something I cannot give you – I am prevaricating, because I know not what to think of it."

"Surely you do not still believe Miss Elizabeth Bennet to dislike you?"

Darcy's mind quickly returned to the thoughts that had plagued him during his journey home the night before. Why had Elizabeth taken the trouble to speak to him at the end of the evening? She had indicated that it related to his letter, but had said it was not its content…

"Fitz?"

"There is nothing I can tell you of solace, other than I exchanged some dialogue with the lady quite cordially."

Georgiana frowned at him. "Is that so very out of the ordinary?"

Smiling ruefully, Darcy nodded. "Somewhat. Our conversations have generally been a little fractious."

"And-" his sister hesitated, "and was there nothing else of note?"

Darcy thought for a moment. He knew perfectly well that she meant in relation to his acquaintance with Elizabeth, but as there was little he could offer her, he had no alternative but to alter the direction of the conversation. "I made the acquaintance of Mr Gardiner. He is a fine gentleman."

Just then, the gentle chimes of the carriage clock on the mantel caused a welcome interruption, and seeing Georgiana throw it a quick look, he got to his feet.

"Come, Georgie. Mrs Annesley will be awaiting you, and I must away to my study for a while."

He smiled faintly at her pout as she got reluctantly to her feet and patted her reassuringly on the shoulder as they both walked towards the door.

"No amount of conjecture will provide you with the answers you seek. Go – distract yourself with something far more constructive, and I will see you anon."

Georgiana bit her lip. "Forgive me, Fitz. All I would wish is for you to be happy."

"Of this I am aware. Do not concern yourself over me, my dear. I will be well."

Reaching up to place a kiss on his cheek, Georgiana gave him a quick smile and preceded him out of the door and up the stairs to find her companion.

Once she had disappeared from sight, Darcy continued down the hall to his study, but he found himself unable to take his own advice. For a while he settled behind his desk, attempting to read the day's newspaper, but nothing could interest him. Tossing it aside, he turned his attention to one or two matters of outstanding business, but these were relatively straightforward and easily disposed of and soon he was able to put them aside; the pile of invitations he did not even register, such was his disinterest in them. He stared about the room and then stood up, walking over to the window and gazing thoughtfully out over the garden, bathed now in strong sunlight.

Though he had derived some comfort from seeing Elizabeth again, Darcy could not shake the feeling that he needed to go somewhere out of London. Their coming across each other in Berkeley Square Gardens had been purely a coincidence, but within hours it had led to an evening in company. He could no longer be blind, as he had been, to the likelihood of further meetings, and, likewise, Elizabeth should not have to suffer his continued presence. She must have thought herself to have escaped from Kent and all its associations, and yet here he was, in danger of hounding her every step, especially given Bingley's intentions with regard to her sister.

What should he do? From their conversation, it appeared that Elizabeth's stay in Town was likely to only be of short duration, possibly a matter of weeks, thus all he required was a temporary escape. Pemberley was too far away to attempt such a brief sojourn, and besides, he was needed more in London at this time of year; nor would it be fair upon Georgiana to leave her so soon after returning from Kent. For a fleeting moment, he recalled Bingley's invitation to join him at Netherfield before dismissing it out of hand. If Elizabeth should return home sooner than anticipated, the situation would be worse than ever.

Turning away from the garden, Darcy silently surveyed the room, seeking a distraction for his thoughts, but none came. All he could think of was Elizabeth at the recital – an Elizabeth who had appeared to be carrying an air of diffidence that sat ill upon her. Yet she had not hesitated to make conversation with him, both during the intermission and afterwards... the recollection of Elizabeth's approach at the end of the evening and her attempt to speak to him caused him to frown.

That damned letter; it clearly troubled her. Though he had gained the satisfaction of her now knowing of Wickham's true character, he regretted that he had ever taken such a selfish step as to write it. All he had thought of was to defend himself – he had given little consideration at the time to how it might affect her, and clearly it disturbed her yet.

Muttering an oath under his breath, Darcy forced himself to move, heading back out into the hallway. There were no servants in sight; the house was eerily quiet for the time of day.

Restlessly, he roamed around, pausing to look into the small music room to see if his sister had yet repaired there for her daily practice, but it remained empty. With a sigh, he turned on his heel and headed back down the corridor towards the drawing room, but before he could enter, the front door was opened from outside and Colonel Fitzwilliam stepped into the building.

Welcoming the distraction as much as he did his cousin's safe return, Darcy walked towards him with a smile.

"An early start?"

The Colonel nodded, shrugging his travelling cloak from his shoulders and handing it to the footman who had materialised at his side, along with his hat and gloves.

"I have endured worse ones, Darce, but it is more the hardship upon my stomach that I suffer from than the early rising. There are no good breakfasts to be had between Brighton and Town, it is truly quite shocking."

"Then do you wish for a meal?"

Fitzwilliam shook his head emphatically. "Indeed no. The reason I know there are no good breakfasts to be had is because I sampled not one but two during my journey. Needless to say, I managed to partake of a substantial amount of sustenance, but none of any quality!"

"Then shall I order some tea? Or do you wish to refresh yourself first?"

The Colonel met his cousin's look with an unusually serious eye. "I am not sure tea will be strong enough, but permit me a few moments for a quick wash and brush up, and I will join you in your study; there is something I would impart to you – in private."

It was a little under a quarter of an hour later that the Colonel entered the study, closing the door firmly behind him before turning to face his cousin. Darcy, who had just thrown open the full length windows overlooking the garden so that the warmth of the morning could permeate the room, turned to look at him over his shoulder. A glance at his cousin's grave mien was sufficient to make him turn to face him.

"What is the problem?"

The Colonel grunted and headed for the tray of spirits.

Darcy frowned. "It is not yet eleven. Is the news so dire?"

Pouring himself a measure, the Colonel turned to face his cousin and raised his glass to him before tossing the liquid down his throat. He grimaced at the taste before saying, "It is the lack of news that concerns me."

"You are worrying me."

"I am worrying myself."

Colonel Fitzwilliam turned to refill his glass and pour one for his cousin, and once they were both in possession of a drink, they walked with unspoken agreement out of the open doors onto the terrace and down the steps into the garden. Glancing at the windows behind them, the Colonel nodded his head in the direction of the bottom of the garden and Darcy fell into step behind him, a sense of growing unease intensifying with every step.

Once they had reached the seclusion of an old stone bench nestled against the far garden wall, they sat down side by side and for a few moments savoured their drinks in companionable silence.

Darcy let the liquid burn a trail down his throat, and leaning back against the wall he closed his eyes briefly, welcoming the warmth of the sun upon his face. His cousin was not prone to exaggeration; nor was he generally excitable or indulgent of drama. Something was amiss, and deep within he felt he had a sneaking suspicion of the cause. Opening his eyes again, he sat up.

"What has he done this time?"

The Colonel coughed on his drink and sat up also. Clearing his throat, he turned to eye Darcy.

"So you comprehend who the deviant is that drew me to Brighton." The words were matter of fact. "By all accounts, he left his regiment under cover of darkness on Monday night. He must have got wind of what was afoot, for he was under covert investigation and likely to have been taken into custody within four and twenty hours – hence my original summons to Whitehall."

Darcy blew out a breath. "So – tell me. Other than desert his post, what *has* he done?"

The Colonel got to his feet and paced to and fro for a moment, before casting a sidelong glance at his cousin. "Apart from the usual: the massive debts unpaid, the gaming – he is up to his neck in it – there is the matter of some indelicacy concerning a fellow officer's daughter, who is but fourteen."

"Damn the man. What is his predilection with innocent young girls? He is a danger to society and should be permanently confined."

"Had I arrived before he could abscond, that is precisely where he would be, secured by a weighty padlock. However, that is the question. Where is the fiend now? Where has he flown and in whose company would he seek protection?"

"To be certain, his best chance of concealment will be in Town, will it not?" Darcy paled as he spoke these words. "You do not think that he will attempt to seek out Georgiana?"

The Colonel shook his head reassuringly. "Put yourself at ease, Darce. Even Wickham has sufficient sense to realise that he has burned his bridges there. Had he not got the memory of your last meeting to remind him, he is not so foolish as to imagine that Georgiana could be taken in by him twice. That is the only solace we have – once bitten by the snake, one does not return for a second painful encounter, which is all the protection his victims have."

"But what is being done? He cannot be left free to stalk the innocent."

The Colonel shrugged his shoulders. "There is little I can do at present. My hands are tied by my profession; I am not instructed to hunt him down, there are others on that path even as we speak. I was called in to oversee his arrest, and once it was known he was gone, my presence was merely required to record the incident and report back to my commanding officer on the situation."

"Would that I had taken some action over him before now. It is clear that no respectable group of people is safe from him. What damage might he next inflict, damn him?"

Colonel Fitzwilliam shrugged again, and having drained his glass indicated that they head back towards the house.

"One thing we can be certain of – he is not stupid enough to return to anywhere he has been before. His reputation always follows him; once he has departed a neighbourhood, his vices become clear. Indeed, his current predicament has only resulted in his flight because they came to light so precipitously."

Darcy followed his cousin down the garden mulling over his words, hoping that it was right to trust in them. He could not help but recall the last place Wickham had been before heading to Brighton.

Chapter Ten

As THE SOUND OF church bells tolling the hour resonated along Gracechurch Street, echoed softly by the drawing room clock, Elizabeth glanced up from the page she had been endeavouring to read. Several attempts had failed and, conceding defeat, she replaced the marker and put her book aside. Jane remained intent upon her embroidery, settled into the window seat so as to capture the best light, and looking over at her sister, Elizabeth sighed. The sunshine beckoned and she longed for the afternoon's delight: a picnic in Southwark Park. Mr Gardiner had promised to end his week early so that the four of them might enjoy several hours exploring the maze and the arboretum before partaking of the victuals being prepared even now by the cook.

Getting to her feet, Elizabeth headed for the door, and when her sister looked up from her work gave her a smile. "I am just going to speak to Aunt." Jane nodded and returned her attention to her stitching, and Elizabeth gently closed the door behind her and headed down the hall to her aunt's sitting room.

Poking her head around the door, she was unsurprised to see Mrs Gardiner bent over her writing desk, studying what appeared to be a ledger of accounts. She looked up as her niece peered into the room, however, a warm smile spreading across her features.

"Do you need me, Lizzy?"

Elizabeth shook her head reluctantly. "No, Aunt. Forgive the intrusion. I was merely —" She sighed, but before she could continue, Mrs Gardiner beckoned her into the room.

"You are restless, are you not?" and at her niece's nod, she smiled understandingly. "At home you would long have been outdoors, I do not doubt. But come — tarry a while whilst I complete my calculations. I shall enjoy the company."

Elizabeth walked over to where her aunt sat. "I do not disturb you?"

"The interruption is not unwelcome, my dear. I derive little enjoyment from the household accounts and yet it is not often that I am presented with a distraction to allow me to put them aside. Let me just finish this page, and I shall be done for today."

Elizabeth turned to survey the small sitting room. There were several paintings on the walls that she had been familiar with ever since she was a young child. Many were landscapes of varying country, a few held buildings or water features, and it was quite apparent that they were done by the same hand as the painting hanging above the hearth in the chamber upstairs.

She walked over and studied one of them for a while: a stark landscape of sharp rocks and crags. The hand that had captured them, whilst clearly no master, was an accomplished one, and as her eyes roamed over the view, Elizabeth could almost feel the breeze and imagine the silence. The scenery, as it was in the other paintings around the room, was rugged and masterful, quite unlike any of the southern counties with which Elizabeth was familiar, and she determined to ask her aunt about it.

Turning slowly around, her eye was caught by the long table holding the array of miniatures, and Elizabeth smiled as she walked over to observe them, her eye immediately caught by the more recent ones of herself, Jane, Serena and Nicholas, taken two summers ago at Sutton Coker. She traced a finger over the beloved faces before her, recalling the occasion with pleasure, trying to determine if they had altered much since they were taken.

"There. I am done." Mrs Gardiner had come to stand beside her. "Why, that is most singular!"

Elizabeth glanced at her aunt, whose gaze was fixed upon the miniatures. Shaking her head, Mrs Gardiner laughed and walked over to the cupboards that framed the chimney breast on the opposite wall, her accounts book tucked under her arm.

"What is singular, Aunt?"

Mrs Gardiner unfastened the lower door and placed the book inside before turning to face her niece with a smile. "I looked over those miniatures only the other day, and I could have sworn that one of them was missing – yet, now I see it quite clearly!"

"Perhaps one of the maids had moved them around when dusting."

"Perhaps. But no matter, it is most definitely there now. Well, Lizzy, what can we do to amuse you until your uncle returns?"

"Will you tell me a little something about these paintings?" Elizabeth waved her hand around the room, for there were several on the walls of varying sizes. "I can see they are by the same hand, but I cannot make out the signature." Elizabeth laughed ruefully. "I confess that they are as familiar to me as those at Longbourn, yet I have shown a shameful lack of curiosity about them over the years!"

Mrs Gardiner accompanied her over to the fireplace where the largest painting hung. "It is not your fault, Lizzy, if paintings hold little interest for you. One either has a natural love and interest in something or one does not, and to make pretence of it is not an admirable trait."

"I must own that I am not necessarily an avid admirer of portraits. I find them stiff, so unlike life. But these landscapes have been captured by a skilful hand – one can almost see the grasses moving and hear the birdsong."

"I am glad that you like them. My mother was the artist, and she was no painter of portraits." Mrs Gardiner laughed and glanced over at her miniature collection. "And nor is her daughter, it would seem, though I do profess to an interest in the occupation that she did not."

"I believe your talent improved along with the behaviour of the models! We hardly gave you fair chance in our early days."

"Aye, that is true." Mrs Gardiner turned her attention back to the painting that hung above the fireplace. "This particular scene is a favourite of mine. It is the view towards Lambton from our garden at Seavington Place."

Following her conversation with Mr Darcy on the prior evening, Elizabeth studied the painting with renewed interest, conscious as she now was that her aunt's former home was so close to Pemberley.

"I like it. I like it very well. That church spire and a hint of rooftops down in the valley – it looks a pretty place to have grown up, Aunt."

"Indeed it was. I missed it dreadfully when we first moved away. Now that Papa is restored to his home, I look forward very much to visiting him. I hope that I might still find some acquaintance in the area."

"And is this not similar to the one in our chamber? I detect some resemblance, I am certain." Elizabeth turned and indicated the one she had been studying when her aunt had joined her.

Mrs Gardener pursed her lips in thought for a moment. "I believe that is one of a pair, for we have a similar one in ours. Mama was particularly fond of an outbreak of rocks known locally as the Edge. It was, as I recall her telling me, devilishly hard to scale with a drawing pad and pens, but she would sit on the top there and sketch away to her heart's content, and then come home and turn her pencil drawings into paintings."

They both stared at the vista for a moment longer as Elizabeth acknowledged the irony of being entranced, unbeknownst to herself, by the scenery of Derbyshire, a county with which she had no familiarity at all; then, Mrs Gardiner clapped her hands together and exclaimed, "I almost forgot!"

She hurried over to the dresser on the far wall and tugged at something that rested against the wall behind it, retrieving a canvas covered parcel that she quickly unwrapped before holding it up for Elizabeth to see. The picture was of smaller proportions than those they had been discussing, but it had charm nonetheless. It showed an area of striking, park-like gardens, with a water cascade tumbling down the hillside, a decided contrast to the untamed beauty of the other landscapes. It was so skilfully rendered that Elizabeth felt she would be able to feel the coolness of the water should she touch it.

"How lovely. Why is it not on display?"

"It has only recently arrived. My father sent it down from Lambton; he said that he came across it when they were renovating some of the rooms and thought that I might like to have it for my collection. Mama painted it when they were first married. I thought you might find it of interest, for it is but a small part of the grounds at Pemberley."

Elizabeth's eyes widened and she studied the picture with awakened interest.

"How was your mother able to capture such a likeness?"

"Living but five miles away, my parents used to frequent the park whenever there was the opportunity, so beautifully situated as the grounds are. My mother took many a likeness there, though this is the only one that I possess."

"It is quite beautiful; and the fall of water is very unusual. Have you seen it yourself, Aunt? The original?"

Mrs Gardiner nodded and placed the painting on a nearby table.

"Oh, yes. When I was but a young girl, we went on more than one occasion for a walk. I have seen it in every season, though you will appreciate that it was some years past, and at the time the late Mr Darcy was the master, not the gentleman that you are acquainted with."

Unwilling to allow her thoughts to stray in that particular direction, Elizabeth moved around the room, studying the familiar landscapes that hung on the walls with renewed interest.

"I have travelled so little, Aunt. The southern counties are all that I am familiar with outside of books. This scenery is so dramatic – there is something untamed about it that appeals to me."

Mrs Gardiner turned to look at her niece with a fond smile and then ushered her towards the door. "Have you forgotten that you are to accompany us on our travels to the Lakes in the late summer? I am sure you will find them very much to your liking. Indeed, we may well combine a trip to Lambton with that journey and make some stay with my father before heading further north. I am certain you would find Derbyshire fascinating."

An almost instantaneous agreement was upon Elizabeth's lips, but she held it back and gave her aunt a smile instead as they walked out into the hall, intent upon re-joining Jane in the drawing room. She could only hope, should such a plan come to fruition, that by the end of the summer she would have consigned all thoughts of a certain gentlemen to oblivion. If the mere word Derbyshire was sufficient to restore his presence fully to her consciousness, how she would fare visiting his home county she could not imagine.

Having returned to the study from their brief sojourn in the garden, Darcy threw himself into the high-backed chair behind the desk whilst the Colonel walked over to the side table and deposited the empty glasses next to the decanter. A quick glance at the clock confirmed the progression of the morning, and before Darcy could prevent it all concern over Wickham vanished as his thoughts turned to Elizabeth and what she might be doing. To be certain, the weather being so much fairer than the day before, the likelihood was that her inclination would be for a walk, but whether she might be permitted to indulge it, he knew not. Idly, he picked up a pen from the blotter and rolled it between his fingers, his mind drifting.

"Now that we have wasted precious time discussing a certain worthless cad, perhaps we can turn to something more pertinent."

Darcy looked up at his cousin, a brow raised in question.

The Colonel rolled his eyes and grunted. "It will serve you no purpose, Darcy."

"What will?"

"The air of evasion, disinterest, bewilderment – call it what you will."

"I do not understand you, Cousin."

With another grunt, the Colonel dropped into the chair opposite the desk and eyed Darcy with a smirk.

"Do you not have something you might wish to share with me?"

Darcy's gaze narrowed as he met Fitzwilliam's eye, and he reached forward slowly and placed the pen in the pot that held several others. He was not ignorant of his cousin's purpose, but he was intrigued as to how he might have received word of any of Darcy's movements during his absence so soon upon his return.

"Perhaps you could inform me as to what it is I wish to share."

"Hmmm – nice manoeuvre, but you forget that I am the strategist of the family. You have to be up early to catch me out. Besides which, I believe part of your reluctance to speak is due to the fact that I was right and you were wrong."

Darcy sighed and leaned back in his chair. "Then let us get the gloating over and done with. Enlighten me as to what triumph you have scored this time."

With a satisfied smile, the Colonel sat forward, resting his elbows on his knees, keeping a keen eye on his cousin's face.

"The very thing you said would not happen has taken place. You have seen Miss Elizabeth Bennet."

Chapter Eleven

THE RECOLLECTION OF THE moment when Elizabeth had spoken his name brought Darcy slowly upright in his chair, but he attempted nonchalance.

"And how did you manage to discover that?"

"I am not at liberty to reveal my sources, old man. Sorry."

Darcy shook his head. "Oh no, you do not fool me. You have seen Georgiana."

"Damn, Darce, you do not play the game well. This could have run for at least another ten minutes!"

"Well?"

"Well, what?"

Darcy blew out a frustrated breath. "For pity's sake. Just tell me what you know."

The Colonel got to his feet and walked over to the fireplace, then turned to face his cousin.

"You may rest easy; I know very little, and it was not by design. Georgiana happened to leave her room as I headed upstairs earlier. We had barely exchanged greetings before she announced that she had made some new acquaintances the day before."

Conscious of his cousin's gaze, Darcy shifted uneasily in his seat.

"So – tell me. Now that you have met her in Town, and she has made the acquaintance of your sister, how do you plan to proceed?"

Having expended far too much time and energy torn between anticipating further encounters with Elizabeth and finding a way to ensure she did not have to endure his presence again, Darcy had no answer to this. He could not see that there was any way forward by design; it seemed the Fates would do with him as they chose.

"Do not," forestalled the Colonel as Darcy opened his mouth to respond, "tell me that there is no plan. You have met her once by coincidence and must own to the strong likelihood of a recurrence."

Darcy frowned; it seemed that Georgiana had not completely revealed yesterday's events and that Fitzwilliam remained ignorant of his attendance at the recital. Thankfully, his cousin continued without waiting for a response.

"Should another encounter take place, you will have the perfect opportunity to present yourself in a better light. Even if you remain stubbornly convinced there is no merit in attempting to win her, surely you would gain some solace from knowing that you had altered her opinion of you?"

Darcy could not deny the sense of his cousin's words, much as he wished to negate all likelihood of continuing the acquaintance; yet, there were underlying factors of which Fitzwilliam was ignorant. Elizabeth had approached him, not once but twice. His cousin would doubtless construe this as a positive indication of her opinion of him. What he did not know was what Darcy was privy to: she endeavoured to speak to him of his letter, certainly her sole motivation for essaying any contact with him... his train of thought stalled suddenly as he was revisited by that which had haunted him throughout his restless night. What purpose was there in even considering the direction of his acquaintance with Elizabeth, when she and Harington had in all likelihood come to an understanding?

Weary of such speculation, Darcy got to his feet and joined his cousin by the hearth.

"I have no plan, Fitzwilliam. I cannot see any profit from ordering intentions that could only lead to disillusionment on the one hand, and irritation on the other." He hesitated. "I have been considering removing myself from Town on a temporary basis – until the ladies return home to Hertfordshire, that is."

The Colonel frowned on hearing these words, but before they could take their discussion further, there was a knock on the study door and on Darcy's response, Pagett entered the room, bowing solemnly before informing them that Miss Bingley had arrived to visit Miss Darcy and that Miss Darcy had requested that Mr Darcy be advised of the situation.

The Colonel snorted as Pagett backed himself out of the door and closed it reverently behind him. "A cry for help if ever I heard one. Come, Darce, let us go to the rescue."

Somewhat relieved at the interruption, Darcy could not help but smile at his cousin's gloomy expression, and followed him out of the room intent upon easing his sister's discomfort.

Almost an hour later, stirring restlessly in his chair, Darcy had failed miserably in his attempt to shut out the voice of their visitor. Bingley had returned from his appointment within minutes of them joining the ladies, but his recent lack of sleep seemed to have caught up on him. He found the heaviness in his eyelids difficult to combat, and the drone of Caroline Bingley's voice looked set to send him into oblivion.

It was therefore with a sudden sparking of interest that Darcy heard a name mentioned that roused him from his drowsiness and brought his attention immediately to the conversation now taking place between Bingley and his sister.

"The Haringtons? Pah! They have more money than sense!"

Bingley shook his head. "They cannot be too lacking in sense, or they would not have amassed such a fortune!"

"But they socialise outside the *ton* – and they dine with all and sundry."

Finding his attention now well caught, Darcy sat up straighter in his chair. Bingley, who had been seated opposite his sister, had at some point got to his feet and now stood in front of her.

"Do not exaggerate, Caroline. You imply they have neither taste nor discretion, yet they are guilty of nothing more than choosing their acquaintance on personal merit over the size of their pocket book."

Caroline sniffed and turned her shoulder to him, but she continued to address the room at large.

"They mingle with far too many people from a society lower than theirs. They have any number of acquaintances amongst people of *business*. It undermines their position, and must thus have a detrimental effect upon those who associate with them by return."

Bingley laughed, though Darcy could detect no humour in his face. "Nonsensical! If you wish to hold that opinion, then please at least do me the favour of keeping it to yourself. The Haringtons are old acquaintances of mine; James was a good friend to me at university, and I will not have you make derogatory remarks about them in my company."

Caroline gave her brother a conciliatory smile as he walked away and resumed his seat. "Now, Charles. Do not take offence. I would not have spoken of them had you not raised the name. It is not as if you were not cognisant of my opinion; but you must own they eschew all the protocols of their position. Why, they do not even keep a house in Town!"

"And what of it? Mrs Harington has always had a predilection for Bath, and that is where their 'town' seat is and always has been. If they come to London at all, they are perfectly content with the comforts of *Grillons*. Besides, you were sufficiently keen on the connection once; their wealth and status impressed you greatly when I first made Harington's acquaintance."

"That was before I learned of their tendency to fraternise with those of lower rank, after which I could see no value in the connection." She turned her eye on Darcy suddenly, who started and tried to assume an expression of disinterest. "The Haringtons would do well to emulate the Darcys."

Bingley laughed once more. "Well, I can vouchsafe for a similarity in many ways."

Darcy frowned, unsure of his friend's meaning, but catching his cousin's eye and seeing his enjoyment of the sibling exchange, he remained silent and let them continue. Georgiana, in the meantime, gazed from Bingley to Caroline with what appeared to be wary fascination.

Caroline began to protest, only to be forestalled by her brother.

"The Haringtons' wealth and their properties and land are of equal standing to that of my friend, as is their position in society in terms of the age of the family and its connections."

"But there the similarity ends! Do not be so tiresome, Charles, in your attempts to persuade me otherwise. Mr Darcy's father did not marry a nobody of little fortune; and neither Mr Darcy, nor his predecessors, would deign to socialise with those who are not their equal. He will not take men of business to his dining table, nor will he welcome tradesmen to his family seat." Caroline turned her eye upon her subject. "You are entirely too discerning, Sir, and indeed have the breeding and good sense to know your position and to do your duty to it." With these final words, she inclined her head regally in Darcy's direction and then sat back in her seat with a complacent smile.

The tone of conviction and indeed pride with which Caroline Bingley pronounced these final words dropped into a silence of profound proportions. Bingley was quite clearly at a loss of how to curb his sister's tongue, Georgiana appeared to be struggling to fully comprehend her meaning, Colonel Fitzwilliam eyed Darcy with blatant amusement at her tirade and its implications and the man himself, at whom it was all aimed, gazed from one to other of the room's occupants as if seeking some form of divine intervention.

In all honesty, Darcy had to own to feeling chastened, striving to reconcile himself to the fact that she was far too close to the mark. He had indeed been raised to believe in his superiority: of fortune, family name and rank. Had he not denigrated the Bennets, dismissing them and all their local society as being beneath him? Had he not scorned their relations in trade, yet now been forced to accede that his judgement was at fault? Before his consciousness could travel any further down this path, he realised that his sister had risen to her feet to cross the room, and he gave her an encouraging smile.

"Brother?" She began, "I would very much like to pay a call this morning."

Darcy's eyes narrowed. "Where would you wish to go?"

"I would like to call upon… upon Mrs Gardiner and her nieces."

This affirmation caused a momentary confusion for Darcy's conflicted feelings as he fought the desire to be in Elizabeth's company, cognisant as he was of his intention to do right by her and stay away. He was soon distracted, however, by the appearance on Caroline Bingley's face of a puzzled frown as she looked from her brother to Darcy, before fixing her gaze upon Georgiana. "But surely you are not acquainted with such people?"

Bingley threw Darcy a quick glance, but his hesitation was almost imperceptible and when he spoke he did so in a firm manner. "We had the good fortune to run into Mrs Gardiner and her nieces yesterday in Berkeley Square, Caroline, and later we had the even greater fortune to accompany them all to a recital."

Darcy winced and looked warily at his cousin, awaiting his reaction to this piece of information.

"But Sir, you cannot permit Miss Darcy to call at an address in *Cheapside*! It will not do!"

Darcy turned back to Caroline Bingley. "Will not do for whom? I believe your brother has managed to visit there and emerge unscathed, as have you. Did you not pay a call there yourself?"

"I must own, reluctantly, that I did, but I shall not do myself the disservice of repeating the offence, and I cannot condone your permitting Georgiana to go."

Unable to muster a polite response to this, Darcy got to his feet and walked over to the window.

"Fitz?"

Turning, he looked down at Georgiana, who had come to his side and whose countenance once more expressed that determination countered with anxiety that she had been deploying so effectively of late. Yet before he was forced to make a decision that on the one hand satisfied his sister's wishes but on the other would no doubt be the opposite of that desired by Elizabeth, Bingley spoke.

"If you wish to call, Miss Darcy, I shall be delighted to accompany you. What say you, Darcy? Shall you sanction the visit – or will you do better than that and join us?"

Darcy looked down at Georgiana. "Fitz, please? It is very kind of Mr Bingley to offer to accompany me, but I would so value your company. I am not yet proficient in paying calls alone, and though I found Mrs Gardiner and both her nieces charming, my apprehension will be less if you are with me."

He held his sister's gaze for a moment, mindful of the unspoken plea in her eyes. The temptation was a sore trial, but the sudden recollection of Elizabeth's attempt to speak to him regarding his letter was the incentive required to enable him to come to a decision that he hoped would suit all concerned.

"Then let us go," he said firmly. "Miss Bingley, you will excuse us, I am sure."

It seemed to take a moment for Caroline Bingley to realise the portent of Darcy's words, but she got rapidly to her feet as a concerted effort was made to vacate the room and seek outdoor clothes. Georgiana, in her haste, was the first to escape, but the others were not so fortunate.

"But – but Mr Darcy! Surely you do not intend..."

"*Caroline!*" Bingley turned on his heel and glared at his sister. "You have made it abundantly clear that you have no desire to revisit the neighbourhood. I will escort you to your carriage," and when she hesitated, pursing her mouth as if another objection was about to burst forth, he added loudly, "Come!" and took her arm and ushered her from the room.

Hearing a chuckle from behind him, Darcy turned around, still somewhat dazed by the pattern of the last few minutes of his morning. His cousin grinned and gave him a prod in the back, encouraging him towards the drawing room door.

"Mind if I tag along too, Darce? It would be ill-mannered of me not to call upon Miss Elizabeth Bennet as you are making the journey, and I would like to meet her relatives. Besides, you have told me nothing of this recital yet, and I am all ears."

Darcy preceded him out into the hall. "And thus you shall remain, Cousin. I refuse to discuss anything of the sort in front of Bingley; nor do I wish to debate the matter further with Georgiana."

A look of cunning, unobserved by Darcy, crossed the Colonel's face as they made their way towards the stairs, and he said quietly, "Aha. So she has attempted to drag from you the events of the evening. Do not think you can thwart *me* as easily, Darce."

Darcy threw his cousin a silencing look as Bingley fetched up beside them, having just closed the door on Caroline Bingley's retreating back.

"My apologies, gentlemen. My sister oversteps the mark at times."

Darcy patted his friend on the shoulder as they turned to mount the staircase in search of their outdoor clothes. "Think nothing of it, Bingley. We have a relative of our own who enjoys nothing more than to express her opinion, regardless of whether it is to the taste of her audience."

He turned his head, expecting the Colonel to be in full agreement with him, only to find that he remained at the bottom of the stairs.

"Fitzwilliam? Do you still wish to join us?"

"I shall be with you directly." He waved them on with his arm. "I am just going to send a servant to bring the carriage about," and he turned on his heel and walked away down the hall.

Chapter Twelve

SOME FIFTEEN MINUTES LATER, Darcy eyed his cousin resignedly as he mounted his horse. An excited Georgiana had been settled into a small phaeton, the hood adjusted so that it sheltered her from the sun, and Bingley had happily taken the reins. As the carriage moved off along the street, the Colonel threw Darcy a smug look, guiding his mount so that it fell into step beside him.

"Nicely manoeuvred, Cousin."

The Colonel nodded. "I like to think so. Not only have I pleased my young cousin, who is delighted at having the opportunity to ride in the new conveyance on such a lovely day, but now we have the solitude of a four-mile journey to ourselves so that we may consider our plans."

"I am curious – how did you encourage Bingley to take the seat?"

"Ah, yet another piece of inspiration: I suggested that he might be the best guide, being the only one of us who has yet ventured there!"

Darcy shook his head. "I endeavour to encourage him to control his own actions, yet you steer him to suit your purpose."

The Colonel snorted. "I would not concern yourself. I do not think he has regressed; he merely saw the wisdom of being guide, having travelled that way before. Besides, he is in fine spirits, is he not? The way he strove to handle his sister – I did not know he had such firmness inside his genial frame!"

Darcy was silent for a moment as they entered the busier domain of Berkeley Square. He knew his cousin's purpose was to continue the discussion that had been interrupted, and he felt the time opportune to alert him to certain pertinent facts, the hope being that it would silence him on the topic of plans henceforth.

"I suspect his defence of the Harington family stems from more than the length of the acquaintance. I believe he expects to become kin; his sister's attitude towards them will be as damaging to him as her behaviour towards the Bennets if she is permitted licence to continue as she is – perhaps more so."

The Colonel threw him a puzzled glance. "Kin? I thought Bingley enamoured of Miss Bennet. Is there a Harington sister too, who has taken his fancy?"

"No – there is no sister, as far as I am aware, and Bingley is as committed to Jane Bennet as any man can be who has not yet declared himself."

"Then what is your meaning?"

"Miss Elizabeth Bennet. This Harington – he and she seem destined for one another."

Darcy felt the ache in his breast tighten as he uttered these words but he was determined to make the situation clear to his cousin.

The Colonel slapped his forehead. "That is it!"

"I beg your pardon?"

"That name – a fair prospect. The lady was called into question over shortening her stay in Kent, and Harington was mentioned. Our aunt pressed her quite soundly on the matter before drawing the conclusion that he would be an excellent match for her." The Colonel grunted. "I must own, Miss Bennet bore her onslaught as well as you might imagine; yet I had no notion that there was some truth in it." He peered over at Darcy intently as they rode. "Is there, and if there is, how is it that you know this on so short a re-acquaintance? When last we spoke – which was barely eight and forty hours ago – you believed her enamoured of Wickham."

"Bingley." The Colonel threw Darcy a questioning look, and he shrugged, attempting to ignore the weight in his chest as he absorbed his cousin's words. "He implied even after that first evening at Gracechurch Street that there was something – a particular bond – between Harington and Miss Elizabeth Bennet. And this was reinforced by something that happened yesterday."

Silence reigned for a moment as they navigated their way through the congestion of a junction, but as they set off at a reasonable pace along Piccadilly, Darcy, knowing full well that his cousin would not let the matter rest there, continued his explanation.

"To cut a long story short, Harington and Miss Elizabeth Bennet's acquaintance stems from childhood, and in their youth they used to regularly correspond – until they were caught out. Bingley has every reason to believe, from something that took place yesterday, that they are exchanging letters even now – you know what that must mean."

The Colonel whistled. "I am sorry, Cousin; more sorry than I can say. So though she championed Wickham, she was not fool enough to fall for him. Well done, Miss Elizabeth Bennet. For that I am relieved – are you not?"

"Indeed, it is a mercy to be thankful for."

"I suppose there is no chance this Harington will turn out a villainous character that you could likewise warn her against? You know – sort of like a hero, protecting her honour?"

"Do not be fatuous, Fitzwilliam."

Darcy urged his horse forward in an attempt to draw nearer to the back of the phaeton carrying his sister. He had no desire to further a discussion about Harington and his closeness to Elizabeth. His cousin, however, kept pace with him.

"So – Miss Bingley would have it that the Darcys are the epitome of superior breeding, to be emulated by all of similar rank."

"The woman is deluded."

"She was not that far from the mark, Darce. You have had a tendency to do that."

"I know. I am haunted daily by facets of my character that I have long upheld as admirable but now see entirely differently, and this is all down to one woman."

The Colonel grunted. "She is a remarkable one, to have you so altered."

"That is of little comfort in the circumstances."

"No – I am sure it is not."

Darcy threw his cousin a quick glance.

"I cannot believe I have been so blinkered. Mr and Mrs Gardiner are most genial. Making their acquaintance has been both a pleasure and humbling. They are refined, intelligent and display manners that far exceed those of many of our acquaintance."

"I look forward to meeting them. Now – how is it that you attended a recital?"

For a moment, Darcy said nothing as his thoughts returned swiftly to the previous evening. Then, he signed. "I went under duress."

"That I can believe! Do you not always attend social events under duress?"

"Perhaps. On this occasion, however, I was determined to stay away for Miss Elizabeth Bennet's sake."

"Yet you went along..."

Darcy shrugged his shoulders, glancing over at his cousin again before looking away. "Bingley. He forced my hand. He would not go if I did not."

"Ah! And having been forced, how was it?"

Reflecting on his earlier response to Georgiana on the very same subject, Darcy shook his head, but knew his prevarication would hold little sway. His instinctive desire to put an end to this questioning was nonetheless assisted by their arrival on Haymarket which they needed to negotiate before heading east along the Strand, and thankfully, the subsequent congestion and its associated noise and distraction, combined with the need to concentrate upon keeping their mounts under control, left no time for further conversation.

The announcement of their callers caused no little surprise to the three occupants of the Gardiners' drawing room.

Getting hastily to her feet, Elizabeth was torn between astonishment that Mr Darcy had actually called in Gracechurch Street, along with his sister, and a sudden recurrence of her trepidation.

Before she could dwell upon which feeling was uppermost, the visitors were in the room, and, formal acknowledgements having been made, her aunt moved forward to greet them as Elizabeth exchanged a warm smile with the Colonel. He accepted the introduction to Mrs Gardiner in his usual manner before walking briskly across the room to bow formally to her.

"Colonel Fitzwilliam! It is good to see you."

"I echo your sentiments, Madam. I trust you journeyed safely?"

"As you see, Sir!" Conscious that he had glanced towards her sister who stood by her side, Elizabeth recalled her manners.

"Forgive me – Jane, as I have told you, Colonel Fitzwilliam is cousin to Mr and Miss Darcy. Jane is my eldest sister."

The Colonel performed another formal bow. "It is a pleasure to make your acquaintance at last, Miss Bennet."

"At last, Colonel?" Jane looked somewhat puzzled.

"Your reputation precedes you." He smiled at her, casting a fleeting glance in the direction of Bingley, who excused himself from Mrs Gardiner and made his way over to them.

Jane blushed and seemed unable to find a response to this, but as Elizabeth laughed and the Colonel's expression broke into a warm smile, she smiled too, albeit a little self-consciously. It was with clear relief that she turned her attention to Bingley as he greeted her, and as he led her away to a nearby seat, Elizabeth turned her attention back to her companion.

"I trust you also travelled safely, Colonel? I understand from your cousin that you have been away since your return to Town?"

"Indeed I have. My time is not my own to command, unfortunately. Yet I am pleased to be once more sequestered with Darcy and as you can see, I am keen to enjoy what leisure there is whilst I may partake of it."

"Then please, Colonel, take a seat and let me fetch you some tea."

He nodded and took himself off to be seated next to Mrs Gardiner, and Elizabeth walked over to the table holding the tea urn. She had barely scooped several portions of fine tea leaves into the silver pot, however, when she became aware of someone's tentative approach to her side, and glancing up she gave Georgiana Darcy a warm smile.

"You do us great honour, Miss Darcy, in calling upon us."

Taking a further step so that she now stood next to Elizabeth at the table, Georgiana gave a hesitant smile in return.

"I trust it is no intrusion, Miss Elizabeth. I will own the practice of making calls sits ill upon me. I always feel it to be an imposition."

Elizabeth smiled again as she turned the tap on the urn to add hot water to the teapot. "I am sure no one would ever feel your company to be so."

"You are too kind."

With a laugh, Elizabeth shook her head and set some cups upon their saucers before glancing at the young lady at her side.

"Sadly, I am not. Kindness is something you would be wise to anticipate from my sister; I am far more likely to be nothing but honest, and I fear that, unlike within Jane, the two are seldom married!"

Seeing that Georgiana looked somewhat uncomfortable, Elizabeth patted her gently on the arm.

"Pray, give what I say no mind, Miss Darcy. You will discover that I am fond of expressing my opinion; it does not mean what I spout forth is of any value."

She turned her attention to pouring tea for the company and encouraged Georgiana to assist her in delivering them by bringing the sugar bowl and milk jug along, and once everyone was suitably served, she led her companion over to two button-backed chairs near the window, placing their own cups on a small drum table between them. Conscious that Mr Darcy, who sat on the other side of her aunt to his cousin, was in her line of vision, she moved her seat slightly, that she might keep her attention on his sister instead.

"Do you enjoy being in Town, Miss Darcy?"

Elizabeth picked up her cup as Georgiana settled herself onto her seat and took a sip of her tea.

"I must own that I prefer the country, but I am happiest wherever my brother is. I only truly feel at home, be it in Derbyshire or London, when he is with me also."

Touched by the sentiment, and not blind to the testament of proof it gave to the affection between Mr Darcy and his sister – something she would have ill afforded him credit for not so long ago – Elizabeth sighed. "Then you must miss him very much when he is away."

"Indeed, I do, though I do have a companion – yet she is no substitute for Fitzwilliam."

Elizabeth laughed gently. "No – I can imagine that she is not." She studied the young lady before her for a moment, then added, "I begin to envy you, Miss Darcy, and envy is not generally in my nature!"

Georgiana leaned forward. "You do? Might I ask in what respect?"

"It is quite simple; I have four sisters, but no brother."

"But when they marry, you will gain so many!"

"Indeed I will!"

They shared a quiet laugh over this notion as they drank their tea, Elizabeth conscious that her amusement stemmed more from the thought of what type of husbands her younger sisters might bring to the table as brothers. It was not something she felt she could share with her young companion on such slight acquaintance.

Georgiana sighed. "I should so dearly have loved to have a sister."

Conscious that she might well have been such, Elizabeth could not forestall a blush from staining her cheeks, and glancing up the colour deepened as she noted Mr Darcy intently watching their interaction from across the room. She swallowed quickly, returning her attention to Georgiana.

"You are more than welcome to share any of mine," she paused, "Save Jane, whom I must reserve selfishly for myself."

Georgiana looked somewhat taken aback, and Elizabeth laughed.

"Oh Miss Darcy, I speak in jest. Here," she leaned forward and gently removed Georgiana's empty cup and saucer from her grasp. "Let me refresh your cup."

Crossing to the side table, Elizabeth looked anxiously at the clock before glancing in Mr Darcy's direction once more, where he now sat in quiet conversation with her aunt. He had not spoken a word to her since his arrival. Unsurprised though she was by this circumstance, Elizabeth remained determined to speak to him – whether he desired the contact or not. Her only dilemma was how to affect such an opportunity, but here she was aided, unbeknownst to him, by Bingley.

"Mrs Gardiner," the gentleman had risen to his feet. "It is a fine day. I wonder – would it be a presumption to request that we all take a stroll? I believe I noticed a small park as the carriage turned into Gracechurch Street."

Unable to suppress a smile at this attempt to extend his time in Jane's company, Elizabeth lowered her gaze to the tea urn to hide her amusement. The so-called park was merely a triangle of grass and shrubs with two paths dissecting it. A walk around it would take all of ten minutes for even the slowest of gaits.

"You are most welcome, Sir, to explore what greenery the district offers, and I can only apologise for its scarcity. However, you will have to excuse me, as I have preparations to oversee for this afternoon."

Chapter Thirteen

THE DECISION MADE, Elizabeth turned her back on the tea things, and within a matter of minutes everyone was suitably attired in their outdoor garments. Elizabeth once more sported a Spencer of Serena's, a grey silk that blended well with her blue gown; the shortness of sleeve she ignored. It was a warm day, and had she been in Hertfordshire would not have thought to take aught with her but her shawl, and most definitely would have eschewed the gloves and bonnet bestowed upon her most firmly by her aunt. Reluctantly tying the ribbon beneath her chin, she did gain a modicum of satisfaction from stuffing the gloves into her reticule.

They set off along the pavement, neatly coupled: Mr Bingley, as expected by all, escorting a more than willing Jane, Mr Darcy offering his sister his arm and Elizabeth, by default, partnered by the Colonel.

"I understand your recent trip was on business, Colonel. I trust it was successfully concluded?"

He smiled ruefully. "Sadly not. My venture was an edict from above and not of an amiable – or satisfactory – nature. Suffice it to say, I am taking more pleasure from my return to Town."

Unable to enquire further, Elizabeth continued at the Colonel's side, her gaze now turned upon the backs of Mr and Miss Darcy as they walked ahead of them.

"It was a pleasure to make Miss Darcy's acquaintance."

The gentleman at her side emitted a grunt of laughter. "It would appear the sentiment is reciprocated. I can assure you that almost the first words out of her mouth this morning were of you!"

A surge of emotion rushed through Elizabeth that she could ill account for, but uppermost was a burst of pleasure that whatever estimation Mr Darcy now held her in, his sister was pleased with the acquaintance. As the walking party neared the small garden that was their destination, however, she realised that time was of the essence, and determined not to let this opportunity escape her, she gathered her courage.

"I know that it might seem irregular, Sir, but I wish to speak with your cousin about something. Might I enlist your support in an attempt to exchange walking partners?"

"But of course. I am certain Georgiana will be most honoured."

"Colonel…" Elizabeth faltered for a moment. "Forgive me, but it is your other cousin I would speak with – if you do not think he would object."

The silence that followed this statement caused her to immediately regret her words, but before she could seek to redress the situation, the Colonel patted her on the arm and then shouted, "Darcy! Come. You have commandeered your sister's attention too long. She must yearn for some lighter discourse, and it is my duty to discharge it."

Both Darcys had turned to face them, and before anyone could react further, he stepped forward, removed Georgiana's arm from her brother's and replaced it with Elizabeth's.

"Now," he could be heard saying as he marched purposefully forward with his young cousin towards the swathe of greenery that Jane and Mr Bingley had by now entered, "Tell me all about how much you missed me these past four and twenty hours and make it credible. I am in much need of comfort!"

Darcy found himself walking, Elizabeth on his arm, before he had time to perceive the Colonel's intent. He threw a hasty glance at the lady, determined to summon all manner of punishments for his tactless cousin; her colour was high, yet her gaze was earnest, and before he could conjecture any further as to her feelings, she spoke.

"Forgive me, Mr Darcy. I trust the interruption will not have caused your sister any consternation."

Darcy frowned, but then he recalled her approach to him on the prior evening and, keen to have his speculation answered, he shook his head.

"You need not concern yourself unduly. Much as I hate to admit his accuracy, my cousin was not far from the mark. I am afraid that we walked in silence, companionable though it was!"

Elizabeth smiled. "I am glad. I would not wish to unnerve Miss Darcy." Their steps led them into the path that dissected the green lawns on the corner of Gracechurch Street and Cornhill, and Darcy threw her a quick glance. Though she had indicated a wish to speak to him about his confounded letter, she did not seem angry or offended, though she retained the air of diffidence about her that he had detected on the previous evening.

"Are you quite well, Miss Bennet? You are – you do not seem yourself."

She gave a small laugh and glanced up at him, shaking her head before returning her gaze to the path ahead, and he followed her example, but as they made their way past the ornamental plantings, their steps slowed and they turned about. Jane and Bingley had seated themselves on a bench that was furthest from the corner, where the noise of the carriages and barrow boys was less intrusive. Georgiana and Fitzwilliam were stood nearby, deep in conversation.

"Would you care to sit for a while?" He gestured towards a nearby stone bench, and, at Elizabeth's nod, accompanied her over to it.

As soon as they were seated, she spoke. "I beg you will forgive me for demanding your attention, Sir. I had hoped for a word with you last evening, but it was not to be."

"You wished to speak of my letter. I have long been regretting that I ever put pen to paper, and if it continues to trouble you so, then I suggest you burn it, that you might never have sight of it again."

Elizabeth shook her head. "What will you think of me, when I confess that I have perused it so often, I am by way of knowing it by heart? You may feel the content was not written in the best of spirits, but I assure you I have welcomed the self-knowledge that has come with it. But I digress…"

Darcy frowned as her expression sobered, and he suppressed the sudden urge to reach out and take her hand. She glanced down at her lap, then sat up straighter and met his eye with a determined look.

"It will not do. I have very little time to make my confession, and delaying it will not make it any easier to deliver, nor any more palatable a truth."

"Confession? I do not understand…"

Elizabeth got to her feet, clearly agitated, and she spoke gravely but quietly as he rose to stand beside her.

"Your letter – inadvertently, it was left behind in Kent. Oh, do not be concerned," she put out a hand towards him, then it fell to her side. "My carelessness has been rewarded, not punished. The letter is once more within my safe-keeping, and I am confident its content remains known to no one but myself."

Darcy studied her thoughtfully for a moment, certain that her admission had cost her dear, though if no one else had read the letter, the situation was no different to when he had taken the risk of handing it to her. He wondered who had returned it to her, for it must surely have been sent on rather quickly. It was a coincidence, to be certain, hard upon the heels of Bingley's assertion over her leaving a letter of Harington's behind... a sudden surge of hope he could not suppress swept through him. Might this be the one that had arrived yesterday? Was this what had caused him such unhappy deliberation? Determined to know all, he glanced quickly along the path before meeting her anxious gaze.

"Please. Let us be seated." He gestured to the bench from which they had just risen, and he watched her settle upon it once more before resuming his own place. "I would not wish to be impertinent..." he paused as a smile touched her lips.

"It would seem only fair that you repay my own manner in like kind, Sir."

He smiled briefly. "Might I enquire how it was returned to you – how it is that you are certain it fell under no other eye?"

"It was enclosed in a letter I received yesterday from Char – Mrs Collins. I trust her word – she did not read it." Her gaze dropped to her hands where they rested in her lap and she sighed before raising her eyes to his once more. "Yet I would not have you ignorant of that fact – that she knows you have addressed me so. As she resealed it, she happened to witness the signature."

Darcy experienced a rush of relief followed by an insane urge to smile, but he suppressed it, conscious that the rise in his spirits did not stem whence it should. He found he cared little enough for the misadventures of his letter, only that the one returned to her was not from Harington. He glanced at Elizabeth. She was once more staring at her gloveless hands. The situation clearly caused her some disturbance of mind, and he felt his own culpability in the matter.

"Forgive me, Miss Bennet."

She looked up quickly. "Forgive you, Sir? Pray, what is it in all that I have said that leads you to seek my pardon?"

"I put you in an untenable position by writing to you. I knew of course that the attempt should not be made; yet, I was unable to prevent myself from succumbing to the temptation. It was selfish of me, and my action could

well have caused no small amount of embarrassment or worse for you. So yes
– I would ask for your forgiveness."

She stared at him for a moment. "On one condition alone, Sir."

"And that is?"

"That I am able to secure your own for my carelessness."

"That is easily done."

Elizabeth shook her head and, recalling his own feelings towards Bingley
when he had absolved him so easily, though he truly did not think their errors
comparable, aided Darcy in understanding her present demeanour.

"No harm was done. You have faith in the discretion of your friend, and
if that is sufficient for you, then I am satisfied. Let us think on it no more and
trust that the letter need never be a subject between us again. I wish that you
might reconsider the efficacy of destroying it."

Elizabeth shook her head once more. "For all that you may wish it
unwritten, I will stand by my earlier assertion: I am thankful for the
revelations within it and for the self-awareness that it brought. I will never
regret that you sent it, only that you had need in the first place."

Darcy was somewhat taken aback at these words. He stared at Elizabeth,
who held his gaze unwaveringly albeit the colour that had so recently invaded
her cheeks remained high. Then, she sighed.

"To have been so blinded to a man's true nature."

"As well you know, you are not alone in having been deceived by that
man. He is well practised in the art of appearing what he is not."

A movement caught his eye and, seeing that the rest of their party now
made its way towards them along the path, he got to his feet, conscious that
Elizabeth had also arisen to stand at his side.

Yet before they were no longer alone, she said quietly but quite
distinctly, "You misunderstand me, Mr Darcy. Mr Wickham's was not the
character to which I referred." Desperate not to read too much into her
words, he threw her a questioning look, and she added, "I spoke of you, Sir."

Before he could fully assimilate these words, she gave a brief curtsey and
stepped forward to walk with his sister as they all turned to make their way
back along Gracechurch Street.

Darcy stared at Elizabeth's back as his cousin fell into step beside him, a
glow of warmth easing somewhat the ever-present constriction within his
breast. His opportunity for reflection did not prevail, however, for as they

approached the Gardiners' residence the Colonel renewed his efforts to persuade Darcy to pursue his acquaintance with the family.

Despite his pleasure in Elizabeth's words, Fitzwilliam's suggestion fell on stony ground, but with an impatient grunt, the Colonel came to a halt.

"Darcy, if you will not extend the invitation, then I shall. It is a heaven-sent opportunity."

Turning and walking back two paces to re-join his cousin, Darcy frowned.

"For what, Fitzwilliam? I really do not think-"

"Would you like me to draw up a list? For further righting the wrong you did your friend, by giving him an evening in Miss Bennet's company; for permitting your sister more time with Miss Elizabeth – she seems to derive a great deal of pleasure from the acquaintance, perchance you had noticed?" The Colonel inclined his head to where Georgiana and Elizabeth stood at the bottom of the steps leading to the Gardiners' house, deep in conversation. "For aught else – well, I give you leave to be pig-headed about anything else!"

"It is too much to put upon Georgiana. She is not practised in hosting dinner parties, Cousin, as well you know."

"A paltry excuse, Darce, as well *you* comprehend. You are there to host, and what is there even for you to do, pray? Mrs Wainwright will deal with the preparations as competently as she does everything else." The Colonel let out a snort. "If you are so ingrained with duty and require a host*ess*, I shall acquire a gown and slippers of my own!"

Darcy did not respond to this piece of nonsense other than to throw his cousin a look of exasperation. Then, he realised that his sister had excused herself from Elizabeth, who was even now making her way up the few steps to the door, and soon joined them.

"Brother? Is something amiss?"

Darcy threw Fitzwilliam a warning look, but to no avail.

"I am attempting to persuade the stubborn mule to invite the family to dine with us on the morrow. According to Mrs Gardiner earlier, their anticipated outing to the opera has been postponed in the absence of Harington, so they are not engaged."

Georgiana's face lit up, and she fell into step beside her brother as they moved forward. "What a splendid thought! Fitz, should you not step inside and speak with Mrs Gardiner before we depart?"

Darcy looked from one to the other. "I had not – I did not –"

"Well, never mind that; there is no time like the present," countered the Colonel, and he came to a halt by the shallow stairs leading to the Gardiners' front door, where Bingley stood in conversation with Miss Bennet.

"Go on, Darce. Seize the moment!" and he gestured for his cousin to mount the steps.

Elizabeth had been contemplating on the success or otherwise of her confession. Mr Darcy had taken it well, and she was both relieved and gratified by his response and his unexpected apology. She frowned as she recalled this; his consideration struck her anew, and she would have deliberated further on this had her eye not been caught by a movement below her as she espied the gentleman himself making his way up the steps to stand beside her.

"Miss Elizabeth."

"I beg your pardon, Sir." Unsure of his purpose, she felt a little uncomfortable, and he seemed equally ill at ease. "Did you – were you wishing to return inside?"

"No – no, I was not. I – that is, we-" he glanced over his shoulder, to where his sister and cousin remained at the foot of the steps, then turned back to face Elizabeth. "We would be honoured, Madam, if you could extend an invitation to dine with us to your aunt and uncle. I understand that your engagement for the morrow has been postponed, and we are at leisure."

Conscious of a rush of pleasure for the gesture extended to her family and surprise that Mr Darcy should wish to promote a further occasion for their being in company together, Elizabeth did not speak for a moment. Then, she smiled.

"Then the invitation is purely for my aunt and uncle, Sir?"

Darcy narrowed his eyes as she met his gaze with an innocent one. Then, he gave a short laugh and shook his head.

"I would not do you and your sister the disservice. The invitation is for your entire party." He paused. "As I think you are well aware."

"Forgive me. I thank you for the honour. I am certain my family will be delighted to accept. Will you not step inside and speak with my aunt now? That way you will be able to leave us the direction as well."

Chapter Fourteen

THE GENTLEMEN RODE westwards for about a mile, one either side of the phaeton, the Colonel well satisfied with the morning and content to keep his peace at first. As they made their way along the Embankment, however, he signalled to his cousin who fell back to ride alongside him, allowing the carriage to go on ahead.

"Darce?"

"I would rather not talk about it."

"It? I am not certain that you should refer to Miss Elizabeth Bennet in such a cavalier fashion."

Darcy shook his head, but the Colonel merely shrugged at him, and they continued for some distance without exchanging another word. The congestion and noise in the streets was sufficient to prevent any reasonable conversation as they returned along the Strand and up Haymarket, but as they made their way along the further reaches of Piccadilly and neared the quieter thoroughfares of Mayfair, the Colonel's curiosity finally outwitted his patience, and he pulled his mount closer to Darcy's as they turned into Berkeley Street.

"So, Cousin. The lady sought your company. It is a singular action for one whom you profess hates the very sight of you, is it not? What might her approach be towards someone she favours?"

Darcy threw Fitzwilliam a look that expressed itself far more explicitly than words.

"Come now, man. Admit it. She does not dislike you; indeed, from the apparent intensity of your conversation, I would deign to say she liked your company very well."

Garnering no response to this, the Colonel studied his cousin thoughtfully for a moment. "Your silence is very damning, Darce! What, no denial? No prediction of doom and gloom?"

"Enough, Fitzwilliam!" Darcy's retort was mild, accompanied as it was by a reluctant smile.

The Colonel acceded to his cousin's request, introducing a new topic of conversation, but as their party progressed through the Square he could detect a subtle change in his companion. The weary set of his shoulders had begun to lift; the evidence of strain and sleepless nights about his eyes seemed somewhat lessened. It was not that he brimmed with hope or expectation, merely that there was some evident easing of the pain and despondency.

Smiling to himself, the Colonel settled back in his saddle. His anticipation of the upcoming dinner party was as high as could be, and though they had yet to gain an introduction to one another, he sent a silent nod of thanks to Harington for absenting himself from Town for the present.

The party from Mount Street went their separate ways once returned to the house, the Colonel retiring to his chamber to deal with some correspondence, Bingley settling in the drawing room to read the paper and Georgiana seeking out Mrs Annesley.

Darcy, having retrieved the post from the tray in the hall, proceeded to his study, but he had yet to lift the opener from the blotter. His cousin's words had struck a chord, and combined with the sentiment expressed by Elizabeth earlier, he was hard put to move beyond it.

"I would deign to say she liked your company very well."

Darcy could not help but acknowledge a slither of warmth filling him at the notion of being so much as liked by Elizabeth. Though he could not fully accept his cousin's logic, knowing that she had sought him out for reasons other than the pleasure of his company, even he could detect a difference in her manner towards him. There was sufficient sincerity in her expression to assure him that he was not misled: she no longer held him in contempt. Further, from their recent exchange it was apparent that she not only believed what he had written in his letter but that she accepted she had been blinded to his true disposition.

Unable to settle to his purpose, Darcy got to his feet and walked slowly over to the hearth and studied the large painting that hung above it for a moment before turning his back on it and facing the room. He knew full well the futility of anticipating the furtherance of the acquaintance. Despite learning that there was actually no evidence now of an understanding between Elizabeth and Harington, he should not assume her feelings were unattached, and even were they so...

Releasing a breath of frustration, he passed a hand through his hair and then flexed his fingers. Try as he might to put Elizabeth from his mind, she was firmly in situ. Walking slowly back over to his desk, he berated himself for his weakness. Had he not sworn to distance himself, to allow her to enjoy her stay in Town without the constant reminder of him, yet at the slightest influence he had been persuaded to be in her company – and now she was to dine in this very house. How he had come to be in this situation, he could hardly fathom, yet so it was.

Disgruntled, he threw himself into his chair and eyed the pile of post before him. Barely had he lifted the opener, however, when a knock came on the door, and Pagett entered bearing a small salver.

"An *Express*, Sir. The rider was not instructed to await a response." Darcy reached out and took the letter from the tray and studied its direction, as Pagett solemnly removed himself from the room. Breaking the seal, he cast his eyes over the short message contained therein; then, he leaned back in his chair with a sigh, the letter still gripped in his hand.

Having taken much pleasure from their afternoon outdoors, indulging in a fine walk after their picnic, the party from Gracechurch Street had returned home shortly before dinner, and as time was short and the only company that evening their own, they had all agreed to refresh themselves quickly and meet again for pre-dinner drinks in the drawing room before the summons came to table.

Jane, as was often the case, had completed her ablutions before her sister had begun and sat on the bed patiently awaiting her; Elizabeth, who had only now returned from Serena's chamber where she had been restoring the garments she had recently borrowed to their rightful places, hurried to wash her hands and face and then began to take down her hair as she walked over to the dresser.

"I am pleased that you had the opportunity to talk to Mr Darcy. It must have brought you some relief."

Elizabeth nodded. "I am still astounded by how well he took it. He was more than gracious."

"He is a good man."

"Yes – I dare say he is." Elizabeth gave a rueful smile, filled with an unaccountable sense of sadness. "And good men collect others about them." She turned to study her sister. "I no longer wonder at him and Mr Bingley being such close friends."

"Did you?" Jane looked somewhat taken aback.

"Most indubitably. I found it impossible to comprehend that a man such as Mr Bingley could countenance being in company so continually with a man of Mr Darcy's alleged nature." Elizabeth shook her head. "Yet now…"

"Now, Lizzy?"

"I comprehend better their compatibility." She drew in a deep breath and then released it on a huff of laughter. "Come, let us be done with this subject." She turned back to face the mirror. "It hardly answers my desire to put aside thoughts of the man."

"You may be making too fierce an attempt."

Elizabeth laughed. "That is little consolation! If this is the outcome of such concentrated effort, how would I fair if the endeavour was abandoned?"

Jane stood and walked over to the window. "I wonder if you should not adopt some of the philosophy you afforded me lately and accept each day on its own merits." She turned to look out of the window, and Elizabeth sighed.

"Perhaps." She returned her gaze to her reflection for a moment before slowly reaching out to place the pins on the dresser top, but as she took up her comb she happened to glance down at her hand and recalled in an instant the Colonel placing it on Mr Darcy's arm when they had changed walking partners.

A sensation of warmth in her face drew her gaze back to the mirror, and she watched the faint pink invading her cheeks, an echo of the colour that she was certain had flooded them earlier. It was fortunate she had been so determined to say her piece, and that Mr Darcy had suggested they sit, that she no longer be distracted by his closeness… the colour deepened, and conscious of the heat that permeated her skin, Elizabeth raised a hand and placed a cooling palm against it for a moment. She had been thankful for the reprieve, for heaven knew if she would have been able to be sufficiently coherent in her confession otherwise.

Frustrated at the direction of her thoughts, Elizabeth threw the comb down onto the dresser and selecting a piece of ribbon from those draped over the mirror quickly tied her hair back with a neat bow. "There. I am ready."

Jane turned from her study of the street and walked over to join her at the door, and they quickly made their way downstairs as one of the housemaids closed the front door on the back of a departing servant.

The maid turned around, a note in her hand, but as soon as she espied the young ladies she smiled and dropped a quick curtsey before handing the note to Elizabeth who happened to be nearest to her. "This just arrived, Ma'am."

"Thank you," Elizabeth excused her with a nod of her head and glanced down at the note in her hand, only to feel her heart lurch in her chest. She recognised the hand instantly, and then berated herself for seeking her own name upon it. Quickly turning it over to ascertain the seal, she looked up at Jane and frowned.

"It is for Uncle – from Mr Darcy!"

Darcy had passed a pleasant evening with Bingley, the Colonel and his sister, and when the latter had retired and the gentlemen had progressed, as was their habit, to Darcy's study for a snifter of brandy before parting, the conversation turned to his friend and his estate.

Bingley was for Hertfordshire on the following Tuesday and had all manner of questions for Darcy pertaining to the running of his manor. His cousin's suggestion that he accompany his friend, that he might be on hand to answer them as they arose, was silenced with a pointed glare, and for once Fitzwilliam merely shrugged and held his tongue. Unwilling to allow his thoughts or the conversation to stray further in that direction, Darcy changed the subject, and soon after they followed Georgiana's example and retired for the night.

Darcy's hope was for a night of full repose, but even as a clock elsewhere in the house sounded the faint chimes of midnight, he lay yet awake, flat on his back and staring at the canopy above his bed. He had exhausted his deliberations over whether to leave Town or not, his speculation over his cousin's purpose in suggesting he accompany Bingley unanswered.

He closed his eyes, willing sleep to seek him out, but no amount of inclination would turn his thoughts far and soon they were with Elizabeth's family, wondering how his note been received and what would be the outcome.

Gracechurch Street slumbered under a full moon that dusted the white stone buildings with a ghostly sheen and cast dark shadows from every tree and railing. There was little sound, other than a rustling of leaves, stirred by the light breeze, and the occasional neigh of a horse from the nearby mews.

In the chamber she shared with Jane, Elizabeth lay on her side, her eyes gazing into nothingness, but her mind once more a challenge to satisfactory rest as she reflected on Mr Darcy's most recent communication.

Her uncle had taken the proffered note from her as soon as they entered the drawing room, and she had only just caught herself from telling him whence it came. Feeling her skin heat at the memory, Elizabeth stirred restlessly and turned onto her back. How she would have been able to adequately excuse her ability to discern both the gentleman's hand and his seal, she could not think, and she thanked her sister wholeheartedly for the cautionary hand upon her arm which recalled her to herself just in time.

Her instinctive assumption, as Mr Gardiner handed both girls a glass of sherry and then broke the note's seal, had been that Mr Darcy wrote to retract his invitation – that on due consideration, he had decided against its sagacity and that some fabricated intervention would excuse him from the commitment. Yet before she could ruminate further on this, or question the sense of disappointment it engendered, her uncle had looked up with a smile. The note did refer to their invitation to dine, but the retraction was offered to them.

Elizabeth tugged the covers so that they met her chin and snuggled further into the warmth of the bed. Mr Darcy wrote to advise them of two unexpected additions to his household on the morrow – his aunt and his cousin from Kent. Her uncle had outlined the gist of the note in a manner that clearly bespoke his approval of the courtesy extended to them, for Mr Darcy offered them the opportunity to withdraw with grace from the obligation now that the party would be extended. However, he stressed as much as one is able in such circumstances that for his part the invitation stood, and he hoped that they would still wish to partake of it.

Due to the lateness of the hour, Mr Gardiner had determined to send a response at first light, and Elizabeth had been rather taken aback at the depth of her relief when, having debated the matter between themselves, her aunt and uncle had agreed they should very much like to accept Mr Darcy's offer to retain the engagement.

With a sigh, Elizabeth closed her eyes and strove to relax her mind, letting it go where it would, and within minutes she had drifted off into a peaceful slumber.

The arrival of the new gowns brought an air of excitement to the Gardiner household on Saturday morning, yet Elizabeth was almost equally delighted by the return of her old coat and dress, both now dyed a darker shade of their original hue in order to conceal the staining about the hem.

She carried the coat over to the window to observe the effect in full light and then turned to face her aunt with a wide smile.

"It is perfect! Oh Aunt, I am so pleased."

"Your dress would appear to be likewise mended, see?"

Elizabeth walked back over to the table where Mrs Gardiner had been unwrapping the parcels and lifted her dress from the tissue paper. Happy though she was to have both items restored to use, they had taken on a new significance, for she was certain the dress and coat would likely never lose their association with Mr Darcy and his proposal.

With a sigh, Elizabeth acknowledged that yet again the gentleman had intruded upon her thoughts. However, once the maid had been summoned to take the evening gowns away to hang in preparation for Monday, she was able to push aside unsettling images of last Sunday and contemplate the upcoming evening with keener interest.

"What have you a mind to wear this evening?" Jane closed the door upon the retreating backs of the maid and their aunt, who was determined to ensure that the new gowns were treated with due consideration. "It is likely to be very grand, is it not?"

"Mr Darcy's house? I suppose it must be, and as we have been forewarned that his aunt is to be there, we should make every attempt to look our best!"

"What sort of woman is she? When you spoke of her, you were not generous in your praise. Were you in earnest?"

"Unfortunately, I was. Lady Catherine is quite intimidating, and I suspect she will extend little if any warmth towards us."

Jane looked somewhat discomfited, but Elizabeth waved a dismissive hand.

"Pay her no mind. She will be but one of a larger party – though it is imperative you feel at ease in whatever you wear. Let us make use of our dresses from the Netherfield ball, with a change of sash or trim to dress them up. If we match a different colour ribbon to the dressings in our hair, it will create a pleasing enough effect, I believe. Come," Elizabeth turned and headed towards the door. "Let us fetch them now and make some small alterations."

Chapter Fifteen

HAVING ENSURED HIS AUNT and cousin, safely arrived from Kent not an hour since, were comfortably installed in their rooms, Darcy had returned to his study, determined not to dwell upon the upcoming evening, though in truth he could think of little else since receiving Mr Gardiner's reciprocal note expressing their pleasure in honouring the commitment.

He picked up one of the papers, intent on following Fitzwilliam's example where he lounged in the opposite armchair, and within a few minutes, a companionable silence hung over the room, disturbed only now and again by the flutter of paper as a page was turned.

Their peace did not endure, however, for the door suddenly flew open, and both Darcy and the Colonel looked up as Lady Catherine de Bourgh swept across the room towards them. Exchanging a quick look with each other, they put their papers aside and got to their feet.

"Aunt Catherine." Darcy inclined his head briefly as she fetched up before his desk. "Please, do come in."

A smothered snort from the Colonel attracted that lady's stern eye for a second, but then she returned her gaze to her other nephew.

"What is this I hear of a dinner party this evening? Georgiana informs me you are to entertain. Why was I not informed?"

"The invitation was issued but yesterday. At the time, I was unaware of your impending arrival, and even had I been, there was no way of forewarning you. "

The lady frowned. "I do not like to be taken unawares, Darcy. And issuing invitations but one day before a dinner – it is not the done thing."

"Well, it was the done thing yesterday, so there it is," interrupted the Colonel. "Indeed, the spontaneity was most stimulating. You should perhaps try it, Aunt."

"Do not be flippant, Fitzwilliam. It does not become you. Now," she turned back to Darcy. "I trust I am to be hostess?"

"If you wish, the offer is accepted with gratitude."

Lady Catherine inclined her head. "And Georgiana – will she attend?"

"Of course. I believe she will enjoy the experience all the more for not having undue pressure upon her."

She nodded, tapping her folded fan against her palm. "Quite. She will be able to observe and learn from my excellent example." Both her nephews remained silent at this, and she continued. "I trust the guests are appropriate company for one such as Anne."

Darcy frowned. "The company is entirely appropriate. The only detriment is that we now number four gentlemen but six ladies."

His aunt's brow creased in a reciprocal frown. "But that is intolerable! You must invite two more gentlemen at once."

The Colonel chuckled. "I thought issuing invitations with little notice was not the done thing?"

Darcy suppressed the urge to smile and continued. "I have no intention of inviting random gentlemen to dine in my home simply to aid a balanced seating plan. I am certain that, with your expertise in hosting, you will triumph with the given ingredients."

Lady Catherine expressed her opinion of this statement with a loud huff, turning on her heel to walk back towards the door. She paused, however, before she reached it, and both gentlemen schooled their features quickly into blanks as she turned to face them again.

"Who is of the party? I must have names for the placements. Really, Darcy, this is most vexing. I did not anticipate spending the evening in the company of strangers."

"Then you will be delighted to learn that you are acquainted with one of our guests." The Colonel smiled at the sudden interest in his aunt's eye as she walked back towards them.

Darcy threw his cousin a quick warning look, but he could tell that he pretended not to notice.

"Miss Elizabeth Bennet will be attending."

Lady Catherine narrowed her eyes, looking first at the Colonel, then transferring her gaze to Darcy. "Miss Elizabeth Bennet? This is most unsatisfactory."

Before Darcy could object to this incivility, his cousin had responded. "I cannot think why, Aunt. You were content enough to invite the lady to dine at Rosings."

Lady Catherine gave an irritated shake of her head which caused her coiffure to shiver. "In country society, she is not so out of place. Those were somewhat informal dinners, and it was a duty to include the guest of my parson."

The Colonel smiled. "I am certain you will find the lady equal to the occasion, Aunt. Indeed, she will be amongst both family and friends, will she not, Cousin?"

Darcy nodded. "Indeed. Miss Elizabeth Bennet's sister and her aunt and uncle will also be in attendance."

At this, Lady Catherine's eyes snapped angrily and she pursed her lips tightly for a moment. "The relatives from *Cheapside*? Have you taken leave of your senses, Darcy?"

He chose to ignore this slight upon his guests. "And of course, you are acquainted with my friend, Bingley – he will also be here. Along with yourself and Anne, that makes up our party of ten."

The lady snorted indelicately. "That at least evens the balance."

"How so?"

"It is a matter of social standing," she snapped. "Six people of rank and four of little consequence. Our breeding will carry the day."

Riled beyond his limit, Darcy could not let this go, despite his cousin's restraining hand upon his arm.

"Miss Bennet and Miss Elizabeth are the daughters of a gentleman whose family has held that status for many a generation. In this they stand on a par with Georgiana."

Lady Catherine drew in a sharp breath. "Heaven preserve us! You cannot compare their father's social position to that of George Darcy of Pemberley! And what of these – these – *trades people*? Is your home to be thus polluted?"

Darcy's forbearance was at its limit, but he was determined not to lose his temper. "The Gardiners are fine folk, Aunt; fashionable, refined and intelligent. They make excellent company."

The lady glared at him. "You take advantage of my good nature."

Feeling quite out of patience, Darcy shook his head.

"Not at all, Aunt. You kindly offered to host. If you wish to retract, then so be it. I trust you will be content to dine in your room with Anne this evening?"

Lady Catherine's mouth opened but no sound came forth as she stared at her nephew in disbelief.

"Indeed, I believe that might well silence your concerns, Aunt," said the Colonel. "If you and Anne dine upstairs, the numbers return to their original and acceptable balance: four gentlemen, four ladies."

Eyeing both gentlemen with a narrowed glare, Lady Catherine pursed her lips. "You leave me little choice. It is clear that, for Georgiana's sake, I must intervene. I will host your dinner party, Darcy, but do not think I do so gladly or willingly." With that, she turned on her heel and left the room.

Darcy met the Colonel's amused eye for a moment, who shrugged, before both gentlemen picked up their respective papers and settled back into their chairs, the comfortable silence soon in place again.

Their dresses soon altered to their satisfaction, Jane and Elizabeth handed them over to the maid that they might be pressed and aired for the evening before repairing to the drawing room to read the correspondence that had arrived in the meantime.

"Mama hastens me home." Jane blushed as she glanced back down at the letter in her hand. "It would seem that Netherfield is to be opened up. As of yesterday, the servants were all recalled to their duties to ready the hall for the master's return."

"It is fortuitous timing, then, is it not?" Elizabeth laughed as the colour in Jane's cheeks intensified. "That or a strange coincidence. Mr Bingley is not leaving anything to chance on this occasion."

"Oh hush, Lizzy. It does not mean anything, other than the man holding the lease of the property wishes to partake of his manor. For all we know, he comes for naught but the shooting."

Elizabeth shook her head. "For shame, Jane; 'tis May as of yesterday! Any gentleman – and indeed, any gentleman's daughter – should know full well that the season has been over these many weeks!"

It was apparent that Jane could not conceal her pleasure at the news in her mother's letter, even if she did not appreciate the sentiment behind her encouraging her eldest daughter home.

"You will accompany me, Lizzy, when I go?"

Dropping the letter she had been perusing onto a side table, Elizabeth got to her feet and wandered over to the small pianoforte against the far wall. She settled herself on the stool and lifted the lid before responding.

"I believe that I must tarry a week at least in Town. Serena is not due to arrive before Tuesday, and I long to spend some time with her and clearly she with me. I doubt Mama is writing to beg *my* return?"

Elizabeth cast Jane an amused glance before turning her attention to the music on the stand in front of her. She essayed a few scales to warm her fingers and then began to play the light air.

Getting to her feet, Jane walked over and joined her sister.

"Mama suggests that either Lydia or Kitty be sent to Gracechurch Street for a while – she says the girls are trying her nerves." She glanced down at the letter in her hand. "Here it is: *...they constantly vanish for hour upon hour with no consideration for my wants or needs, and even when they do return home, they secret themselves away in their chamber. I can detect nothing from their whispers and giggling when passing by their door. I am poorly used and sorely tried, for what company, pray, is your father?* And then she goes on to repeat her request for my prompt return."

Elizabeth laughed. "Dear Mama! She believes sending them away will cure nerves aggravated by their absence? Besides, what of Aunt Gardiner's nerves? Is there no compassion for her having a house full of visitors all the time?"

"You know full well that I do not suffer from nerves, Lizzy," came their aunt's admonishing voice as she entered the room, and ceasing her attempt to play, Elizabeth turned on her stool to watch that lady cross to take a seat opposite the fireplace. "Now come – what is it that might try them, if I had?"

With a smile Elizabeth got to her feet and walked over to join her aunt, taking a seat next to her.

"Jane has received a letter from Hertfordshire, requesting her presence at Longbourn."

Jane in her turn had come to join them and informed their aunt of her mother's wish that she now return home, but that Mrs Bennet felt it would be beneficial if either Lydia, Kitty or both, join Elizabeth in Town for a short stay.

"Beneficial for whom, I wonder?" mused Elizabeth.

"Come now, Lizzy. You know that I love nothing more than having a house full of my favourite young people, and they do both petition so often and so fiercely for a change of scene. Surely you would not begrudge your younger sisters that?"

"But there is the oddity in it, Aunt. I too have received a letter – from Kitty no less – who declares that neither she nor Lydia has any desire to travel at all, even to Town. I must own to being mystified by such a change in them."

"I am certain that there is a logical explanation," counselled Jane, looking from her sister to her aunt. "Perhaps they have realised that there is plenty of richness to be found in their present surroundings and are learning to appreciate their time at home more."

Mrs Gardiner smiled. "I am sure there is some merit in what you say, Jane. Perhaps you are right, and perhaps they are growing up at last."

"Aye, and perhaps Papa's favourite sow will sprout wings," Elizabeth muttered under her breath, conscious from the smothered laugh beside her that her aunt had heard her, but thankful that Jane's attention was once more with her letter.

The afternoon gradually waned and though there was bustle aplenty amongst the servants preparing for the evening ahead, all remained quiet in the music room at the back of the Darcy home in Mount Street.

Georgiana Darcy sat at her pianoforte, yet for once it held no sway over her attention. She had been left to her own devices: her brother and cousin were ensconced in the study once more, considering a matter of concern that had arisen in relation to some fund or other, and her aunt and other cousin were resting yet from their journey. Mr Bingley had gone to call upon his sisters in Grosvenor Street and her companion enjoyed her daily hour of free time.

Normally, she would have revelled in the opportunity to spend time with her instrument. As it was, her thoughts were entirely engrossed with the upcoming evening. Relieved though she was that there was no onus upon her to take any role in its organisation, she could not help but speculate upon its potential for her brother.

With a sigh, Georgiana got to her feet and walked over to the window and stared out into the garden. Her brother's avowal that there was no future for his acquaintance with Miss Elizabeth Bennet puzzled her exceedingly. Though she had been too wrapped in her own anxiety to notice the lack or otherwise of interaction between them on first being introduced to the lady, and Fitz had reminded her of the futility of any hope for furthering the relationship only yesterday morning, Georgiana's own observations of them during their walk on the previous day seemed to contradict him; yet, her brother was a man of his word, was he not?

With a frown, she turned away from the window and walked slowly back over to her pianoforte and sank onto the stool. She had enjoyed immensely calling on the Miss Bennets. The family was so at ease, made her feel so welcome and most decidedly not the centre of attention, something she could not abide.

How much had she enjoyed speaking to Miss Elizabeth, and how delightful had it been that Mr Bingley had made his impromptu suggestion of a walk! She had observed Fitzwilliam closely, and whatever the topic of his conversation with Miss Elizabeth, there was nothing, even in Georgiana's limited experience, to indicate animosity or dislike emanating from the lady. Indeed, she had seemed quite as if she wanted to be in discourse with him, and they had not appeared to part on indifferent terms. Oh, how she wished she had the nerve to ask Miss Elizabeth what she really thought of her brother. How she wished she might have the opportunity to…

Sitting up straight, Georgiana let out a small gasp of excitement. She got to her feet and hurried from the room, making her way quickly up two flights of stairs to her chamber, intent upon choosing a gown for the evening ahead. This *was* her chance; there would in all likelihood be an occasion – when the ladies separated after dinner, perhaps – that would present her with the chance she sought: to speak to Miss Elizabeth, perchance at some distance from others, certainly without being under the eye of her brother.

Inspired by her realisation and refusing to give any credence to her common sense, which countered with all manner of reasoning as to why she could not or should not attempt such a thing, she opened her door and hurried inside. So consumed was she by her intent that she failed to recall her inherent shyness outside her own family circle and how she might overcome it to achieve her aim.

Chapter Sixteen

THE AFTERNOON HAD finally faded into early evening, and the Darcy home, which had undergone an unprecedented amount of activity throughout the day, rested peacefully at last, candles flickering expectantly in the wall sconces and crystal chandeliers and crackling fires emitting a welcoming glow in every room. The oil lamps hanging either side of the front door shone brightly, along with those built in to the stone gateposts, casting a warm glow over the carriage pulling up at the kerbstone.

Perched on the window seat of her second-floor chamber, Georgiana had been craning her neck for some minutes in expectation of the conveyance that was now outside the house. Jumping to her feet, she pressed her cheek to the glass, her eyes straining in the dim light of dusk to reassure herself that it truly was the anticipated party, before hastily grabbing a silk shawl from the back of a nearby chair and hurrying out of the door onto the landing.

Taking a quick step back from the drawing room window, Darcy turned around. She was here. He was about to welcome Elizabeth into his home.

"Do our guests arrive?"

The Colonel's voice, emanating from a fireside armchair, roused Darcy, and he nodded, conscious that Bingley had turned from the other window, his face wreathed in a contented smile.

"Where is Aunt Catherine?"

Darcy shrugged, his mind full of Elizabeth. "She will be down directly, I am certain."

In the guest suite, Lady Catherine de Bourgh turned away from the window and eyed her daughter stonily.

"Come, Anne. We must do our duty. Keep your distance from these visitors; they are not the sort of company we are accustomed to." She snatched up her fan from the dressing table and turned to survey Anne as she rose from the window seat at the other end of the room. "It is fortunate that our breeding will carry us through. I do not know what Darcy is about; this is all most vexing".

Then, without a backward glance to see if her daughter followed, Lady Catherine barked "Door!" at the maid who hovered nearby and swept herself onto the landing, her heavy brocade gown trailing in her wake.

Darcy paused in the open doorway of the drawing room, causing both his cousin and Bingley to halt also. His aunt and Anne, along with Georgiana, had gathered at the foot of the stairs and Pagett was even now admitting the Gardiner party into the house. He cleared his throat and straightened his cuffs, unaware of Bingley's puzzled look up at him.

The sound of voices drifted along the hallway and, giving his cousin a slap on the shoulders, the Colonel urged him on.

"Here we go then, Darce! Let the latest skirmish commence!"

Darcy stepped forward and acknowledged Mr and Mrs Gardiner before turning to repeat the gesture to both Miss Bennet and Elizabeth. Keen though he was to feast his eyes upon the latter, he strove to remember his duty, and led the Gardiners forward to where his aunt and cousin stood, the young ladies following behind.

"Aunt Catherine, Cousin – permit me to present to you Mr and Mrs Edward Gardiner and their niece, Miss Bennet." Darcy stepped aside, that bows and curtseys might be exchanged, then added, "Mr and Mrs Gardiner, Miss Bennet – this is Lady Catherine de Bourgh, my aunt, and her daughter, Anne."

"It is an honour to make your acquaintance, Lady Catherine, Miss de Bourgh," said Mr Gardiner, a warm smile upon his face.

"Quite so," responded Lady Catherine with a snap of her fan. She let her gaze travel slowly over the newly arrived company, before coming to rest upon Elizabeth, who, having no need of being presented quite so formally, had held back a little.

"Miss Elizabeth Bennet," she intoned with a slight inclination of her head.

"Lady Catherine," Elizabeth dropped a curtsey, before meeting that lady's eye with an expressionless face.

"How unexpected that we meet again so soon after your departure from Kent. I was quite astounded to learn that you were to dine here this evening."

"I cannot profess to return the compliment, Ma'am."

Lady Catherine's eyes narrowed. "I beg your pardon?"

"Knowing of your visit, your dining here this evening caused me no particular surprise."

"I see." The lady drew herself up. "However, you misunderstand me. No compliment was intended."

"Oh, I assure you, Ma'am, there was no misunderstanding." With a smile, Elizabeth dropped a further curtsey.

Lady Catherine pursed her lips, but no comment came forth, and Darcy cleared his throat quickly.

"My aunt and cousin are breaking their journey with us and will continue on their way to Bath in the morning."

As Mrs Gardiner attempted to speak to his aunt of their intended stay in that city, Darcy noted that Elizabeth had turned to Anne.

"Miss de Bourgh." His cousin's paleness was emphasised by the dark colours she habitually wore, this evening being no exception. "I trust you journeyed well?"

Anne looked slightly taken aback, but said shortly, "As well as can be expected."

"Come, Anne, let us adjourn to the drawing room." Before any further discourse could be attempted, Lady Catherine stepped forward and took her daughter's arm, throwing Elizabeth a look of quelling disdain, and with a narrowed glare at Darcy as she passed, she turned and swept her daughter across the floor towards the door through which the gentlemen had come some moments earlier.

"Will you do the honours, Darce?"

Darcy turned towards his cousin and frowned.

"Please excuse my cousin," the Colonel continued. "We do not often let him loose upon society, for he knows not how to behave."

A chuckle from Bingley roused Darcy, and with sudden clarity he snapped to attention.

"Forgive me. A small oversight, I assure you."

Turning back to his guests, Darcy tried not to notice the small smile upon Elizabeth's lips as he spoke to her uncle.

"Mr Gardiner, it is with much regret that I must introduce my cousin, Colonel Fitzwilliam to your notice. I only hope that you will excuse me for doing so henceforth."

At this, everyone laughed, not least the Colonel, who stepped forward and bowed formally.

"Delighted to make your acquaintance, Sir. I had the good fortune to meet your wife only yesterday, when we had the pleasure of calling at Gracechurch Street."

Amidst the general conversation following this introduction, Darcy motioned for them to follow his aunt's example and move towards the drawing room, and as they turned in that direction, Elizabeth walked over to where Georgiana stood twisting the ends of her shawl.

"It is so kind of you to welcome us all into your home this evening, Miss Darcy."

An eager smile spread quickly across Georgiana's features. "Oh no, Miss Elizabeth. Indeed, the kindness is all yours in accepting the invitation at such short notice."

"Then we must be grateful for the cancellation of our plans to visit the opera, must we not?"

"Oh! I did not mean…"

Elizabeth laughed as they too turned to follow the rest of the party.

"Dear Miss Darcy! I am teasing, though I must be honest with you and own that I would always rate a dinner in good company above a night spent watching a group of strangers cavort upon a stage!"

"My aunt says that opera is a refined taste, and that there are few that have the breeding to fully appreciate it. I worry that it makes so little sense to me."

Elizabeth shook her head.

"I must own to being no great follower of operatic pieces myself. Those I have attended thus far have all been of a wretched nature. Whilst I can appreciate a fine tragedy as well as any, I prefer to read of them, and indulge my misery in solitude. Life is too full to be saddened by such things. Bring me a comedy any day." She smiled at her companion as they reached the door to the drawing room.

"Then you truly do not regret the change in your arrangements?"

"Not at all. We are delighted to be here, I assure you." Elizabeth stood aside to allow Georgiana Darcy to precede her into the room, reflecting as she did so that it was indeed no lie.

Some minutes later, the majority of the party seated to their satisfaction, Elizabeth found herself stood by one of the tall windows, the better to look around the room, letting out a sigh a pure contentment as she did so. It was a beautiful space, charmingly dressed with furnishings that bespoke a combination of quality and good taste.

She smiled as she began a study of the contents of a nearby glass cabinet, noting amongst what were no doubt valuable treasures some pieces that were clearly made by the hand of a child and some time ago. Her eye had just been caught by a small, faded marker not dissimilar to the reed stick she had found the other day, though this one had clearly once been painted over by a childlike hand, when she became aware of someone at her side.

"May I offer you a drink, Miss Elizabeth? A sherry or some wine, perhaps?"

Turning around swiftly, she faced her host with a smile.

"Wine would be lovely, I thank you."

Darcy returned with her glass, and conscious that he would likely retreat should she not detain him, Elizabeth spoke immediately.

"You have a beautiful home, Sir."

Elizabeth watched him as he stood awkwardly for a moment before giving a brief smile.

"I am glad that you find it so. Very little has been changed since my mother was alive, so in some respects it may appear dated."

"I believe it has a charm and elegance that transcends fashionable trends. I find it very – warm."

That he was gratified by her words was evident, for his expression was plainly unguarded at that moment. They stared at each other in silence, Elizabeth becoming uncomfortably aware that praise in relation to his home was probably something he was showered with on a regular basis, and feeling foolish for having fallen back on something so mundane, she sought keenly for a change of subject.

Her eyes lit upon a figurine placed upon a nearby drum table, and with a nod in its direction, she said, "I have seen that piece before. My father has a wonderful volume in his library that contains colour plates of sculpture, beautifully detailed sketches, of both life-sized and miniature, such as this. Is it not of Italian origin?"

Darcy followed her gaze to the ornament in question, and he picked it up, weighing it carefully in his hand.

"Indeed it is. It caught my eye the instant I saw it," he looked back at Elizabeth and smiled. "I was on my Tour and had been in Rome but two hours. I had ventured into a back street in an attempt to escape the intensity of the sun, and once my eyes adjusted to the shade, I discovered myself to be in a veritable treasure-trove of a district, thriving with specialist shops and the most wonderful cafes – the aroma of the coffee there I shall never forget!"

Elizabeth smiled, but it faded slowly as a feeling of sadness swept through her. Why was it only now that she realised she could listen to Mr Darcy's voice endlessly? It mattered not what he was saying, merely hearing the timbre of his well-modulated, deep tones was sufficient to give her a sense of satisfaction she was hard put to deny.

"May I?"

With a start, Elizabeth realised he held out the figure, and she quickly extended her palm so that he could place the figurine gently on to it. Against his hands it had assumed tiny proportions, but resting on her own slender one she was better able to study it.

"It is exquisite. One cannot appreciate the detail from a sketch."

She looked up and found Mr Darcy's eyes upon her face rather than the sculpture and smiled tentatively at him before holding the piece out to him, but he did not take it at first. His gaze never left hers and the silence between them swelled for a moment, unimpaired by the other interactions in the room. Then, he too smiled.

"It pleases me that you like it. I have several other pieces by the same sculptor. If there is time after dinner, I will happily show them to you, if you would be interested?"

"I would like that very much."

Darcy took the figurine from her and replaced it on the table; then, with a small bow, he excused himself and walked over to join the company.

Elizabeth took a small sip from her glass, then a deeper one, letting the chilled liquid flow down her throat. For some reason, her heart had increased its rate, and she could feel the tell-tale warmth in her neck.

Then, catching her sister's concerned eye from where she sat beside Bingley, Elizabeth sent her a reassuring smile, and made her way across the room to join the rest of the party.

A half hour later, as the ladies took their places around the dining table, Darcy reflected upon the success of the evening so far, something that should not, but did, astound him. Yet, even as that thought flickered through his mind, he realised that he was a fool to be so surprised. His home was not Rosings; it was he who set the tone here, not his aunt, despite her formidable presence. And here she was, even in her role as hostess, utterly outnumbered by people with manners and social graces that far outshone her own. The irony that Elizabeth's relations could carry themselves in a class above a member of the aristocracy, did not fail to humble him anew.

How was it that he had moved through the world so? How could he not have become aware before now of his own prejudice? How could he have lived in such ignorance of the world beyond his own self-imposed boundaries? This lesson had been too long in coming, and he thanked Elizabeth from the bottom of his heart for the instruction, hard though it had been to accept at the time.

As the first course was laid before them, Darcy ran his eyes down the seating arrangement. To his right was Anne, followed by his other cousin – who was busy pouring a glass of wine for Georgiana on his other side – all part of his aunt's insistence that her daughter would only be safe in such tainted company if seated between himself and Fitzwilliam, and beyond his sister sat Bingley. To his left were Mrs Gardiner, Elizabeth, Jane and their uncle, the latter who had the misfortune to be placed on his aunt's right.

Torn between amusement and embarrassment, he realised that Lady Catherine had achieved her intention with the seating plan, albeit to her own detriment. She had successfully kept the 'trades people' from Anne and Georgiana's sides, but had had to sacrifice herself in the process – he could only hope that Mr Gardiner was of strong constitution. The division of the table, however, was clear to anyone who chose to deduce it, and he only hoped that Elizabeth would appropriate the arrangements to the correct source.

Chapter Seventeen

As THEY SET TO WITH their opening course, the conversation around the table became the typical ebb and flow of any dinner party. Lady Catherine, Darcy noted, had addressed a few words to Bingley who sat on her left, but had not – as far as he could determine – so much as acknowledged Mr Gardiner. That gentleman, however, did not appear in the slightest put out, enjoying a healthy debate with Elizabeth, Miss Bennet – who sat between them – merely smiling and occasionally shaking her head at her sister. He turned to his cousin, Anne, and addressed one or two comments to her, but her response was as short as ever, and he was unnerved by her unwavering stare. Thus it was that he welcomed the distraction of the servants bringing the next course, conscious of a sense of well-being as he observed the Gardiners and their nieces clearly enjoying his hospitality.

"Mr Darcy."

He turned and smiled at Mrs Gardiner.

"The painting there, is that not a view of Dove Dale?"

Darcy glanced over at the large painting which graced the wall above the mantelpiece and nodded. "Yes – yes, it is. There are several views of Derbyshire to be found in the house. I suspect you would recognise many of them."

Mrs Gardiner smiled. "It does not surprise me that you choose to keep some of the landscape nearby even when in Town. I do much the same myself." She returned her attention to her serving for a moment, then looked up. "I was quite heartbroken when I had to leave Derbyshire as a girl."

Though she now appeared focused upon her platter, Darcy was certain that Elizabeth's attention was with their conversation. As such, he was determined to show her that he not lost aught of his civility from the day before.

"To what part of the country did you move?"

"Hampshire, Sir." Momentarily, a cloud crossed Mrs Gardiner's face; then, she smiled wistfully. "I had only recently lost my mother to a sudden and aggressive fever, and my father, who was most sincerely attached to her, could not bear the associations. Thus it was that our manor was let on a long lease, and thereafter I was sent on to school in Winchester."

Darcy studied the lady beside him with compassion. The loss of his own mother was fresh in his mind as he replied, "That must have been a very difficult time."

"It was – yet every hardship has its blessing, does it not? I made the dearest of friends at school – Alicia McHale – or Harington, as she is now."

At this mention of the Harington name, Darcy found his attention well caught. "Nicholas' mother and I formed a deep bond at the time, being of similar background and not entirely… well, let us say that some were not so welcoming as others."

Darcy picked up the wine decanter, waving away a hovering servant, and topped up Mrs Gardiner's glass, welcoming the opportunity to indulge his curiosity so legitimately.

"I understand the Haringtons hail from Somerset – Mr Gardiner claimed an affinity for that county the other day. Can I assume there is a connection?"

Elizabeth's attention seemed to have been caught by Darcy's words, and she was now quite openly listening to their conversation, her eyes upon him. Feeling his throat tighten as his gaze met hers, he took a quick drink from his glass before returning his attention to the lady at his side.

"Yes; the Harington's shipping company was founded in Bristol, and my friend met her future husband during a season in Bath on her coming out." She paused as she too took a sip of her wine, before adding with a smile, "The Haringtons work closely with the East India Company, as does my husband – that was how we met, through the mutual acquaintance."

Before Darcy could respond to this, Elizabeth spoke.

"You are perhaps not aware, Sir, that my mother's family hail from the West Country, hence my uncle's business interests first developing in Bristol. It was, of course, the perfect location for someone intent upon infiltrating the shipping trade."

Darcy's interest quickened the moment Elizabeth entered the conversation, conscious that Mr Gardiner also looked in their direction.

"And do you yet have connections in that city, Sir?"

"Many in Bristol itself – and of course, the Haringtons are but thirty miles distant at Sutton Coker, and that is a strong association yet, as you may well assume, having met my Godson the other day."

Elizabeth let out a small laugh. "Indeed. Nicholas does tend to leave a lasting impression!"

Mr Gardiner laughed as well. "It is fortunate that he does, as he has now absconded!"

"I believe I understood him to return soon enough, Sir." Bingley ventured from across the table and the gentleman nodded.

"Indeed, indeed. And not all our engagements have been postponed in his absence. We had planned upon attending a breakfast on the morrow, in Vauxhall Gardens, and if the weather remains fine, we shall go, for it will be a pleasant way in which to pass the morning."

"Sounds like a capital thing to be doing," said Bingley enthusiastically. "I must congratulate you, Mr Gardiner, on the entertainments you have employed for your nieces. I wonder that they might ever wish for a return to the country."

"Oh, I cannot take all the credit." Mr Gardiner shook his head, smiling. "Nicholas is the instigator of much of the gallivanting that has taken place. He always had an inability to be still as a child, and it seems to have transposed itself as an adult into constantly needing to be out and about and doing things."

"We have been very grateful for everything that he has planned for us." Jane Bennet interjected, with a smile towards her aunt.

"Aye," added Mrs Gardiner, "And it is to be hoped that he does return, as he wished, for our entry to Lady Bellingham's ball was only assured by way of his acquaintance with us."

"Lady Bellingham" interrupted Lady Catherine loudly. "Did you say Lady Bellingham?"

Mrs Gardiner inclined her head. "Indeed, I did, Lady Catherine. Are you perchance acquainted with the lady?"

"She is known to me."

"She is my Godson's aunt, and has very kindly extended an invitation to us to attend a ball at her home on Monday."

Lady Catherine peered down the table at Mrs Gardiner, her gaze assessing. "You are fortunate in your connections, Madam. One wonders what your opportunities – and thus those for your nieces – would be without such an acquaintance. Only the very best of society will be present at Lady Bellingham's ball; there are those who crave the attention of an invitation, but will await it in vain."

Mrs Gardiner smiled pleasantly. "And did your ladyship accept her invitation? Shall we see you there?"

There was silence for a moment as all eyes turned towards Lady Catherine, who opened her mouth once, twice and then closed it with a snap. Conscious that Fitzwilliam, his shoulders shaking with silent mirth, attempted to conceal his amusement behind his napkin, Darcy struggled to keep the smile from his own face.

Finally, his aunt found her voice again. "I – it was not necessary. We are for Bath, after all, on the morrow."

"And do you look forward to your sojourn, Miss de Bourgh?" With relief, Darcy observed Elizabeth take up the conversational reins, and he quickly took a drink from his wine glass.

"I do."

"Is it some time since you were there last?"

Anne seemed somewhat reluctant to enter into conversation, and though she responded, it was with brevity, and before anyone else could venture a contribution, his aunt spoke again.

"You would, of course, not have had the opportunity of taking a Season in that city, Miss Elizabeth Bennet."

"Indeed, you are mistaken, Lady Catherine. I am as familiar with Bath as I am London, and must own to preferring it of the two."

"A Harington influence, I suspect," interjected Mr Gardiner with a smile as he picked up his napkin and wiped his mouth.

From his position at the head of the table, Darcy had an excellent view of the fond look bestowed by Jane Bennet on her sister, and he winced at the happy smile that overspread the latter's features at the mention of the name.

Conscious that the Colonel had thrown him a quick glance, Darcy discarded his knife and fork and picked up his glass, glad to allow the conversation to come and go around him once more as most of those present had something to say about Bath and its splendours. He frowned momentarily as he observed his cousin replenishing Georgiana's glass. It was not uncommon for his sister to partake of some wine with her meal, but he could not recall her ever imbibing more than one serving, yet she seemed perfectly content with Fitzwilliam's actions, taking a sip from the refilled glass even now.

Darcy returned his attention to his setting, and as the meal progressed towards the end of its main course and dessert was served, a change was heralded at the opposite end of the table. Though he could not tell the subject, Mr Gardiner had succeeded in engaging his aunt in conversation, and Darcy was surprised to note that Lady Catherine's expression had lost some of its hauteur. The way she had of looking down her nose as if something unpleasant were at her feet had gone entirely, and her manner of questioning her dinner companion could almost, at this distance, be considered eager.

He suppressed a smile and glanced over at the clock on the mantelpiece, conscious that time had passed swiftly – too much so. It struck him that he would normally have welcomed the ending of a dinner and the separation of the sexes; yet, on this occasion he felt quite the contrary.

"I say, Darce." The Colonel drew his attention. "Shall we flout convention and not separate after dinner?"

Darcy blinked, somewhat taken aback at the suggestion coming so hard upon his own wishes for such a reprieve, conscious that Elizabeth had looked over at him.

"Your company would be most welcome, Sir," Mrs Gardiner interjected. "But I cannot speak for all the ladies, of whom we number so many more than you gentlemen."

Lady Catherine's attention was caught. "What is being discussed, Darcy? I must have my say."

"Fitzwilliam has tabled it that we do not separate after dinner."

"Not separate? Darcy, that is my decision to make, not yours - nor your guests, I might add."

Fitzwilliam laughed. "I am hardly a guest, Aunt."

Lady Catherine turned her beady eye upon the Colonel, and Darcy winced as he saw Georgiana press herself back into her chair as if she would disappear into it.

"It is not what is done in polite society."

The Colonel snorted. "I am perfectly content to be classed as impolite so we can enjoy more time in such delightful company."

"Perhaps it would be best to follow convention," said Mrs Gardiner softly, and grateful for her understanding, Darcy gave her a brief smile as his aunt instructed the ladies to follow her to the drawing room.

The gentlemen stood as the ladies got to their feet, and Darcy fought against the inclination to assist Elizabeth by pulling her chair back, knowing full well that there were servants enough to render that service and that he would only draw attention by doing so.

Before she made to follow her aunt and sister, however, she turned and met his eye, giving him a wide smile and a brief curtsey. Conscious of the increase in his heart rate and the unexpected lurch of his insides, Darcy sat down rather suddenly as she walked away, reaching for the port decanter and pouring himself a hefty measure. So rarely had Elizabeth bestowed a genuine smile upon him, and if this was to be his reaction, he had best hope she did not repeat the gesture too frequently, for the sake of his sanity.

Picking up her cup, Elizabeth reflected on the evening thus far. Dinner had been delightful, though her attention had been torn between overhearing her uncle's dialogue with Lady Catherine and her attempts to not look constantly in Mr Darcy's direction to see how he fared. After all, not only did he have members of her family at his table whose connection he had so belittled, but he also honoured the woman who had rejected his offer of marriage with an invitation; yet, his manners towards his guests had been impeccable. With a contented sigh, she took a sip of her tea and looked around the room.

Georgiana had settled herself on a banquette beside her cousin, Anne, and appeared to be talking sporadically with her. Clearly, Miss de Bourgh was a little less reticent about conversing with her kin, and Elizabeth could not help but wonder if that was the mother's influence or her own inclination.

Seeing that Jane was ensconced on a chair between the two elder ladies and looking quite intimidated, she walked over to join them, sitting down next to her aunt on a velvet-covered chaise.

"That is a part of London that I have no familiarity with."

Lady Catherine's tone was as disparaging as ever.

Mrs Gardiner smiled. "I would be happy to show your Ladyship around, should you ever frequent the neighbourhood."

Biting her lip, Elizabeth hid her amusement at Lady Catherine's indignant expression.

"I am not likely to *frequent* Cheapside, Madam. It is such an inaccessible place, so far from anywhere of consequence. It must be dreadfully inconvenient."

With another smile, Mrs Gardiner inclined her head. "I believe we manage, Ma'am, and bear it as best we can."

Conscious that Lady Catherine's beady eye had lighted upon her, Elizabeth met her look calmly.

"Miss Elizabeth Bennet. So - who is this person, whose absence resulted in your postponement of a trip to the opera? Was it not the very same whose presence in Town caused your inconvenient early removal from the country?"

"I wonder at your Ladyship deeming my departure inconvenient. If it did not trouble Mrs Collins, then who else was affected by it?"

Mrs Gardiner rested a hand upon her niece's arm. "My Godson was called home by his father, Ma'am – an unavoidable situation, but he will return to us shortly."

Having no patience with Lady Catherine and being in no mood for another of her interrogations, Elizabeth gave her aunt an apologetic smile and got to her feet once more, walking over to where the two cousins sat and taking a chair nearby.

Georgiana gave an acknowledging smile, but Anne de Bourgh merely looked at her, and Elizabeth remained silent as the two ladies continued their dialogue for a moment, but when Georgiana paused to reach for her cup, Elizabeth turned to address her cousin.

"Are you a great reader, Miss de Bourgh?"

The lady studied her without responding for a moment, but then she shook her head.

"As you see," Anne indicated her spectacles, "My eyesight is not good. But despite this, I would say I am a keen observer."

She stared most pointedly at Elizabeth, who then said, "And do you enjoy London when you visit?"

"I take pleasure from any change of scene, albeit the company oft remains the same." Anne sighed. "Yet I must own it is a liberation to be rid of the obsequious little parson for a while."

Elizabeth released a small burst of laughter, but the lady cast her a conscious look, some colour flooding her sallow skin.

"I beg your pardon, Miss Bennet. That was unforgivably rude. I forget he is your cousin."

"Would that I could do likewise! There is no need for apology, Miss de Bourgh, for it is certain you could not find him any more an oddity than I do." Warming to the woman slightly, Elizabeth indicated the pianoforte close by. "Do you play?"

"I have – practised, in my companion's room. I find I am in no-one's way in that part of the house."

Biting back a laugh, Elizabeth's eyes met Anne's and for the first time, they exchanged a genuine smile.

Turning to the girl sitting opposite, Elizabeth's smile widened. "Miss Darcy – would you play something, if your cousin turns the pages?"

Two pairs of eyes viewed Elizabeth with no small amount of alarm, but she looked from one to the other encouragingly.

"We are but a small party here, all ladies. I will sing, if you like, though you may regret it!"

Elizabeth waited; Anne de Bourgh looked over at her young cousin, who pulled at her silk shawl nervously.

"Come, Georgiana. I have not heard you play in an age. Let us see if I can adequately follow the music to turn the pages at the right time, and we can be assured that no one will detect our errors for Miss Bennet's voice will be adequate distraction."

Laughing at this, Elizabeth got to her feet and smiled reassuringly at the still hesitant Georgiana.

"There, Miss Darcy. You have nothing to fear, for your aunt and mine shall be so astounded by the sound of my voice they will not even notice that I am accompanied."

Chapter Eighteen

THOUGH HE HAD ALLOWED his aunt her own way over the separation of the parties, Darcy had no intention of allowing it to be of any duration and, with the mutual agreement of the others, the four gentlemen were soon making their way along the hallway to join the ladies in the drawing room.

Darcy had been much entertained, and his cousin well amused, by Mr Gardiner's recounting of what had so successfully tamed their aunt during the latter half of the meal. Renowned within the family for her predilection for the saving of money and the cutting of expenses, she had come to realise that the 'tradesman' sat beside her had access to resources that she currently paid through the nose for and, more than that, could acquire things that she had to do without during these uncertain times in Europe.

The intimation from Mr Gardiner in response to a question from Bingley, that he could perhaps procure some excellent supplies through his connections, had been sufficient for her to feel him worth paying some court to.

As they approached the doors to the drawing room, Darcy stood aside that his guests might precede him, and as he did so his eye was caught by a tall, slender figurine resting on a side table in the hall. He recalled Elizabeth's interest in the statuette they had examined earlier, and as he turned to follow the others into the room, he determined to do as he had promised and offer her a chance to see some of the other pieces the family had collected.

It was apparent to Darcy the moment they entered the room that Elizabeth had just finished singing, and it seemed that his sister had been accompanying her. Disappointed though he was to have missed the opportunity of seeing them perform, he was highly gratified to see Georgiana and Elizabeth sharing their amusement over something that had clearly not gone to form; even his cousin, Anne, looked amused at their exchange.

He walked over to stand beside Mrs Gardiner, who, having joined the other ladies in applauding the impromptu display, now turned to him with a smile.

"Your sister plays delightfully, Mr Darcy. What a pleasure it is to have heard such a talent."

Darcy smiled in return.

"I am pleased that she felt able to perform." Then, he recalled Georgiana's imbibing of a little more wine than was her habit, and he wondered if that had given her the necessary courage. He lowered his voice somewhat. "She finds her aunt a little intimidating, I am sorry to say."

"Well, I can assure you that she acquitted herself admirably on this occasion – though I cannot say quite the same for Lizzy. She has a very pleasing voice, but she has a sense of fun that sometimes overrides her reason."

Darcy frowned but Mrs Gardiner smiled.

"She has just been adding a few of her own words to a popular song, Sir, much to the amusement of your sister and her cousin, but I suspect less so to your aunt!"

A glance at Lady Catherine's rather indignant expression was sufficient for Darcy to see that Mrs Gardiner was correct in her surmising, but in no humour to allow his aunt to express her displeasure, he turned to the company in general.

"I am taking Mrs Gardiner to see some of the paintings. Would anyone care to join us?" He turned to Elizabeth before anyone could respond, adding, "Miss Elizabeth – if you accompany us, there will be opportunity to see some of the figurines we discussed earlier."

It was soon settled that they both would accompany Darcy, and Georgiana quickly put herself forward to be one of the party, the remainder all being comfortably settled with their coffee, and soon they were walking along the first floor landing where Darcy showed them several watercolours of Derbyshire, along with a couple of family portraits of earlier generations of Darcys.

Some time later, having progressed to the second floor and leaving her aunt to admire a large painting that depicted the village of Lambton, something she studied with great delight, Darcy and Georgiana showed Elizabeth a wall-mounted presentation case that was filled with miniature sculptures, some of which were similar to that which she had admired in the drawing room earlier.

"They are so beautiful. How can you bear to not have them out on display?"

Darcy shrugged his shoulders, watching as Georgiana closed the glass doors of the cabinet. "There are just too many of them! I find that there are too few safe places to put them in the main rooms, so I tend to let them each take their turn in rotation."

"There is more space at Pemberley, of course," added Georgiana as she turned to face them both. "But some of the rooms have such grand proportions, and miniatures such as these... well, the setting does not do them justice, does it Brother?"

"Indeed not." He turned to smile at Mrs Gardiner who had come to join them.

"There is one other painting I would like to show you if you would care to follow me?" He led the way back along the landing, but Elizabeth lingered, taking one last look at the exquisite pieces of marble behind the glass frontage, and Georgiana waited for her.

Finally, with a sigh, she turned away.

"Forgive me, Miss Darcy. They are so beautiful; I could gaze at them for hours. You are most fortunate to be able to see them whenever you wish."

Georgiana looked a little culpable as she fell into step beside Elizabeth.

"I am afraid I do not really think about them, or remember to look at them as often as I perhaps should."

Elizabeth shook her head.

"Of course you do not. I am equally negligent of every ornament and painting at Longbourn! It is perfectly natural when one is surrounded by something to not pay it the interest of new eyes!"

They had reached the stairs now and both Mr Darcy and Mrs Gardiner had long disappeared; however, there was a lady just arriving on the landing and Miss Darcy introduced her to Elizabeth as Mrs Annesley, her companion. Liking the smiling countenance of the lady, Elizabeth greeted her warmly, telling her how well Miss Darcy had played for the ladies after dinner.

It was clear that Georgiana was embarrassed by this praise, but Mrs Annesley's smile widened, and she congratulated her charge on her increased confidence before wishing them both a pleasant evening and continuing on her way along the landing.

They hurried down both flights of stairs then and caught up with the others just as they were making their way along the main hallway towards the back of the house. They both paused, however, so that Mrs Gardiner could study another painting, an aspect that she was adamant she recognised but could not put a name to, and despite Mr Darcy's offering to tell her, she insisted on being allowed a moment to try and remember for herself.

Thus it was that Elizabeth continued along the hall with Georgiana, who led her into the small music room, saying that she wished to show her the pianoforte that she practised on every day.

The moment they entered the room, however, the young girl turned to her guest and said earnestly, ""My brother has told me a great deal about you."

"He – er, has he?" Elizabeth laughed ruefully. "I cannot pretend to hope that any of it was favourable." Feeling somewhat uneasy, she glanced about the room for a diversion.

"Oh, on the contrary, he thinks very highly of you."

Startled at the girl's words, Elizabeth's eyes flew to her face. "I am certain there are many he would hold in esteem."

"Are you?"

"Miss Darcy!"

"I do beg your pardon. I do not mean to make you awkward, nor to trap you into saying things that you would not. But – please forgive me – there is something that I wished… that I must ask you."

Elizabeth essayed a smile. "You are making me quite uneasy!"

"Do you – do you *like* my brother?" Georgiana spoke quickly, anxiety clearly writ upon her face.

Elizabeth stared at her. "Like him?"

"Yes. What I mean to say is – I do not wish to cause embarrassment or offence; I do not wish you to say what you do not feel. I just cannot understand… and it does not seem as if…"

Reaching out, Elizabeth touched Georgiana's restless hands. "Your beautiful shawl will be a rag if you persist in twisting it so."

"Please say you do not hate him!"

A profound silence followed these words, but seeing Georgiana become distressed, Elizabeth forced a smile.

"No, Miss Darcy. I can say, with my hand on my heart that I do not hate your brother. He is a good man. Clearly, he is an excellent brother to you!"

"You do not seek to pacify my feelings? You speak the truth?"

Astonished though she was by this unprecedented interrogation, Elizabeth nodded quickly.

"I do. I do not dislike him. I will admit that there was a time when I did not understand him as well as I do now. But I can say with all honesty that I... I do like him."

"And do you find him handsome?"

"Miss Darcy!"

Thankfully, at that moment Mrs Gardiner entered the room, followed by the gentleman in question. He frowned when his eye met his sister's, and Elizabeth could not fail to notice that he paled suddenly, his gaze moving quickly to meet hers; no doubt he would detect the colour that had risen so recently to her cheeks, but Elizabeth could only let out a sigh of relief that her private discourse with his sister had been forestalled.

Keen to reassure him, however, that whatever he might be thinking, nothing was amiss, she smiled at him.

"This is a beautiful room, Sir. I believe if I had a room such as this to practice in, my talent at the instrument would have progressed further than it has."

Mrs Gardiner laughed. "And I believe that would only ever be the case should you have an instrument out of doors! My niece, Sir, since her earliest days, has found every excuse to be outside rather than in, and it does somewhat hamper her ability to practise!"

With a smile, Darcy held the door ajar for the ladies, and soon Elizabeth found herself in the masculine domain of his study. Full of curiosity, she forbore from staring around too much, conscious that it would be ill-mannered to do so, but it took all of her will power to look at nothing but the wall he directed their attention to.

Leaning against his desk, Darcy watched Elizabeth staring at the watercolour of Pemberley in its glorious setting, backed by tree-covered hills, the golden stone bathed in sunlight. It had been done by a master hand, and was incredibly like; he derived much comfort from its presence during his periods of residence in Town, though it caused him no end of homesickness at times.

Mrs Gardiner asked a few questions of Georgiana, but Elizabeth remained silent, and when she finally turned to face him, her expression was unreadable. Realising that the evening really had reached its conclusion, he sighed before straightening up and leading the small party back out into the hallway. He watched his sister attach herself to Mrs Gardiner as they walked along the hall towards the drawing room, fairly certain her purpose was to delay him from questioning her about what it was she had been saying when they were interrupted…

"Mr Darcy?"

He glanced down quickly at Elizabeth.

"Forgive me, my mind was wandering."

She smiled up at him and then cast a quick glance along the hall towards the retreating backs of Mrs Gardiner and Georgiana.

"We are most grateful for your inviting us into your home, Sir. I wished to thank you for the warm hospitality you have extended towards my family this evening."

"It has been a pleasure." Darcy hesitated. "I must own that, much as I admire your aunt, my respect for your uncle has reached new heights since I discovered his ability to tame Lady Catherine."

She laughed. "Indeed. My aunt has often said that he should have been a diplomat. I am certain that years of practice with his siblings gave him much experience of how to handle unmanageable women...oh!" she broke off, blushing. "Forgive me; that was unpardonable. I meant no offence towards your aunt, Sir."

Darcy could not help but laugh, both at the sentiment and her appalled expression.

"Truly, Miss Bennet?"

"Truly, Sir! The slight was directed towards my own aunt and, wrongly of me I am sure, my mother."

They began to walk in unison along the hallway to join the others.

"There is some similarity in our experience of aunts, then. We each have one of whom we are proud, and one whose behaviour can sometimes cause embarrassment."

Elizabeth nodded. "My Aunt Gardiner, as you have seen for yourself, is refined, charming, intelligent and well-mannered. My Aunt Philips – well, suffice it to say, there is little similarity other than their sex!"

Darcy smiled but made no response – we could well recall Mrs Philips, found as she so often was hand in hand with Mrs Bennet, and two very silly sisters they were for grown women. However, if there was one lesson Darcy had learned, it was not to criticise the family of others when there were members of his own who could draw equal censure.

"You have another aunt, then, Mr Darcy? Other than Lady Catherine?"

"Indeed. The Colonel's mother. She and Lady Catherine are like each other as day is to night."

They had almost reached the open doors to the drawing room, but instead of standing aside so that she could enter ahead of him, Darcy stopped and, putting out a hand, touched Elizabeth's arm. She stopped too, glancing down at his hand resting on her glove, and he removed it quickly.

Every time they met, he feared he might never lay eyes upon her again; she was his last thought before sleeping, and the one he awoke to. Now that the time for saying goodbye once more approached, he felt he could not bear it, yet he knew not how to prolong their stay.

Conscious that Elizabeth observed him quietly, he roused himself to speak. "And so you are for Vauxhall?"

"Yes – for the breakfast. If the weather remains fair, it will be most pleasant." She paused. "Is it – do you – have you ever been?"

Darcy shook his head. The temptation to tell her he would be there on the morrow, if only she would ask him, that he would go anywhere with her that she solicited of him, was so strong that he had to bite his lip to prevent the words spilling out.

They stared at each other in silence for some seconds. The urge to reach out and touch her face possessed him, and involuntarily he took a step closer to her. The voices in the drawing room were becoming ever louder, but he refused to heed them and held his breath, only to release it in a rush as she spoke.

"Well – should you determine to break your fast there, I think you would find the seating near the pond enjoyable, and the gardens themselves are particularly inviting for a stroll."

"Darcy! There you are. Come, it is time to farewell the guests."

Lady Catherine's appearance in the doorway was not unexpected, and with a sigh he gestured to Elizabeth to precede him into the room where he found everyone on their feet and making their way towards the door.

There was all the usual confusion as hats, coats, cloaks and canes were distributed and the guests took their leave. For Darcy, it all seemed to happen in a rush, and barely had the door closed upon them before Lady Catherine gave voice to her opinion, culminating with, "They have their uses, these trades people, Darcy, though I must strongly advise you against admitting them into your home in such a manner, and at the very least, restricting your interactions with them to your study and matters of business. This dining in such company – it is not to be borne."

With as much patience as he could muster, Darcy steered the lady towards the stairs, allowing her to further vent her feelings before wishing her a good night's rest and thanking her for her assistance with the evening. He watched Georgiana as she followed her aunt and cousin up the stairs, knowing she would pause at the top to wave at him before disappearing along the landing. His curiosity as to what she had been saying to Elizabeth when he had interrupted them he could stem for the present.

As he turned to re-join the gentlemen for a nightcap before retiring for the night, Darcy ruminated instead upon the merits of early summer in the city, and how he could justify to his cousin and Bingley his sudden desire to indulge in an outdoor breakfast.

Chapter Nineteen

CAROLINE BINGLEY WAS most seriously displeased. Her brother's determination to seek out Jane Bennet and renew the acquaintance, after the trouble taken by herself and Mr Darcy to sever all connection, was really quite intolerable. Now Charles seemed to spend every conceivable moment in the country girl's insipid company, and what was equally frustrating, the impertinent sister had also resurfaced.

How Caroline regretted her precipitous declaration of refusing to ever set foot in Gracechurch Street again. Having to leave Mount Street so that the Darcys could pay their call had been galling, and Caroline had been ruminating on the repercussions even as the carriage pulled away from the kerbstone. How could Mr Darcy answer for visiting in such a neighbourhood?

The fact that the Bennet sisters and their Cheapside relations had dined at Darcy's home on the previous evening further disturbed Caroline. Her exclusion from these events brought her little solace, even though she eschewed the company, and meant that no opportunity had arisen to discuss with Mr Darcy this dangerous re-acquaintance of her brother with Jane Bennet. She was certain that he must be as appalled as she and thus had determined to accompany Charles on every possible occasion to prevent him from doing something incredibly stupid.

As for Miss Eliza Bennet, she was an aggravation, but nothing more. She had been conscious of Mr Darcy's notice of the girl during their stay in Hertfordshire, but did not fear he would make a fool of himself over her. She knew full well his opinion of the Bennet family, and though intrigued by her, he was no simpleton and knew his duty to his family.

Thus Caroline had determined to secure the earliest opportunity to speak with Mr Darcy regarding her brother, and it was this resolution that saw her up and about at an hour far earlier than was her wont, intent on joining the gentleman in the local church.

A tinkle of bells from the carriage clock drew her attention to the passage of time, and she hurried from the room, casting a glance at her reflection in each mirror that she passed as she made her way down the stairs.

Caroline's appearance in the hall at such an early hour was no doubt the reason for the rather startled look upon the features of the maid as she hurried past her to open the door to a liveried servant.

Elizabeth scooped up her shawl and a straw bonnet and made her way down the stairs, just as the bells of the nearby church tolled the hour of ten. She stopped as she reached the hall and sat down on the bottom step, the bonnet held listlessly in her hands. They had agreed as a family to forego the morning service at St Clements and to attend evensong instead, that they might enjoy their morning in Vauxhall; however, the reminder of it being Sunday brought back a flood of memories and with it an uprush of emotion.

Her mind was all confusion. Images of Mr Darcy, from his rain-soaked visage in the copse to his earnest gaze as he spoke to her last evening assailed her, and as Elizabeth's insides twisted in what had become a familiar sensation, she recalled her conversation with Georgiana Darcy, and that young lady's question: did she find him handsome?

With a soft sigh, Elizabeth acknowledged that she did. Though it had taken their physical encounter to open her eyes and see once more the fine figure and countenance that she had noted on the first night of their acquaintance, she could not deny that, as often as she had thought of him these past days in relation to her growing understanding of him and his character, she had also been drawn to his appearance.

She knew herself to be achingly aware of his touch, and the slightest gesture or facial expression caught her attention instantly. Elizabeth was suddenly reminded of the moment in the hallway on the previous night, when Mr Darcy had placed his hand upon her arm to stay her progress, and a tell-tale warmth filled her cheeks. *Can there be so much awareness in a man's touch… that it turns one's head?*

"There you are!"

With a start, Elizabeth looked up and saw Jane peering round the drawing room door.

"Am I delaying everyone?" Relieved at the interruption, she got to her feet and joined her sister, dropping her shawl and bonnet on top of Jane's on a chair near the door.

"Uncle has gone to have the carriage brought about and Aunt had forgotten her compact. She will be down directly." Jane walked over to the window. "It is a beautiful morning. We are fortunate with the weather."

Elizabeth stood in front of the fireplace, her eye caught by what she now knew to be one of the late Mrs Seavington's paintings. Doubtless, like all the others, it was a Derbyshire view, and she tilted her head aside a little as she considered it, wondering if it bore any similarity of aspect to those she had been shown at Mount Street the night before. Conscious that Jane had come to stand beside her, she reached out and took her sister's hand and squeezed it, before releasing a sigh.

"Lizzy?"

"Hmmm?"

"Aunt Gardiner said that you saw a painting of Pemberley."

Elizabeth nodded, her eyes yet fixed upon the landscape before her. "Indeed, we did."

"May I ask what you thought of it?"

Elizabeth shook her head wistfully. The beauty of the property had quite overwhelmed her, and likewise, so had its proportions – so much so, she had been left without words. Letting out a huff of laughter, she turned to face her sister.

"Why, that of all that property, I might have been mistress and what a fearful mess I should have made of it!"

"Do be serious, Lizzy."

"Oh, but I am. Perfectly so. It was not a house, or even a manor. It was a veritable mansion! And the acreage must be substantial."

"It must have – I cannot conceive what must have passed through Mr Darcy's mind whilst showing you his family home, after all that has gone between you."

As this was precisely what had passed through her own mind at the time, Elizabeth gave a rueful smile. "You feel too much for all of us, dear Jane. Do not be so concerned; Mr Darcy did not seem to confer any especial connection to showing us the painting."

"But do you not wonder... about if..." Jane's voice trailed away, as if she were unsure of how to ask the question, and Elizabeth threw her a loving glance before saying, brightly.

"Oh yes. I do wonder – if it would not have been the perfect place for a game of hide and seek!"

Jane shook her head, but as their aunt joined them at that moment, the subject was put aside as they all turned to make their way out to the front of the house where Mr Gardiner awaited them.

Within a half hour, they were safely delivered to Vauxhall Gardens and joined the throng of people heading for the pavilion where various refreshments were on offer and, having secured a table and some chairs, they were soon settled in the warm sunshine, a waiting-boy on his way to collect their order.

It took all of Elizabeth's will power to not continuously look about her and not eye each new figure on the path with eager interest. She had no reason to anticipate Mr Darcy's presence this morning, yet she could not help from hoping for it. Had he understood her meaning the night before? Elizabeth sighed as yet another group of people passed by and, excusing herself from her party, she rose from the table and walked over to the iron railings that bounded the large boating pond at its centre.

The attempt to distract herself was unsuccessful, however; albeit to the casual observer she was fascinated by a flock of geese presently coming in to land upon the water, her thoughts had returned swiftly to the pleasures of the previous evening.

"Good morning, Miss Bennet."

At the sound of the gentleman's voice, she sent a silent but heartfelt thank you up above before turning to face Mr Darcy, unable and indeed unwilling to suppress her smile of welcome, a smile that widened as her eyes finally rested upon him. He looked particularly fine to her this morning, and she was more than taken with his hesitant smile.

She curtseyed in response to his formal bow, conscious of a deep sense of satisfaction.

"Good morning, Mr Darcy. Have you come, then, to partake of the fare?"

For a second he looked a little awkward; then, shaking his head, he said, "No – no, I did not."

Elizabeth raised a brow, and he added, "I must own that I came solely to partake of the company."

She could not help but smile at this.

"Then I, for one, am most gratified that you did." He met her eye with more confidence, and the hesitant smile that had greeted her became a full one.

Conscious of her pleasure in having drawn such a smile from him, Elizabeth indicated the table where her family were seated, and they both turned to walk towards it.

Striving to bring her feelings under control and unsure precisely what was happening to her, Elizabeth drew in a deep breath and blew it out slowly as they reached the table. Bingley had seated himself beside her sister and her aunt and uncle were clearly engrossed in conversation with Georgiana Darcy and the Colonel. It was only as Mr Darcy pulled out a chair for Elizabeth to sit on that she became aware of the final member of their party: Caroline Bingley stood to one side, the disdain apparent upon her face for all who cared to look.

Caroline's plan had almost been thwarted, but good fortune had favoured her. A note had arrived for her sister advising that Charles must renege on his commitment to call that morning due to an unanticipated engagement: a public breakfast in Vauxhall Gardens.

Though she could not discern from this that any formal arrangement had been made, Caroline was convinced her brother's sole incentive was to seek out Miss Bennet, prompted by something that had happened during dinner the previous evening. As she was keen to speak with Mr Darcy as soon as possible regarding her concerns, she was not prepared to sacrifice the opportunity, however little the excursion was to her taste. Thus it was that she had penned a hastily composed note expressing a keen desire to join her brother and had it despatched forthwith to Mount Street, that he might know to collect her on his way past.

The Hursts had evinced some surprise when Caroline had partaken of a hearty breakfast, but she had no intention of consuming a morsel of food during this ridiculous outing. Her distaste for the anticipated company notwithstanding, she and nature had a longstanding indifference to one another and, as such, she refused to eat out of doors when all manner of airborne insects might land upon the fare.

Thus, once the waiting-staff arrived with their order, everyone but Caroline set-to with their meal of pound cake and fruit loaf, the gentlemen settling for tea whilst the ladies indulged themselves with hot chocolate.

Caroline strolled around the table, making a circle of their group and pretending to ignore them whilst at the same time listening avidly to the conversation as she passed by.

"Come, Caroline, will you not sit?"

Her brother's voice hailed her, and she moved her parasol to her other hand as she answered him.

"I prefer to walk, Charles."

"Well, you are making me dizzy, circling us all like a great vulture."

There was a smattering of laughter at this, and Caroline threw Elizabeth a sour look where she sat next to the Colonel. Being likened to a bird of prey was not the image she aspired to, that of a refined woman, able to exhibit the air and manner of walking that befitted someone of Mr Darcy's own rank and status.

Yet the gentleman appeared not to have noticed the exchange, deep in conversation as he was with Mr Gardiner.

Resuming her walk, Caroline threw her brother an angry glance as she passed him, a pointless gesture as his attention had long returned to Jane Bennet.

Some time later, fully replete, the party rose from their table as one. Caroline, who had spent the past hour on her feet and wished for nothing more than a seat upon which to rest them, found their professed intent was to walk through the gardens for a while.

As everyone busied themselves with shawls and parasols, hats and gloves, Caroline fulminated on how best to achieve her objective of speaking to Mr Darcy. Edging near to where he assisted his sister, she let out a meaningful sigh.

"I am somewhat weary, I must own," she said, to all intents to no one in particular but with her gaze fixed upon the back of her target.

Turning to receive her shawl across her arms, Georgiana looked at her with concern.

"Perhaps you should rest here, Miss Bingley," she suggested. "You will be able to recover whilst we stroll."

Caroline repressed the urge to roll her eyes at the girl's suggestion and forced a smile.

"You are so thoughtful, my dear, but I would not forsake the company on such a fine morning. I merely have need of an arm to assist me."

Mr Darcy, who had by this time offered his one arm to Georgiana, then turned and offered the other to Caroline, as she had known he must, who grasped it willingly, despite the fact that she had hoped to be his only companion.

Fate continued its kindness, however, for they had gone but a few paces when Georgiana stopped and turned to her brother.

"Fitz, may I go on ahead? I would like very much to talk to Miss Elizabeth Bennet, and she is currently walking alone up ahead."

Darcy's gaze, which Caroline was quick to notice was even now fixed upon Elizabeth Bennet, moved rapidly to his sister. They seemed to exchange a look she could not fathom, her curiosity intensified by Georgiana saying, "I will do as promised."

Caroline's eyes moved to Darcy's face, but he merely gave his sister a faint smile.

"Off you go, then."

Thus it was that Caroline, now transferred to Darcy's right arm, was able to secure the moment she wished for and, walking slower than was her usual manner, managed to draw the two of them a few paces behind the stragglers of their party, namely Charles and Miss Bennet.

"I welcome this opportunity to speak with you, Sir. I trust you are as alarmed as I over recent developments."

Darcy threw her a quick look before returning his gaze to the front.

"I do not understand you."

Caroline uttered an irritated 'tsk' and swung her parasol aside that she might look properly at him. "After all our efforts, Sir, *this* is what we are confronted with." She waved a gloved hand at the couple ahead of them.

"On the contrary, Madam, I am not alarmed. I am gratified to see that the damage we both inflicted upon your brother is in a fair way to being mended."

Caroline stumbled, and she tightened her grip upon his arm as she righted herself, her parasol wobbling precariously for a second.

"You are *gratified?* Surely you do not condone it?"

"I do condone it. I have confessed my interference to Bingley, and I have tendered my apology. I am fortunate that he is of such a forgiving nature."

131

"But – but," she struggled to formulate words that fully expressed her feelings, and they walked in a strained silence for some distance. Then, she turned a fiery glance upon her companion. "But their connections – their lack of dowry –"

"Miss Bingley," Darcy came to a halt and turned to face her, and she perforce had to release his arm and stop too. "They mean nothing to your brother. If he wishes to pursue the acquaintance, you should wish him happy."

Caroline observed him in astonishment. "But we are of like minds on this!"

"We were, Madam, but no longer."

"But the family!"

"You would do well to consider your own family before paying mind to any other. Surely your brother's happiness is of paramount importance?"

Caroline stared at him aghast. "But not to the detriment of *mine*!"

Chapter Twenty

THE REMAINDER OF THEIR PARTY had come to a halt near a coppice of beech trees and, finding his conversation with Caroline Bingley distasteful, Darcy increased his pace and she was, perforce, obliged to keep in step with him.

In no humour to spend any further time in discussion of Bingley and Miss Bennet, he determined his best protection would be in numbers, and as she was the only person not currently walking with a partner, Georgiana now being stood in conversation with Mrs Gardiner, he walked forward before he could have any qualms about it and offered Elizabeth his spare arm.

Her surprise was quickly concealed, and he struggled to suppress a sigh of contentment as she accepted the offer and turned to step into pace with them. He sensed rather than saw her glance up at him.

"Your sister tells me that your aunt and cousin were seen safely on their way this morning."

"Yes – yes, they were." Darcy refrained from sharing with his walking companions just how relieved he was at their departure. His aunt's manner he was somewhat inured to; what he had found most unsettling was Anne, whose eyes seemed to be upon him with far too much frequency for comfort. What passed through her mind was anyone's supposition, for she spoke to him as little as ever, and it was with no little relief that he had wished them both a pleasant stay in Bath and waved them off.

Caroline Bingley looked up at Darcy with a smile. "Lady Catherine de Bourgh has such a refined air, Sir. It is her inherent elegance and her perfect good manners that place her above the rule."

The sudden turning away of Elizabeth's head and the slightest increase in the pressure of her hand upon his arm gave Darcy to understand her amusement at this notion of his aunt, but before he could muster any response, Bingley hailed his sister.

"Caroline! Do come. Here are Mr and Mrs Williams, and they are asking after you most particularly."

With a huff of displeasure, Caroline excused herself from Darcy, giving Elizabeth nothing more than a cursory nod of her head, and they both turned to resume their walk without her.

"We all enjoyed our evening at your home very much, Sir."

"No more so than I." He paused, trying to think of something to discuss – anything. Walking with Elizabeth on his arm like this was a cruel comfort, her nearness both enticing and daunting him as one.

"I found your collection of figurines quite delightful. Would you tell me something of your travels in Europe?"

He threw her a quick glance, smiling faintly. "It would be my pleasure. Do you have a particular place that you wish to hear of?"

"No – no, I would have you tell me what you think I would most like to hear."

Darcy's lips parted to respond, but the faint echo of those words being exchanged between them on an earlier occasion drew a frown.

"Forgive me." Elizabeth glanced up at him. "I am teasing you."

Suppressing the urge to place his other hand on top of hers, he shook his head.

"I wonder at my surprise. I am clearly not the quick learner that I used to be."

Elizabeth smiled. "Well then, Sir, I shall have to instruct you further. Now – tell me about Italy. You mentioned Rome to me last night and it has whetted my appetite to hear more of that country."

More than willing to oblige, Darcy began a rambling account of his travels during his Tour, of his journey through France, *"fields of sunflowers, row upon row, their heads all turned up to face the sun,"* and onward into Italy.

"And did Rome impress you the most of the cities you visited?"

For a moment they continued in silence as Darcy's thoughts flew back to those few months when he had been on the Continent. His father had not yet passed away and the burden of Pemberley, of raising Georgiana, had not yet fallen upon his young shoulders. Then, he roused himself.

"No – no it did not. It is a beautiful city, do not mistake me, but the one that touched me most profoundly was Florence."

Elizabeth glanced up at him as he said this, and he met her look openly. He had not reflected upon this period of his life for so long and was astounded at how much pleasure there was to be drawn from the simplicity of walking with her on his arm and telling her of such things.

"And are you prepared to share with me its attraction?"

"I am more than willing to tell you, though I must own that on first acquaintance, the beauty of it left me quite without words."

At this Elizabeth's smile widened, and he met her eye with a questioning glance.

"Then, Sir, must we blame the splendours of Florence for your tendency to reticence?"

Darcy smiled ruefully, acknowledging the hit. "Indeed. Did you not notice the rather splendid watercolour of the Uffizi on the wall of the Meryton Assembly Rooms?"

Elizabeth laughed, and the pleasure at having caused her to do so filled him so swiftly it almost took his breath away. Conscious of the tightening of the familiar band about his chest that seemed his constant companion of late, he swallowed quickly and returned his gaze to the fore.

"It is a beautiful place, with splendid architecture, especially the places of worship. And at noon, the bells from all the churches would chime — some deep, others lighter, all tones, echoing up into the surrounding hills — you could even hear them when at Boboli."

"Boboli?" Elizabeth seemed to be testing the pronunciation as she questioned the word.

"The Boboli Gardens — most decidedly my favourite place to linger. They are built into a hillside overlooking the city, a stunning prospect as the sun begins to lower in the sky, with its terracotta roof tops set against the distant mountains."

"What was it that so appealed to you there?"

"I am not sure I can say precisely. The solitude, perchance; finding abundant nature so close to the city — there were ponds fully stocked with a myriad of fish, and the purity of the bird song was unsullied by the sound of carriages thundering past! To be certain, many of the trees were full young, with only twenty years' growth upon them, but one could imagine how they might appear to future generations."

"And would you like to return one day? To see how they fared?"

"Without a doubt." He looked down at Elizabeth; if she only knew how much he wished he could take her there, show her the beauty of those gardens. He was certain she would derive even more pleasure from it than he.

"And what of the wildlife? Did you see any rare species?"

Darcy shook his head. "Nothing in particular, though there were many small lizards scurrying underfoot. At a distance they appeared brown and plain, but upon closer inspection, I found them to have bright eyes, a symmetry to their form and a fine grace to the their limbs and-"

He broke off, and they both stopped walking as a somewhat out of breath Caroline Bingley materialised at his side. "Oh Mr Darcy! How brave you are to face such creatures."

Darcy chose not to dignify her comment with an answer, turning back to Elizabeth. "If you were fortunate, you could catch one with your bare hands – they are very small and fit in my palm quite easily."

With a gasp, Caroline paled and grasped his arm. "Oh Sir! You did not… you could not let it climb upon your hand! It would be most terrifying!"

Darcy's lips twitched, but he maintained his sombre visage as he removed her grasp from his coat sleeve and placed it on his arm as they began to walk again.

"On the contrary, Madam. I have met members of the human race who terrify me more."

Before long, the walking party had completed a leisurely circle of the gardens, and, at Bingley's persuasion, they found themselves a large table and settled down, prepared to enjoy a final cup of tea before separating for the remainder of the day.

Elizabeth felt some relief at being able to distance herself from Mr Darcy. Much as she had appreciated walking with him, listening to him talk, it was that very enjoyment that unsettled her. Conscious as she was that every touch seemed to agitate her senses more and more, she had been torn by the sensations inspired by walking so closely at his side and the realisation that these stolen moments of companionship were merely hinting at something she had lost. As it was, she took a seat on the opposite side of the table to Mr Darcy, failing to appreciate at the time that this afforded her a full view of his person instead.

The conversation milled around her as the servants poured tea for everyone and a plate of biscuits was passed around, and, her eye caught momentarily by Caroline Bingley swatting futilely at a fly that seemed to be in earnest contemplation of her reticule, she smiled ruefully. Was it possible that a week to the very day that she had spurned the offer of Mr Darcy's hand, she felt some regret? Knowing that this was a futile direction for her thoughts, she roused herself and tried to pay attention to the conversation, which it appeared had turned to their evening out on Monday.

"We are to attend a ball at Lady Bellingham's – she is my Godson's aunt on his father's side."

Mrs Gardiner addressed the Colonel, and he nodded. "Ah, yes. I recall it being mentioned last night."

Mr Gardiner turned to the gentleman at his side. "Will you be attending, Mr Darcy?"

Elizabeth glanced at him quickly, surprised to find his eyes upon her as he replied, "I am not very fond of dancing."

"That was not the question, Sir."

There was a burst of general laughter and Darcy smiled.

"No, indeed it was not." He glanced at Mr Gardiner. "I will own that there is a strong likelihood I have an invitation at home."

"A strong likelihood? You do not know, when the ball is but four and twenty hours hence?"

The Colonel snorted.

"Darcy has yet to address the vast pile of invitations that clutter his desk since his return from Kent. He moves it around a little, occasionally shuffles it. Sometimes, I believe, he even adds to it. But that is the sum of it."

Mrs Gardiner smiled kindly. "You do not enjoy the social scene in Town, Mr Darcy?"

"No – I confess I do not."

Caroline Bingley swivelled in her seat to look at Mrs Gardiner. "In general terms, perhaps not, but Mr Darcy's enjoyment of society depends very much upon the inducement, Ma'am. Let us say, some *invitations* will be more welcome than others."

Bingley laughed. "Do not be such a snob, Caroline!"

Amused at Caroline Bingley's presumption in speaking for Mr Darcy, Elizabeth could not resist saying, "I do believe that Lady Bellingham is considered the highest level of society, is she not?"

Mr Gardiner grunted. "Indeed, she is. And lest anyone be unsure, she can be certain to remind them of it with alacrity!"

Caroline's gaze had narrowed, and she turned to her brother.

"Charles, I trust you accepted *your* invitation to this ball?"

Bingley laughed with genuine amusement.

"Accept? Indeed, Caroline, I would gladly do so; however, I was not invited. You did not hear Lady Catherine last night. She echoed Miss Elizabeth's sentiments – only the very cream of society garners the attention of Lady Bellingham."

Mr Gardiner turned back to Mr Darcy.

"Well, Sir, I regret that I shall not be able to enjoy your company. There are very few men I can anticipate spending my time with at a ball, and I had hoped that you might help relieve me of the tedium."

"My dear! You will be required upon the dance floor at least twice!"

"But what of the rest of the evening? A man must have some conversation!"

A light-hearted dispute began between the married couple as everyone began to gather their belongings and then turned to make their way along a wide, tree-lined avenue towards their respective conveyances. Elizabeth was engrossed in her thoughts, struggling to accept that this time, she and Mr Darcy really were going to be saying goodbye. With Jane heading for Longbourn soon at their mother's persuasion, there would be no inducement for Mr Bingley to seek them out in Town, even had he not been intent on returning to Netherfield himself. Thus the likelihood of them crossing paths was substantially reduced and...

"Miss Bennet."

Rousing herself from her speculations, Elizabeth turned to find Mr Darcy at her side once more, and she looked up at him expectantly.

"Forgive me." He spoke hurriedly and glanced over his shoulder before returning his gaze to her. "I am experiencing a small dilemma; I would not wish to offend you."

Puzzled but intrigued, Elizabeth smiled at him as they walked on. "Come, Mr Darcy. We have both proved ourselves adept at causing each other offence at one time or another! Let us be done with apologies and deal openly as best we can."

He nodded, but his expression remained serious. "If I were to... should our paths cross once more during your stay in Town, be it a - er - ball or other gathering where dancing was the form, we would all meet as established acquaintances."

A tremor of anticipation rippled through Elizabeth. Was he contemplating attending a social event that was allegedly against his inclination?

"I have yet to discern the affront, Sir!"

He smiled briefly. "I would be expected to invite all the ladies of that party to dance – indeed, it would be an honour, not an obligation."

"It would?"

"Surely you cannot imagine that I have any objection to this?"

Elizabeth laughed. For some reason, her heart felt lighter than it had all week. "Mr Darcy, I am quite certain you have every objection. However, I remain yet unoffended."

"Do you doubt the sincerity of my pleasure in the acquaintance of your family?"

"Sir, it is not the connection that I believe you object to, but the dancing!"

"Ah, but there is a certain caveat over my desire or otherwise to dance."

"Will you enlighten me – or might I be offended?"

Smiling, Darcy shook his head. "I am not fond of dancing per se, it must be owned. But my objection tends to lie not with the activity but with the choice of partner. On this occasion, I would have no cause for complaint."

Elizabeth threw him a quick glance. "So what is it, Sir, that makes you fear causing offence?"

For a moment he said nothing, but she was conscious that they had both instinctively slowed their pace, falling back a little way from the others who had even now arrived at the carriage stand.

Then, he cleared his throat. "In the present circumstances, I fear it may be a punishment for you to stand up with me; yet should I do you the service of not asking for your hand, that the obligation not be forced upon you, it may cause more of an affront than if you had to endure my company for a set." He looked uncomfortable, and Elizabeth felt her throat constrict with compassion as he continued. "My endeavours to give you distance these past days have come to naught."

"Your consideration is appreciated, Sir. Should you – if we should ever chance upon each other in such a manner, then be assured that I would accept the former over the latter, if it is all the same to you? You may well be no devotee of dances, but I assure you, I am none too fond of sitting them out!"

For a moment, there was silence as they came to a halt near where the carriages stood, and then he smiled and inclined his head. "Then I am glad I sought your opinion on the matter. I hope that you enjoy the remainder of your stay in Town."

Dropping a quick curtsey, Elizabeth eyed him thoughtfully as he bowed his leave before turning to hand his sister into their conveyance. Their conversation this morning, coupled with the attention he had bestowed upon her at his home the previous day, presented facets of him that had heretofore been concealed, revealing a side of him that he was adept at keeping hidden from those outside his immediate circle. What frightened her was how much this aspect of him appealed to her.

Thus it was that she was thankful when her sister hailed her, and within minutes she was ensconced in her uncle's carriage and on her way back to Gracechurch Street; her mind, however, remained in as much disarray as ever.

Chapter Twenty One

SUNDAY AFTERNOON PASSED SLOWLY in Mount Street. Having enjoyed a leisurely meal, the occupants of the house went their separate ways, Georgiana and Mrs Annesley settling themselves in the summerhouse with their books, Bingley paying his postponed call upon his sister and her husband and the Colonel taking up residence in Darcy's study with the previous day's paper.

Unable to settle, Darcy prowled the hallway, seeking a distraction that would prevent his mind from drifting towards Elizabeth, but to no avail. He entered the small music room, only to be reminded vividly of walking in upon his sister and their guest on Saturday.

With a rueful smile, he recalled his conversation that morning with a rather abashed Georgiana, who had confessed to allowing her conversation with Elizabeth to drift into somewhat delicate territory, though precisely what that meant, she had begged him not to ask. Darcy had respected her wish. It was obvious from her mortified expression that she regretted whatever it was she had been endeavouring to achieve, and Elizabeth, though her colour had been high, had not seemed particular perturbed by it. He had, however, extracted a promise from Georgiana not to attempt anything similar in future, and she had consented willingly.

Withdrawing from the room, he walked along the hall again, but every picture that he passed reminded him of the previous evening. Impatiently, he ran a hand through his hair and turned on his heel, heading back towards the rear of the house where he eyed the slightly ajar door to his study for a moment, but knew that the papers would hold little sway over his recalcitrant thoughts, and he walked instead to the window that overlooked the garden.

He and Elizabeth had reached a rapprochement. His relief that the antagonism surrounding his rejection was a thing of the past was countered by the fact that the more time he spent in her company, the deeper his feelings for her became. Was it really but seven days since that awful confrontation in Kent? If only… if only he had seen himself clearly before that, how altered things might now have been.

He leaned against the sill, staring unseeingly out into the garden. His conversation with Elizabeth preyed on his mind, compounded by a frustration with himself for his lack of will power. He had determined to free her from the oppression of his presence; he had also committed to proving that he could be selfless and put the wishes of others before his own. Yet barely had he joined his cousin and Bingley on the previous evening, when his friend had made the suggestion of attending the breakfast at Vauxhall. All he had had to do, as though the temptation had not been eating away at him, was agree to accompany him.

Frustrated with his inability to control his thoughts, Darcy straightened up and turned around. Perhaps he could lose himself in one of the books that had been delivered on the previous day. With this in mind, he set off along the hallway once more and walked into the drawing room. He had, however, barely settled himself into a chair near one of the long windows, open to let the warm summer air pervade the room, when the door opened and the Colonel came in, a newspaper in his hand.

"What the devil is going on?"

Darcy blinked and sat up straighter in his seat as he eyed his cousin warily. "Nothing. Why?"

Colonel Fitzwilliam walked over to a neighbouring armchair and threw himself into it, dropping the paper to the floor.

"It is akin to being on Piccadilly. How is a man to concentrate on his reading with you clattering up and down the hallway like a steed that has lost its way?"

With a sigh, Darcy closed his book and dropped it onto a side table. "My apologies, Cousin."

Conscious that Fitzwilliam eyed him closely, Darcy got to his feet. His cousin had displayed considerable constraint over the past four and twenty hours, having made little comment about the previous evening or the visit to Vauxhall earlier that day. With resignation, he suspected that this reticence was about to end, and thus he was unsurprised at the next words to be spoken.

"Miss Elizabeth Bennet seemed quite welcoming of your notice this morning. Come, man – even you cannot deny it."

Darcy shook his head and turned to look out of the window.

"The only reason her attention was with me was down to the absence of Harington. Do you honestly believe that, had he been one of their party, she would have paid me any mind? Besides, it is impossible to draw any inference from it, as there is nothing to compare it to."

The Colonel shrugged. "I disagree. I compare it to Kent, and the contrast could not be more striking."

Continuing to stare out of the window, Darcy was assailed by the image of Elizabeth when he had discerned her stood by the railings near the boating pond...

"Darce?"

With a start, he turned back to face his cousin.

"You are miles away," his gaze narrowed. "About four miles distant, to be precise."

Darcy released a frustrated breath.

"I told you I should have removed myself from Town. Four consecutive days, Fitzwilliam – she must deem there to be no escape from my company – an unwanted suitor hounding her every step, but with Harington due to return on the morrow..."

"Then you have not considered attending this ball?"

Darcy walked over to the pile of books he had inspected earlier and idly opened the cover of the one that lay on top. "I will not lie – I have considered it." He let the cover fall shut and turned to face his cousin. "What sort of fool am I?"

"And Harington?"

"I have yet to see them interact – when I first met him, the gentlemen and ladies held separate conversations, and then he was gone from Town." He ran a hand through his hair, feeling somewhat uncomfortable with the subject matter. "Bingley, may I remind you, is confident of their being – if not a clear understanding – at the very least, an attachment there."

The Colonel got to his feet and walked over to where Darcy stood. "And have there not been misunderstandings a-plenty of that nature? Perchance you should endeavour to judge for yourself. I have yet to make the man's acquaintance. It would not be a bad thing, Darce, for us to attend. It is better to know for certain, whether Bingley's conjecture is truth or supposition. You may find it hard to differentiate, but I could be an unbiased observer."

Uncomfortable though the notion was of seeing Elizabeth with Harington, Darcy knew there was sense in his cousin's words. He could not countenance, however, once again putting himself consciously in her way when he had vowed to avoid her.

His silence provoked a further comment from the Colonel. "Is she not worth the attempt?"

Darcy lowered his gaze and studied his booted feet for a second. Without question, she was – it was more a case of, was the attempt worth it. Was there anything to gain by observing her with Harington, other than further heartache?

He raised his eyes to his cousin. "I vowed to keep out of her way."

"She does not appear to mind your being *in* her way." Darcy grunted, but Colonel Fitzwilliam continued, "Besides, these encounters – none have been of your making. You said Bingley forced your hand on Thursday; Georgie instigated Friday's call, and I will willingly take full praise for Saturday's success. As for this morning, why, that was Bingley's suggestion."

"And had he not done so, I would have."

"Truly?" The Colonel grinned and slapped Darcy on the shoulder. "Well done, old chap!"

Darcy glared at his cousin, who merely laughed.

"Come. You need distraction. Let us round up Georgie and see if she wishes to join us for a walk in St James Park. It is too fine a day to remain cooped up inside and some time yet until evensong."

Elizabeth dropped her pen onto the writing desk in her aunt's sitting room and leaned back in her chair, releasing a frustrated huff of breath. A glance at the clock confirmed that which she knew full well: the afternoon was well progressed, and she had yet to write her letter, a task she had set herself earlier, leaving her sister and her aunt to enjoy each other's company in the drawing room whilst her uncle retired to his study for a while.

She stared at the parchment in front of her for a moment; the opening lines were traditional enough, thanking Charlotte for her letter and trusting that she remained in good health. Beyond that, she seemed completely unable to progress. What could she possibly say regarding Mr Darcy's letter? After all, that being the sole purpose of her friend's missive, she could hardly fail to acknowledge it.

Chewing her lip, Elizabeth leaned forward and rolled her pen to and fro on the blotter. Then, with renewed determination she picked it up, dipped it once more in the ink well and set it to the page.

"As you will ascertain, I am safely arrived in Gracechurch Street, and I am able to report that Jane is in much improved spirits. I thank you, also, my dear Charlotte, for the safe return of the letter you so kindly forwarded to me. There is no need for concern, I assure you. The message being conveyed necessitated the use of correspondence at the time. It is of little consequence, but I do appreciate your care in both protecting my privacy and returning the letter to me so promptly that I had yet to detect its absence."

She sat back in her seat once more and re-read her words carefully, trying to determine if they sufficed to satiate any remaining curiosity on the part of her friend whilst not entirely deviating from the truth. The recollection, however, of both the letter and its manner of return, coupled with Mr Darcy's noble acceptance of her confession, would intrude, and knowing she had little inclination to continue, Elizabeth got to her feet, tossed the pen onto the desk and walked over to the window.

Gracechurch Street was a busy thoroughfare, rarely devoid of traffic, and for a moment she watched the activities in the street in an attempt to regain her train of thought. It was a futile activity, and she acknowledged this with a rueful smile. Mr Darcy had been in the back of her mind for most of the afternoon as it was; the penning of her letter merely brought him to the forefront.

With a sigh, she turned her back on the outside and walked slowly across the room, sinking down onto the chair, her eye scanning the few sentences she had penned thus far. It was sufficient for the recollection of Mr Darcy's recent behaviour to return in full force, most particularly the memory of their conversation before parting that morning. Whatever his intent, whatever conclusion he came to, the consideration that he had given the matter should they attend an occasion where dancing was involved touched her deeply. She had accused him of a selfish disdain for the feelings of others – yet this was a blatant indication that he considered her own to an unprecedented degree.

Before her thoughts could expand upon this notion, the door opened and Jane entered the room.

"Have you finished your letter?"

Elizabeth shook her head. "It is proving more challenging than I anticipated."

Jane walked over to stand beside her, her workbasket clasped to her chest.

"As you will see, I have barely begun." She folded the piece of parchment before placing the pen in the pot with several others. "Though it is long overdue, it will have to wait for another day; I find my mind too easily distracted from its purpose."

"Charlotte would not expect you to reveal the letter's content, surely?" Jane walked over to the dresser on the far wall and opened one of its many cupboards.

"No. No, I am certain she would not. Yet I am not blind to the fact that whatever explanation I give, it will not satisfy her."

Elizabeth got to her feet, slipping the unfinished letter into her writing case. "Is Aunt Gardiner asking for me?"

Having stowed the basket away, Jane closed the door and turned to face her sister. "She is gone to have a cup of tea with uncle in the garden. She suggests that we join them. It is a beautiful afternoon; I said that I would look in on you." She hesitated. "Lizzy, I have spoken with our aunt and agreed with her that, if uncle is in accordance over the use of the carriage, I will return home to Longbourn once the ball is over."

"How soon after?"

"Aunt thinks Wednesday would be the earliest." Jane walked over to Elizabeth, her countenance uneasy. "You do not mind if I leave you behind? I know you are waiting on Serena."

Elizabeth shook her head. "I am more than content to tarry awhile in Town, Jane. You go home to Mama and enjoy the local neighbourhood!" She laughed as she saw the tinge of pink invade her sister's cheeks. "And do not fail to keep me well informed of all that occurs in my absence, for I am certain there will be much to tell."

"Oh do hush, Lizzy. I am hopeful that my removal to Longbourn might ease some of the pressure upon you, though."

Elizabeth frowned. "How so?"

"With Mr Bingley gone from Town, there is less likelihood of you running into his friend."

"That is true, but you must not think I could not endure it for your sake!" Elizabeth forced a smile, refusing to own the sense of dissatisfaction that filled her at such a notion. "I shall miss you very much, Jane, though I am pleased you return home in such improved spirits." Elizabeth paused. "I do believe you have spent more time in Mr Bingley's company of late than in your entire acquaintance in Hertfordshire!"

Jane blushed becomingly, but she smiled as she turned towards the door. "One could perhaps say the same of you and Mr Darcy."

Not wishing to pursue this, Elizabeth quickly followed her sister. "Come, let us be done with such talk of gentlemen, Jane!" She extended a hand to her sister which was taken with alacrity. "We shall indulge ourselves in the fresh air and take some tea!"

They made their way out into the hall, intent upon seeking their aunt and uncle's company for an hour until it was time to prepare for church.

Chapter Twenty Two

FOLLOWING A BRIEF AMBLE around a small part of St James Park, a service at the local church and a leisurely evening meal, Darcy escorted Georgiana to her chamber for the night.

The fresh air, undemanding company and gentle exercise had helped to ease the conflict in his head, and as he closed the door behind his sister, he came to a decision on that which had haunted him all day. Turning on his heel, he headed back down the stairs into the now deserted hallway. He could hear Fitzwilliam through the slightly ajar doors into the drawing room, expounding upon something to Bingley and, knowing he had but a few minutes grace, he picked up a nearby candelabra and walked as quickly as the flames would permit down the hall to his study.

Closing the door behind him, Darcy walked over to the desk, placing the candelabra in the centre and, for the first time since his return to Town, he took hold of the pile of invitations that he had been ignoring and threw himself into his chair. He stared at the lettering on the first envelope, though he did not absorb the words. His mind was more agreeably engaged, recalling the smile upon Elizabeth's face as they had parted company earlier that day. He knew it was ridiculous to hope for the best of outcomes from this renewed acquaintance – there was Harington to consider, after all – but despite that, he could not fail to be comforted by their interactions over the past few days.

The sudden screech of an owl from outside the un-curtained window startled him out of his reverie, and returning to his purpose, he sat forward in his seat, placing the pile of parchment upon the blotter and began to sift through them, discarding each invitation as it failed to offer what he sought, until finally, he came to it – an elegant if somewhat over-adorned envelope, heavily embossed in gold lettering and bearing the Bellingham crest.

Barely had he broken the seal, however, when a rapid knock upon the door followed by the opening of the same revealed his cousin, with Bingley hard upon his heels.

"What the devil are you playing at, Darce? You were to re-join us post haste to indulge in a glass or two before retiring, yet here you are fetlock-deep in paperwork!"

Bingley raised a brow at the papers strewn across the desk, but the Colonel's gaze now fixed upon what Darcy held. "But not business paperwork, I suspect! Would that perchance be an invitation, Cousin?"

Bingley frowned but must have noted the resigned look upon his friend's face for he soon made the connection, adding, "To a ball?"

"Being held on Monday evening?" continued Colonel Fitzwilliam.

Darcy leaned back in his chair, the invitation still gripped firmly in his hand. He eyed his interrogators narrowly for a moment, then gave a rueful smile and tossed the card onto the table where it was immediately snatched up by the Colonel, Bingley peering over his shoulder so that he too could read it.

"You are considering attending, then, Darce? It is a little late to be accepting, but I am certain your presence would be welcome whatever the notice."

Darcy studied the fingers of one hand with a deliberate air of nonchalance for a second; then, he looked up at his cousin, conscious that Bingley was completely in the dark as to why he might wish to attend such an occasion.

"I thought that I might... look in on the evening."

Bingley's eyes widened. "Are you quite serious?" Darcy fidgeted in his seat, anticipating some awkward question or other, but to his surprise his friend looked equally discomfited. "May I make a request of you, then?" He was a little pink in the face, but raised his chin determinedly. "It is just... as you know, the Bennet sisters are to attend the very same ball, and I would wish – I should like to – well, if I cannot dance with Miss Bennet myself, then I would welcome the knowledge of who else has the good fortune to do so."

Bingley looked a little shame-faced once he had admitted this, and his gaze dropped to his feet.

The Colonel threw his cousin an amused glance and held the invitation back out to him, tapping his finger at the base.

Reading it, Darcy smiled. "I believe I have something better to offer you. Would you care to attend as my guest? It is stated quite clearly here that I may take one!"

Bingley's mouth opened and closed once as he stared from his friend to the Colonel and back again.

"I would be delighted." He hesitated, then looked to the Colonel. "Do I take your place by accepting?"

Colonel Fitzwilliam laughed and shook his head. "On the contrary, Bingley. I have an invitation of my own – yet I had not anticipated making use of it."

"Capital!" Bingley's smile was infectious. "And yourself, Colonel? Will you attend now and bring a guest?"

"I thought perhaps your sister, Bingley…" the Colonel let out a shout of laughter at the appalled expression that crossed both Darcy and Bingley's faces. "Well, perhaps not."

"Good heavens, Colonel! One moment Darcy offers me an evening of unrivalled pleasures, then you attempt to sabotage it in one fell swoop." Bingley blushed. "Forgive me. I am being ungenerous towards my sister."

Darcy shook his head, trying to suppress his amusement, something the Colonel was happy to indulge in, and Bingley took the opportunity to bid them both goodnight.

Conscious that the Colonel studied him closely from the doorway, Darcy raised his gaze from the invitations now scattered untidily across his desk.

"I trust you intend to secure Miss Elizabeth Bennet's hand for a dance, Darce."

"I would hope that I may have that pleasure."

"Come, man. It was blatantly obvious today, even you must own, that she no longer has qualms over your company."

Darcy struggled to suppress the sensation of hope that had been attempting to surface during the afternoon. He knew he needed to keep his rising spirits in check, to not make any assumptions.

"We know Harington is due to return. As I mentioned before, I think you will find that the ease with which we have been able to converse is down to his absence."

The Colonel merely grunted at this, muttered "Harington be damned" under his breath and bade his cousin goodnight.

As he closed the door, Darcy returned his attention to the invitations. Which other of these occasions had Elizabeth secured an invitation to? What else might she be planning to see or do that he too could attend?

Conscious suddenly that such action was completely contrary to that which he had avowed earlier, Darcy dropped the envelope he currently held back onto the pile and sat back in his chair as if the action of distancing himself from the desk would remove the temptation to scour the contents. Had he not deemed it selfish in the extreme to attempt to throw himself in her way? Yet – yet were things not different now? Was it not true that there was a certain enjoyment to be gained from her company, and, if he was not mistaken this time, was she not also deriving some pleasure from their interactions?

Yet still there loomed the shadow of Nicholas Harington.

Monday morning passed in a leisurely manner, and the ladies of Gracechurch Street were enjoying a last cup of breakfast tea in the dining room when a servant entered bearing the post on a tray.

Having passed an envelope to each of her nieces, Mrs Gardiner sat back in her chair to open the first of several letters, and a restful silence settled over them as they each turned their attention to their correspondence.

Intrigued to see that she had received a letter from Mary, normally the least communicative of her sisters, Elizabeth smiled as she broke the seal, but before beginning to peruse its contents, she sat back in her seat for a moment, reflecting.

Her eyes had closed upon pleasant thoughts the night before, and she felt well rested, perhaps for the first time that week. That the progression of her relationship with Mr Darcy was paramount to the improvement in her spirits she no longer bothered to deny. Whatever its implications, she was sufficiently content to know that it pleased her.

Detecting a soft sigh emanating from Jane as she turned her letter around to read the writing that crossed it, and realising that her aunt was likewise engrossed, Elizabeth turned her attention to the letter in her hand, settling back in her seat to enjoy its contents. It was but a moment later, however, before she leapt to her feet with an exclamation.

"What is it, Lizzy? What is amiss?" Jane eyed her with concern from across the table.

"Oh no." Elizabeth looked quickly from her aunt to her sister and back again. "Dear Aunt, I beg your permission to send an *Express* to Papa."

Mrs Gardiner stood up, dropping the letter she had been reading onto the table, and hurried to her niece's side.

"Whatever is it, my dear?"

"Mary has written of what is meant to be a secret. Lydia, it would seem, has formed an attachment to someone – a strong and rapid attachment. But Mary – bless her for her indiscretion – disapproves strongly and writes to express her dissatisfaction as she can speak of it to no one at Longbourn." Elizabeth looked over at Jane. "It is Wickham. He is back in Meryton, and though Mary knows not of his true nature, she is disapproving of what she sees in both his and Lydia's conduct."

She studied the letter further, biting her lip as she read on, anxious to know it all. When she had finished, she looked up and sighed.

"It would seem that Mary is as duped as Lydia, did she but know it. Wickham has alleged that he is there *'on a mission of secrecy'*, some covert business that behoves him to hold his counsel as to his purpose." She glanced at the letter once more, seeking a sentence that had struck her forcibly. "Apparently, it is for this reason that he presently is not wearing his red coat – though this seems to have detracted little from his charms in Lydia's eyes."

Jane frowned. "I cannot conceive how his regiment would have sent him to Meryton, of all places, on such serious business."

Conscious of her own sense of disquiet and no little confusion over Wickham's intent, Elizabeth shook her head. Then, her eye caught the pages still held in Jane's hand. "Is your letter not also from Longbourn?"

"It is from Mama."

"So soon after her last?"

Jane shrugged her shoulders. "She would apprise me of all and any news pertaining to Mr Bingley's imminent return to the neighbourhood."

"And what of your letter, Jane? Is there any word on this matter that seems to be causing such concern to Lizzy?" Mrs Gardiner patted Elizabeth on the shoulder as she sank back onto her chair.

She writes," Jane studied the letter further, and as she read she grew paler before raising a troubled face to her sister and aunt. "Oh dear. What is to be done? She is lauding the likelihood that I shall not be the first of her daughters to become betrothed! She is implying that Lydia is close to an understanding with someone, but says she is not at liberty to say who for there is some delicacy in the matter."

Conscious that delicacy had never prevented their mother in the past from letting slip some juicy gossip, Elizabeth felt her insides tighten with anxiety. If Wickham had so successfully persuaded her mother to keep quiet, then his hold upon her and Lydia must be very secure. She turned to her aunt who had remained standing at her side.

"Dear Aunt, please may I write this instant? I know that I was unable to disclose my understanding of Wickham's true nature to you the other day, for risk of revealing some confidential detail, but please trust me in this: Papa must be warned of his character before it is too late – heaven help us if it is even now so. Mary indicates that he lodges with Aunt Philips, and Lydia will have far too easy access to him if this is so."

Mrs Gardiner hastened to reassure her. "I confess I do not fully understand the matter, but I can see that you are both uneasy, so of course, my dear, write your letter directly, and I will make arrangements for the *Express* rider."

She turned to the door, her nieces following in her wake, intent upon doing as she instructed.

By noon, the *Express* was on its way to Hertfordshire, and there was little Elizabeth could do but speculate. She had no high anticipation of a response from her father. Whether he would act upon her advice to him, constrained as she was to not reveal her source or the full evidence of her allegations, she knew not. Their only other hope was Jane's return to Longbourn on Wednesday and a reliance on her ability to reinforce Elizabeth's concerns with Mr Bennet and keep a watchful eye on their youngest sister.

Realising that at present she had done all that she could, Elizabeth strove to focus on other things, and she was thus aided by her aunt who joined them just then in the drawing room, where Jane and Elizabeth had now settled to pass the afternoon before beginning their preparations for the ball.

"You appeared to be having an absorbing conversation with Mr Darcy yesterday, Lizzy. Is his company growing on you?" Mrs Gardiner settled herself upon a chair near the hearth, but Elizabeth so welcomed the interruption that she glanced over from her position on the window seat.

"A little." Then, she laughed ruefully. "I must own that it does. He is not only an interesting man – intelligent, well-educated and... even intriguing, but also has demonstrated a depth of understanding, of consideration for the feelings of others that I initially gave him little credit for. I find his company grows upon me very well."

Staring out of the drawing room window once more as she was, Elizabeth failed to see the look exchanged between her sister and aunt.

"Then you will not be disappointed to learn he is to attend the ball?"

A jolt of anticipation shot through Elizabeth, and she turned fully to face her aunt, unable to conceal the pleasure this news brought her.

"It is certain?"

"Did you think that he might?"

"He – the possibility was touched upon."

Her aunt glanced at Jane before returning her gaze to Elizabeth. "Mr Bingley is to attend as his guest. Your uncle received word from Mr Darcy not this half hour since."

Elizabeth got to her feet and walked over to join Jane on the couch as a light rap on the door heralded the entrance of a maid bearing a note for her aunt.

"Well, it is certainly a day for news!" Mrs Gardiner raised her head from reading the note. "Nicholas is safely restored to the Pulteney and will call at six with his carriage."

With a smile, Elizabeth picked up her book from the side table. "I am glad he is come back, or I might have had to forego the first dance."

"Yes – he was quick to secure your hand, was he not?"

"I am grateful for the attention, Aunt." Elizabeth laughed and threw her sister a quick glance. "For I cannot imagine for a moment that Mr Bingley would have asked me."

Jane's cheeks coloured as she met her sister's teasing eye, but she could not help but smile in return.

"Perhaps not," conceded Mrs Gardiner, "and I would not have you in want of a partner for the all-important opening dance." She gave her younger niece a speculative glance, and Elizabeth hoped she was not likely to mention Mr Darcy again, but to her relief, her aunt got to her feet.

"Well, my dears, I must attend to some domestic matters before we adjourn to make our preparations for this evening. I leave you to your own devices and will send you some tea to enjoy whilst I am gone."

Chapter Twenty Three

IT WAS BUT FIFTEEN MINUTES later that the drawing room door opened to reveal the maid once more, a small tea tray balanced on her palm.

Jane having offered to see to the pouring, Elizabeth returned to her book, but try as she might, it could not hold her attention, and she cast it aside with relief as her sister walked over to hand her a cup.

"Is aught amiss, Lizzy?"

Elizabeth shook her head and took a sip from her cup. "No. It is merely that I find myself torn between worry over what is afoot in Hertfordshire and anticipation for our evening. I am certain I should be more concerned with the former, yet it is the latter which would consume my thoughts." She gave her sister a small smile. "I do wonder at Mr Darcy's attendance. Though he implied he may well consider it, he has made it clear that such gatherings are not to his taste." She frowned, recalling their conversation yesterday. "I cannot begin to comprehend why he might willingly place himself in my way."

"I think you are too hard on yourself, as you are on Mr Darcy."

"Me? Too hard on Mr Darcy? Never!"

"Be serious, Lizzy. As I have mentioned previously, I do not think he has an aversion to your company, nor is his admiration for you transitory."

Elizabeth blushed, conscious that this notion gave her a combination of pleasure at the indication of a continued affection and confusion over why such a situation could be so gratifying for her. She took another sip from her cup, a pensive expression settling upon her features.

"He did own that he had endeavoured to keep out of my way." Elizabeth threw Jane a glance. "It would seem you had the right of it; any distancing I perceived was done for my benefit over his."

"Yet when you have had the opportunity for discourse, it did not seem as if either of you had any aversion to it – certainly not on Saturday evening, nor yesterday at Vauxhall."

Elizabeth nodded slowly. "I would have to agree. I am finding that I enjoy his company of late – due I am sure to my understanding his character better and shedding my own blind prejudices... yet – yet, it would not do for him to believe that my feelings for him have changed so materially as to..." Elizabeth paused and bit her lip, throwing her sister a conscious look. "Oh Jane – I do not know *what* I mean. Am I more concerned that he might be encouraged afresh by our interactions, or that no amount of encouragement would ever induce him to consider me good company again?"

Reaching over, she placed her cup on a side table and released a heavy sigh; then she began to laugh. "I have a mind that is all confusion; I fear I may be turning into our mother! If I begin to ask for salts, be sure to slap me to bring me to my senses!"

"Dear Lizzy." Jane patted her affectionately on the knee. "You are just thinking too much. I thought you had decided to take each day upon its own merits."

Leaning back in her seat, Elizabeth smiled at her sister. "Indeed. You are quite correct. I shall do as you say. Tell me, have you thought any more upon whether to apprise Mama of your renewed acquaintance with Mr Bingley? Will he himself have returned to the neighbourhood by your return?"

"Yes, he will. When we were walking yesterday, he confirmed that he plans to leave Town in the morning." Jane smiled wistfully. "To know that he will be in residence there when I return is a comfort beyond any other, but I do so fear Mama's reaction. Indeed, I have thought of little else, but have come to no conclusion. As time is passing, I believe I shall trust to fate and keep silent for now."

"Very wise. The least said, the better, where Mama and eligible young men are concerned!"

Jane laughed, then sobered somewhat. "Dear Lizzy, do not tarry too long in Town. I shall have need of your company and counsel before long, I am certain."

Elizabeth leaned over and hugged her sister tightly.

"I will see the week out at the very least, I suspect. I am popular, am I not? You, Serena and even Nicholas all seem to seek my ear at the moment!"

"You will miss Nicholas when you return home."

"Aye, that I will. He is the brother I never had!"

Jane gave her thoughtful look.

"Do you – Lizzy, did you never think – about Nicholas, I mean – that he might be the ideal partner for you?"

Elizabeth stared at her sister, her suspicion over Nicholas' purpose in wishing to speak to her returning, but then she shook it aside. "Never! Be serious, Jane. We are too alike to suit each other in a relationship as serious as marriage!"

"But it would be a good match for you. He is rich, to be sure, but more importantly, his character is known to you. He is a very good man – and you are entirely compatible."

"Jane, why are you speaking thus? You know that I would seek a marriage of mutual affection just as much as you."

"But you have affection for Nicholas."

Elizabeth shook her head. "Not the right sort."

"I am concerned – should Mr Bingley... if he – if he does declare himself, Lizzy, and I leave Longbourn, I would suffer for knowing you were there yet. Mama does not appreciate you."

Elizabeth laughed again, but it sounded rather hollow. "Indeed she does not! What a travesty! But Papa, I believe, does. One cannot have everything."

"You would do well to think, Lizzy, about the happiness to be derived from being wed to someone you know and trust, even if the love you feel for them is of a platonic nature at first."

Unable to deny the logic of this, Elizabeth sighed. Then, she shook her head.

"It is pointless to consider it, as no offer has been forthcoming. What would be the purpose in my thinking about the future in that way, anticipating whether a marriage between us could work, when it may be the furthest thing from his mind?"

"How can you be so certain that it is so?"

Elizabeth hesitated. How could she? They did have a great deal in common, and had long been the best of friends. There was nothing fake about their camaraderie. Nicholas had been trying to speak privately with her ever since she arrived, and was it not he who had petitioned his aunt for Elizabeth's early removal from Kent?

"Lizzy?"

Elizabeth turned to her sister and smiled. "Forgive me, Jane; I am miles away. Let us not pursue this direction. Come, time is passing on; we should begin our preparations for the ball."

As Jane summoned the maid to retrieve the tea things and order some hot water for bathing, they made their way up to their room; yet Elizabeth could not help but ruminate further upon her sister's words. The thought of Nicholas considering her in any light other than that of a friend unnerved her. What would she do should he ever extend the offer of his hand? To reject him would be difficult and definitely unwise, for it was indeed a good match for her. Having turned down Mr Collins and Mr Darcy, could she justify rejecting a man whom she knew well and both admired and respected?

With a sigh, Elizabeth owned the truth of it – no, she could not. And what of Nicholas? If his affections were genuinely engaged, would it not cause him immeasurable pain to have his application refused?

In an instant, she recalled Mr Darcy's expression during their heated exchange. The anguish in his eyes she would never forget, nor the distress she had felt in causing it, despite her low opinion of him at the time. How would it feel to deliver such a blow, albeit with kinder words, to someone she loved as she did Nicholas? Would she, for his sake and that of her family, accept him with an affectation of pleasure, that she might never inflict such unhappiness upon her dear friend?

Elizabeth swallowed uncomfortably. She feared she knew the answer – she had no choice but to do the right thing. Yet what of Serena? By not hurting one friend, would she bring despair upon the other, even though her refusing to marry Nicholas would not make him any likelier to transfer his feelings to Serena?

Following Jane into their chamber, Elizabeth hurried to the dresser where she began unpinning her hair, keen to distract herself from such disturbing thoughts, thankful for the interruption of a servant bearing the hot water, and she picked up a bathing towel determined to close her mind to such musings. She would not dwell on what she could not control. She had no notion of what it was that Nicholas wished to speak of, and speculation would not make it any clearer. With that, she pushed all thought of him aside and turned her attentions to her sister and their preparations for the ball.

Some time later, their bathing complete and hair suitably dressed, Elizabeth tried to remain still as Jane fastened the tiny buttons that secured the back of her dress.

"They are beautiful gowns, are they not?" She studied the fall of the heavy silk from the delicately constructed bodice, delighted with the fluidity of the fabric and the richness of its colour. "Madame Eliza is quite the talented seamstress. The beading is so skilfully rendered."

Her ministrations complete, Jane came to stand beside her sister. "It is exquisite, is it not? The colour becomes you very well, Lizzy."

Elizabeth turned to study her reflection in the looking glass. "I must own, Jane, that though I will never hold a candle to your beauty, I cannot recall ever a moment when I have been quite so satisfied with my appearance!"

They turned to face each other, both smiling widely, and Jane shook her head. "You do yourself a disservice, and you do look beautiful this evening."

"Aye, well," turning back quickly to tuck a recalcitrant curl into place, careful not to disturb the tiny silk roses that had been made from the same fabric as her dress and painstakingly positioned in her hair by her aunt's maid, Elizabeth pulled a face at her reflection and then turned to her sister again. "You will outshine me, as you have always done, and I shall exhibit no jealousy, but simply be immensely proud. Your gown is splendid, Jane, but it only enhances your natural beauty."

Blushing, Jane turned to the bed to retrieve their evening cloaks. "Oh hush, Lizzy. 'Tis too much praise."

"Impossible! One cannot praise you enough! I am certain Mr Bingley will agree with me. I shall ask him his opinion so that you will see I am right!"

Jane looked quite shocked as she handed Elizabeth her cloak and gloves. "You would not dare!"

With a laugh, Elizabeth shook her head. "No – I would not. But the temptation is delicious!" Her expression sobered suddenly, and as they moved towards the door, Jane threw her a worried look.

"What is it?"

"'Tis nothing. I was simply reminded of Mary's letter – the word temptation was liberally spread throughout, as you might imagine, with her quoting the good Book at me. Still, we must accept that she may have done us all a great service with her indiscretion." She threw Jane a glance as they made their way out onto the landing. "I am intrigued by what has drawn Wickham back to the neighbourhood, though – I find his tale of being there under orders of such secrecy hard to credit."

"But he must have a purpose – and perhaps he is genuinely in love. Mama seems quite adamant Lydia will be wed soon."

"I believe he will do no such thing."

Jane frowned as they made their way down the stairs. "But then, what is his interest in her? Mary implied the attachment was mutual, did she not?"

They had reached the hallway, and Elizabeth turned to look at her sister.

"Dear Jane. What do *you* think?"

Jane raised a hand to her mouth. "Oh, surely not. Lydia would not be so foolish."

Elizabeth rolled her eyes. "Based on the past sixteen years, I think we would be the fools to expect any better of her. I only hope that Papa accepts the truth of my letter and steps up to the mark."

"Did you trust to a response from him?"

"Not particularly, and as it may have brought confirmation of his doing nothing rather than his doing something, I am at least freed that disappointment for this evening." They moved towards the drawing room, but before joining their aunt and uncle, Elizabeth met Jane's eye seriously. "I shall have to accept that I have done all that I can for today, and rely on you to carry the point if need be on Wednesday."

Jane nodded fervently, and with that, Elizabeth pushed open the door, to be greeted by their aunt and uncle's delighted effusions over their appearance as they awaited Nicholas' arrival to convey them all to the ball.

Chapter Twenty Four

HAVING DISPOSED OF THEIR outdoor attire and endured a typically brusque reception from Lady Bellingham which she countered with far more composure than she felt, Elizabeth accepted Nicholas' arm, smiled at Jane as she accepted the other, and turned to follow her aunt and uncle towards the ornate staircase.

Bellingham House was a formal and austere building from the exterior, but its interior bordered on the grotesque. The main entrance hall, a vast and lofty chamber, suffered from an excess of ornamentation, from the mouldings to the ceiling cornices. A double staircase, its elaborately carved banisters likewise encrusted with gilt, swept upwards in two semi-circular rises, and enormous brass chandeliers, suspended from the uppermost ceiling to a variety of heights, cast a blazing glow of light upon proceedings.

"You would think they were expecting company," whispered Elizabeth to Nicholas as they started to mount the first steps, inclining her head towards the endless row of footmen who stood, one per stair, each holding a golden tray laden with goblets of wine.

Nicholas let out a grunt. "Not at all. I can assure you my aunt always has them stood as such. She need never want for thirst that way."

Laughing, Elizabeth craned her neck as they continued to make their way, along with the other guests, up the grand staircase. The floor above was open on all sides to the central staircase, circling it with small balconies currently filled with guests partaking of their arrival drinks, the rise and fall of their voices echoing as they rose up into the domed ceiling several floors above. Large stone candelabra were built into the balconies, all burning fiercely, and the light was so bright that it was not possible to distinguish the faces beyond, putting everyone in shadow instead.

When they finally reached the mezzanine, Nicholas was hailed immediately by those around him, and releasing his arm Elizabeth stepped over to one of the carved balconies to look back down towards the entrance hall which was awash with every possible colour of gown; jewels flashed in the candlelight and feathers waved as heads were nodded in greeting. Elizabeth smiled. There was much to observe, yet her eye sought not to admire the other ladies' gowns but rather to seek the figure of a certain gentleman, and she allowed herself the luxury of scanning the crowd below for Mr Darcy, soon rewarded as he entered the foyer, accompanied not only by Mr Bingley but also the Colonel.

Feeling her heart pick up its pace, she stepped back quickly from the balcony and turned around, accepting with alacrity a glass of wine from a tray that was currently being offered to her party and taking a long, cooling drink.

"Mr Bingley has arrived." She addressed her sister with these words, and Mr Gardiner looked over and smiled.

"Excellent. And does his friend accompany him?"

Elizabeth nodded. There was a strange constriction within her throat, and she doubted she could have uttered the words 'Mr Darcy' if her life depended upon it at that moment. She took another hasty swig from her glass, but before she could venture to add that the Colonel was also of the party, two of the three gentlemen arrived at the top of the main staircase and there was a flurry of greetings as Bingley welcomed Harington's return and introduced him to Colonel Fitzwilliam before both gentlemen turned to greet the Gardiners and finally both Jane and Elizabeth.

"Miss Bennet. Miss Elizabeth."

Elizabeth greeted them with a smile, but could not help her gaze from drifting over their shoulders.

The Colonel, catching her eye, seemed to look at her rather thoughtfully for a second before saying, "Darcy got waylaid, poor devil. Hazard of the family name, I am afraid."

Bingley grinned and offered Jane his arm which she took immediately, causing his smile to widen further. "And the family estate! We had gone but ten paces across the lobby before he was approached!"

Mrs Gardiner smiled. "You do not seem particularly concerned for your friend's welfare, Sir."

"I do not know what he is about," laughed Bingley. "It is not his habit to tolerate too much fawning, but he seems to have acquired a taste for it of late!"

"More likely a taste for forbearance, Bingley," the Colonel interjected, and Elizabeth smiled, conscious that his gaze was still upon her.

"You were all for rescuing him on Thursday, Sir." Mr Gardiner drew a little closer, his wife upon his arm, that their party might not be separated by the crush of people around them. "Do you not provide the same service on all social occasions?"

"Indeed, I would, if it were welcomed. I think, however on this occasion, he was perfectly content with the intrusion."

Elizabeth was flustered and uneasy. Conscious of the need to keep a clear head, she placed her wine glass carefully on a nearby side table, determined to secure a glass of water from the next servant who crossed her path, an action she immediately regretted as the man in question appeared at the top of the staircase – for Mr Darcy was not unaccompanied.

Watching her as he seemed to be, Elizabeth was not surprised that the Colonel quickly discerned her interest in something behind him and looking around he waved at his cousin to attract his attention before turning back to face her.

"Darcy would appear to have been persuaded to escort a young lady up the stairs. How charming to be of as much use as a hand rail!"

The general laughter this entailed was sufficient distraction for Elizabeth to take herself to task. Yet to her further disquiet she realised that the person upon Mr Darcy's arm, and who showed no sign of relinquishing it, even on the level floor of the landing, was none other than the young lady he had escorted back to her seat at Thursday's recital.

"Ah – it is Clarissa." Nicholas, who had been busy greeting the many acquaintances of his family who were in attendance, had returned to their circle, and following his gaze, the party turned as one to regard Mr Darcy's companion.

Bristling with curiosity, yet refusing to acknowledge the quite blatant tremor of jealousy that passed through her, Elizabeth smiled at Nicholas as he came to stand by her side.

"And should that enlighten us, Boy?" Mr Gardiner threw his Godson a resigned look and shook his head at him.

Nicholas laughed. "Forgive me, Uncle." He glanced around at the small group of faces. "Lady Clarissa Mallen. She is quite the heiress. My aunt would secure her for myself or one of my brothers, given her own way. She does love to bring another title into the family through one form or another."

Bingley laughed at this, but Elizabeth felt even more unsettled. Rich, titled and beautiful and completely at ease in the superior society to which Mr Darcy belonged – how much more suitable was this lady to be with him than she – and why did this knowledge induce such feelings of sadness and, if she were to be truthful with herself, envy? It was not in her nature to be so, and it was hardly as if she had welcomed the gentleman's addresses when they were made. What could it possibly matter to her where his interests now lay?

Mrs Gardiner threw her Godson an admonishing look. "Now, Nicholas, there are ladies present. Let us have none of this talk, please."

"I beg your pardon, Aunt." Nicholas bowed in Mrs Gardiner's direction and turned an apologetic smile upon Jane and Elizabeth. "My tongue has run away with me." He turned to the Colonel and Bingley, adding, "But I must own that, beauty though she is, Lady Clarissa is entirely too tall for my tastes; I would rather not have a partner in life who is so easily able to look down upon one by virtue of their height as well as their fortune!"

The gentlemen laughed at this, though Jane looked rather uncomfortable, and seeing the look her aunt gave Nicholas, Elizabeth shook her head at him and, feeling completely out of sorts, turned to request some water from a nearby servant, almost wishing, quite irrationally, that she had never come to the ball at all.

Having done what he felt was his duty, and trusting that he had appeared to tolerate it with good humour, Darcy bade farewell to those around him. Securing the hand of Lady Clarissa Mallen, the daughter of some slight acquaintances, for the first dance had seemed full of good sense. Assured though he was from his conversation with Elizabeth that she would accept the invitation to dance should he offer it, he had no illusions that she would be available for the first set, and to stand to one side watching her with Harington... he was haunted yet by Bingley's conviction of an understanding between them. Should that not actually be the case, he could not deny that his friend felt there was a closeness and familiarity there, and Darcy was not looking forward to observing it, despite the sense of his cousin's avowal that he ought to determine the truth of it for himself. The distraction of having to dance with someone with whom he was little acquainted would be the perfect antidote to enduring a difficult half hour.

Free at last, however, to finally join the group who most drew his attention, he crossed the landing to where his cousin and Bingley were making a loud party of it in one of the semi-circular balconies, and greeting everyone as quickly as possible, he soon discerned that Harington had indeed returned to Town and was securely ensconced at Elizabeth's side. The ease with which they had been able to stand together, to converse and to spend time in each other's company over the past few days was clearly at an end. It was out of the question that he walk over there and stand beside her and expect her to transfer her attentions to him. Indeed, there was a distinct wariness upon her features as she acknowledged his presence. Perhaps she feared he might impose himself upon her company in front of Harington and that it would be awkward.

Determined, therefore, to ensure that no such situation arose, and equally committed to causing Elizabeth as little embarrassment as possible, he stayed where he was between Bingley and Mrs Gardiner and soon was engaged in a gentle discourse with that lady.

However, it was not long before there was a general movement towards the ball room, and as the party turned and made their way forward towards the impressive entrance, Darcy found himself near to Elizabeth, and determining that he must take the chance whilst it was presented, he bowed to her.

"Miss Bennet. You look," he hesitated, taking in her appearance fully for the first time. "You – are you well? You look," he swallowed hard. "You look very well indeed."

A hint of her usual smile formed for a second, but it faded rather quickly, and he frowned. "I am quite well, Sir, I thank you."

He found it difficult to concentrate, stood alone with her on the landing. She had quite taken his breath away with her appearance now that he was able to study her more closely, and he struggled to find something commonplace to speak of.

"I – er, I trust you are looking forward to this evening. It seems nothing has been spared in the preparations." He waved a hand at the splendour around them, garish though it was to his eye.

Elizabeth laughed lightly. "I am sure it will be a success. Lady Bellingham would hardly permit it to be otherwise."

Darcy smiled. "She is quite the harridan. I recall her putting the fear of God into many a person when they made their first venture to *Almacks*."

"Yes – Jane is quite intimidated by her." She studied him for a moment, then added, "I am glad you decided to make use of your invitation, Sir."

Darcy acknowledged her allusion to the conversation of the previous day with a short bow. "And... may I secure a dance?"

"I am thus far only engaged for the first set."

"Then the second?"

She smiled. "With pleasure, Sir."

Noticing that the remainder of the party had long disappeared into the cavernous ball room, along with Harington, Darcy offered her his arm and indicated that they follow, relieved when she took it though her slight hesitation was apparent. He felt his heart clench with disappointment that their recent rapport should be so affected.

"I see Harington returned safely."

Conscious that she threw a quick glance up at him, he turned to look at her, but she withdrew her gaze immediately.

"Indeed. He arrived back in Town this afternoon. He is to spend but eight and forty hours here, though, before he is obliged to return to the West Country." She paused. "And you, Sir? Are you settled in Town for the foreseeable future?"

They had arrived at the tall double doors into the ballroom now, which were folded back and fastened to the wall with ornate brass fastenings, and Darcy paused on the threshold.

"I believe so." He scanned the mass of people as the couples forming the first dance began to take their places and, conscious that the musicians were tuning their instruments, he had little option but to escort Elizabeth to where he could see Harington engaged in a lively discussion with what were clearly some close acquaintances.

He turned as they joined him, and thanked Darcy for bringing him his partner. Darcy tried not to notice how swiftly Elizabeth dropped his arm and took Harington's and as the gentleman bore her away to find a place in the line, he turned on his heel, unwilling to watch them further and keen to distance himself from the dance. He had gone but three paces, however, before he was brought up short by the presence of Lady Clarissa, who curtseyed and smiled at him.

"Our dance, I believe, Sir?"

With carefully concealed resignation, he held out his arm and turned to walk back over to the line of couples, thankful that the room was vast, and that two sets had formed. With determination, he led his partner to that which did not contain Elizabeth, and standing opposite Lady Clarissa, his back to the other line of dancers, he tried to focus his attention upon her and not upon the dances that would follow.

Chapter Twenty Five

THOUGH SHE HAD BEEN handed over to Nicholas with little delay, Elizabeth struggled to overcome the customary disturbance of her equilibrium that being in such close proximity to Mr Darcy provoked of late. As she and Nicholas took up their positions and awaited the opening bars of music, her mind was likewise in turmoil. She had lately come to accept that she and Mr Darcy were getting along better, to the extent that she enjoyed any time spent in his company; yet she failed to comprehend how this could lead her to feel so out of sorts over his paying attention to another lady – for there was no denying she could think of little else.

What did it signify that he had secured Lady Clarissa Mallen for the opening dance? Had he been taken with her on Thursday? Had he actually attended this evening in anticipation of seeing her? It was perfectly feasible that the ball had been spoken of at the recital when he had been escorting her back to her seat.

Elizabeth released an involuntary, irritated mutter. Was the woman incapable of getting herself anywhere without the aid of a gentleman's arm? Yet her mind would not be distracted by such trivialities. With an irrational level of discomfort, she recalled her anticipation of Mr Darcy's being at the ball, his words from the previous day hinting that it might occur. Had he known all along that he considered it, that he might see Lady Clarissa again?

As the music swelled around her, Elizabeth endeavoured to push aside such unsettling thoughts. The dance began, and once it had been in progression for some minutes, the couples making their pattern of steps to the side as they made their way nearer to the top of the line, she caught Nicholas' eye upon her, his gaze uncharacteristically serious and intent.

The distraction of Mr Darcy and her tumultuous thoughts over that gentlemen threatened to destroy what was left of her composure, and conscious that she owed her friend better attention than this, she pulled herself together.

"Forgive me, Nicholas. My mind is off a-wandering. Tell me about your trip to Sutton Coker. Was it a success?"

He shrugged his shoulders. "Time will tell. I successfully put my signature to several weighty legal documents, that much I will say."

Elizabeth smiled. "And when do you propose taking up residence at your estate?"

There was a pause and Nicholas cast his eyes about the room before returning his gaze to hers.

"It depends."

"Upon?"

"An unresolved matter."

"You are being mysterious!"

"Not intentionally."

Elizabeth laughed and shook her head at him. "Secrecy does not become you, Nicholas! I understand you better than that!"

A conscious look crossed his features, and as they made another series of steps along the dance, he said, "I know you do. In truth, I cannot answer until we have talked, for your response may have a bearing on that decision." He paused, and Elizabeth felt the edges of concern over his purpose return.

Frowning, she cast a quick look to her left and right. Jane and Bingley were engaged in a gentle dialogue to one side of them; two strangers were likewise intent upon each other's conversation on the other, and she turned back to Nicholas as he said urgently, "Lizzy, truly, I must speak with you. Please, may we find an opportunity?"

The intensity of his gaze reminded her in force of her deliberations over his intent and she swallowed quickly. "This night?"

"I have waited too long for the chance to speak, and my remaining time in Town is now so short… please…"

Concerned at the unusual seriousness of his demeanour, and conscious that she owed him the chance to speak, she nodded. "Of course, Nicholas. I would do anything for you."

A look of relief swept across his features, and he appeared to become more like himself, his smile quickly returning. "Are you free after our dance?"

"No. I am secured for the next pair with Mr Darcy." Unable to suppress a flutter of expectation, Elizabeth drew in a deep breath. She could not detect that gentleman's presence in their line from her position, and could only surmise that he and his lovely partner were in the set behind them. "But thereafter, I am not engaged."

"Then may we take advantage of it? My patience is at its limit."

Elizabeth frowned once more as the lead couple swept between them, his words intensifying her disquiet. Her conversation earlier with Jane was fresh in her mind, and she studied the young man opposite, watching her reactions in a way that was wholly out of character.

"Of course – though I think in this crowd," Elizabeth gestured with her arm at the throng of dancers, "we will struggle to find a sensible place for private discourse."

Once again, a hint of Nicholas' normal smile returned as his spirits seemed to rise. "Do not fear, Lizzy. I have known my aunt's property quite thoroughly since childhood. I know precisely where to find the seclusion that I seek!"

A final few moves to the side brought them both to the top of the line, and as they stepped forward to grasp each other's hands, Elizabeth could not help but laugh at the way Nicholas waggled his eyebrows at her before they set off down the dance together.

Though her rising anxiety over what it was that Nicholas wished to seek a private audience over still hovered on the edges of Elizabeth's conscious, she found she was able to push her concerns aside as the opening dance ended and they entered into the next. Her anticipation of dancing with Mr Darcy superseded everything, not merely because she wished to expunge the memory of the last time they had danced, when her opinion of him had been so different, but because she wished to savour every moment of it.

Once the set was concluded, she allowed Nicholas to lead her across the floor to where the gentleman stood with his partner, conscious once again of the discomfort that swept through her as she saw him paying the lady such a depth of attention that he did not seem to perceive their approach.

"Darcy!" Nicholas' voice, however, caused him to look over his shoulder and, taking his farewell of the lady, he turned to face them as they reached his side. "I present your partner for the next set."

Before either of them could speak, Nicholas had transferred Elizabeth's hand from his arm to Darcy's and with a bow and a departing, "Take good care of her, Sir," he left them together.

As Mr Darcy led her back towards the centre of the room to take their place amidst the other couples, Elizabeth concentrated on her feet. As always, their closeness affected her senses, and she felt a little too warm for comfort, conscious as ever of the feel of his arm under her hand. It was, however, with reluctance that she released him as he took his place opposite her, and as she met his eye, she realised that he looked somewhat out of sorts himself. Thus, she determined to put aside her own concerns and attempt to put him at ease and smiled at him, pleased to see that he reciprocated.

Conscious as she was of her heightened colour, she made an effort to breathe steadily, aware that his gaze was now fixed upon her. Elizabeth was unsure as to why it mattered so much that she create a better memory for them both. Unfortunately, the remembrance of Netherfield, of the antagonism she had felt for him at that time, of her championing of Wickham and her insolence towards Mr Darcy, would intrude as they stood waiting for the dance to begin, and with a sudden rush of disquiet, she recalled the *Express* she had sent to her father and the genuine risk that her family was currently under.

Fortunately, distraction was swift as the musicians finally began to play the opening bars of the dance. Placed as they were in the centre of the line, it would likely be some ten minutes before they would reach its head, and conscious that the couples upon either side of them were even now engaged in some trivial chatter, Elizabeth took comfort from their preoccupation and spoke up.

"Are you enjoying the ball, Sir?"

He did not answer at once, and as the music swelled around them and the first movement of the dance took place, Elizabeth found herself unable to look away from his intent gaze as they crossed the dance with their neighbours and returned to their original places.

"I am now."

Conscious of a burst of pleasure, Elizabeth smiled widely at him. "Then was the first set not to your liking?"

He shook his head as they crossed the dance again. "No – no, it was not."

As they stood opposite each other once more, he made a negating movement with his hand. "It was the perfect example of why I do not, in principle, enjoy dancing."

Elizabeth laughed, her heart suddenly lightened. "And pray tell me, was it the music or the dance itself that failed to deliver on this occasion?"

"Indeed, Madam, it was neither. It was the company."

A little shocked at this confession, Elizabeth struggled not to let out a burst of laughter at the appalled expression that suddenly crossed his features.

"Forgive me," he said quickly as they crossed over once more. "I mean no slur upon the lady."

Elizabeth studied him thoughtfully as the dance continued around them and, as soon as the opportunity presented, she said, "It was the unfamiliarity with your partner that was the issue, rather than the partner herself?"

He nodded. "I do not find dancing conducive to meaningful conversation, and when what discourse there is to be had is with a stranger…"

Elizabeth felt she understood perfectly his feelings. She had learned that he was not fond of exchanging pleasantries, and thus having to make conversation for the sake of it was not in his nature. She recalled the ease with which they had conversed on the previous day when walking, and sighed as she waited for the two couples to her right to perform their moves.

Yet as soon as she and Mr Darcy had stepped up to their new position, he fixed her with his eye, saying, "I trust your family remain in good health, Madam. It must be some time now since you saw any but your eldest sister."

Reminded instantly of the perilous situation at home, Elizabeth bit her lip in consternation, a sense of unease permeating her skin, and she could not help but stare back at her partner, completely unsure as to what to say.

"Miss Bennet?" Observing his frown as they stepped across the dance, she sighed and, as soon as they were once more in position, she said as quietly as possible but that he might still hear her:

"Forgive me, Sir. They are well enough, as far as I can tell."

"Yet you seem out of spirits now that they are mentioned."

She could not deny it; with sudden clarity, she realised she had no wish to prevaricate with him, and without thinking of the consequences she hurried into speech.

"Mr Darcy, with your familiarity with my family, I fear you will not be surprised by the circumstances I am about to relate…" She hesitated and threw an anxious look at those around them to ensure they were sufficiently occupied before meeting his concerned gaze. "I received a letter this morning from one of my sisters." They crossed the dance again, and then she continued. "It would appear that the gentleman whose character we have discussed of late has returned to Meryton."

Observing how Mr Darcy paled as she spoke these words, Elizabeth faltered, but conscious that they were moving ever closer to the head of the line, she persevered. "I believed him to be in Brighton, with the Regiment. I cannot understand how he came to be there, but so it is."

He shook his head, but she suspected more at himself than at her. "I must own that I knew he was not," and at her questioning glance, "Some intelligence from my cousin – though we knew not where he had gone."

"You, Sir, will understand my concerns over his return to the neighbourhood. What is worse, he is lodging with my Aunt Philips in Meryton. Lydia and Kitty had petitioned Papa for him to be housed at Longbourn – *that* he did not agree to, though I can imagine Mama's protestations and what it cost him to stand by his decision."

"Then there is hope…"

"No, Mr Darcy. My father may well comprehend that to accept a single young man into a house where three young ladies reside does not make for good sense, but to exert himself to prevent them from visiting my Aunt Philips or Meryton… he will savour the peace he has secured for himself and trouble himself not with what he cannot observe."

There was a pause as they once again crossed with their neighbours and moved along, now only one set of couples from reaching the head of the line, and as they stood opposite each other once more, Elizabeth swallowed hard as she registered the seriousness of her partner's countenance.

"This is grave indeed."

"I have told my aunt some of what you shared with me, though obviously not that which was confidential." He blinked but said nothing. "She supported my desire to send an *Express* to Longbourn, but I do not believe that it will have any material effect upon Papa, for there was little I could reveal in support of my allegations against the man concerned. I fear he will be relishing the improved spirits within the household, which will secure him the peace and quiet he craves, and will not concern himself with what he will consider hearsay."

A silence settled upon them both, and as they had now reached the top of the dance, they made their reverse pattern of steps without speaking. Once more in position, however, Elizabeth took courage and looked at her partner, only to feel her heart sink at the shuttered expression that now guarded his face. Conscious that this must be quite the distasteful conversation, she could not help but reflect he probably enjoyed this dance even less than the first set and that it was likely on a par with that of Netherfield.

Chapter Twenty Six

HAVING SET BEFORE MR DARCY the failings of her parents, Elizabeth knew she had worse to reveal: the foolishness of her sister, and before she could lose heart, she broke into speech.

"Mary seemed to think that an attachment had formed between him and my youngest sister. I do not believe Papa to be aware of the nature of the relationship or its rapid progression." Seeing the frown that marred the gentleman's brow, she lowered her gaze, the warmth returning to her cheeks. How ashamed she felt at that moment.

"Miss Bennet." Her eyes flew back to his. "You must remember that they know not what he is."

Touched by the sentiment, that he could even yet attempt to imply the fault was not all with her family, she took some comfort from his words. It was a moment before anything further was said, a more complicated crossover of the dance taking place with the couples on either side of them. As soon as permitted, however, she spoke once more.

"I am deeply concerned, Sir, for the welfare of my family for that very reason. It appears he is there covertly. From my sister's letter, I understand that he is maintaining a low profile, not even making use of a mount, but travelling between Longbourn and my aunt's house solely on foot. I am at a loss as to what more I can do at present."

She could not help the note of urgency from creeping into her voice, but to her dismay she could see that he had withdrawn. His face remained an inscrutable mask, an expression she had plenty of past experience of. He was clearly distancing himself from the matter; from her family; from her.

"I believe you acted correctly, Madam. I do not see that you could have done anything more in the circumstances."

The movement continued for several minutes further and, as a profound silence fell upon them, Elizabeth reflected with growing sadness upon the failure of her intentions. The dance that she had held such high hopes of was over. They both performed a perfunctory second dance to conclude the set, each attempting to maintain a conversation of fits and starts, but the topics were mundane, and Elizabeth could not help but feel his thoughts must be as distracted as her own. As the music finally died away and the dancers acknowledged their partners, Elizabeth could feel a pit of despair settling inside. She sighed as she observed Mr Darcy straightening from his bow, and she took the arm he offered her amidst a tumult of emotions.

They had barely taken half a dozen paces across the floor, however, before Nicholas was before them, and Darcy handed her to her friend with alacrity, took his leave of them both and walked rapidly away.

Watching Mr Darcy leave the room through the double doors onto the landing, as if he could not put distance between them quickly enough, Elizabeth sighed again. Her throat felt tight with emotion; she felt all the shame of what she had so recently confessed, cursing herself for the indulgence.

"Lizzy?"

Startled out of her thoughts, Elizabeth turned to Nicholas with an apologetic smile which he returned quickly before glancing around them.

"Come. I know just the place for us."

They left the ballroom through a further doorway at its end which opened onto the main landing, and Nicholas swept open a tall, heavy door which led out onto a large paved area that ran along the rear of the house, which Elizabeth suspected was built upon the roof of a ground floor salon.

There were two gentlemen smoking pipes near the door, and some couples had come outside to enjoy the fresh air. At the far end of the terrace a group of rather loud young men had gathered, smoking their cigars and causing quite the ruckus as they noisily raised their glasses.

Nicholas, however, did not traverse the terrace, but lead Elizabeth down some narrow stone steps almost opposite the doors they had just come out of which led in turn to a lower deserted and unlit walkway, level with the garden that it overlooked, and they both moved over to the stone parapet that bordered the manicured lawn, that they might benefit from the remnants of light filtering down from the upper terrace.

Feeling quite out of sorts at Mr Darcy's withdrawal and obvious displeasure, Elizabeth was stunned by the sense of loss and despair engendered by the situation. That she had grown to appreciate the gentleman's character of late she had long acknowledged, but to feel so despondent over losing his good opinion was beyond what she could comprehend. It was hardly as if there was any future for their renewed acquaintance… a pervading sense of sadness gripped her, as she accepted that any further chance of building upon their recent rapprochement was gone.

However, there was little time for her to rationalise these new and tumultuous emotions, or understand their significance, for the young man accompanying her, who had for a moment leant on the balustrade and stared out into the inky darkness of the formal garden, had straightened up and turned to face her, and she was immediately struck by his air.

Shocked by the strain etched upon his countenance, Elizabeth caught her breath. Pushing aside all thoughts of Mr Darcy and his ill opinion of her, she recalled her recent concerns for her friend and, seeing now that whatever troubled him affected his well-being, and hating to see him so, she determined to do all she could to alleviate his distress.

Unable to locate his cousin in the card room, Darcy turned on his heel and headed towards the room allocated for refreshments, his head swirling with conjecture and surmise. His priority, he knew, was to enlist his cousin's assistance, and to that end, he had left Elizabeth behind focused on his purpose. Yet ultimately, all he truly wished to dwell upon was that she had confided in him and, alarmed though he was to discover Wickham's whereabouts and deeply concerned about his influence upon the weaker elements of the Bennet family, he could not help but be gratified that she had done so.

He walked into the salon and scanned the crowd of people. There were several parties seated at large, ornately decorated circular tables, and a few groups of gentlemen stood around the sides of the room, some of them slightly more raucous than others as they indulged in their goblets of wine. It was a shout of laughter that drew his attention to the furthest group, and it was no surprise to detect the Colonel in amongst it.

Making his way rapidly across the room, Darcy failed to heed several greetings thrown at him, so intent was he upon his purpose. He needed to speak with his cousin; there was no time to waste if he was to be of assistance to Elizabeth, and he knew that was what he most desired. He cursed his inability to articulate to her that he intended to do something, anything, if he could, though he knew it would have been foolish to make promises he could not guarantee. Warring with this was his regret that he had had to leave her in Harington's capable hands – something he preferred not to dwell upon, nor the proprietary way that gentleman had been hovering to receive her and take her arm upon his own.

"Darce! There you are, man. All danced out so soon?" The Colonel had perceived his approach and raised his glass towards him before downing the contents and coming forward to greet him.

Darcy nodded a perfunctory acknowledgement at the three gentlemen in his company – they were all acquaintances of the Fitzwilliam family, harmless enough in essentials, and boring as hell as far as Darcy was concerned.

"Whatever is the matter?"

Glancing around at the crowd, Darcy motioned to his cousin to walk to the side of the room. They leant against the handrail, backs to the wall, and conscious that the Colonel stared impatiently at him, Darcy said quietly, "I know where Wickham is."

"*What?*"

Darcy threw his cousin a quick glance, not surprised to see the astonishment and concern upon his cousin's face.

"Heaven's above, Darcy, how on earth have you discovered such a thing." The Colonel paled. "He is not *here?*" He looked quickly about the room, his eyes narrowed as he scanned the people milling to and fro.

Darcy let out a humourless laugh. "No – no, he is not. We have no need to be concerned that he might gain entrance to such society. There are those, however, who are not so fortunate, or so protected."

"Look, we must-" but the Colonel never finished his sentence as they were interrupted by a young couple who addressed themselves to Darcy, claiming a slight acquaintance with him from some years back.

Darcy extricated himself as swiftly as he could, but he had barely turned back to his cousin when the three gentlemen with whom the Colonel had been conversing approached. Darcy threw his cousin a frustrated look which he received with an understanding nod of the head.

"Let us find somewhere quieter than here," and with a salute to the group who threatened to surround them, they excused themselves and walked rapidly from the room.

Once back out onto the landing, likewise swarming with people, they both looked about for somewhere to go where they might discuss Darcy's newly acquired knowledge, and seeing a young couple emerge through a door at the end of the hallway they walked swiftly towards it. The Colonel followed his cousin out onto the wide terrace that flanked the back of the house, and they both paused to allow their eyes to adjust to the dim light cast by the torches, nodding a greeting to some people near the door, and stepped forward to stand at the parapet that overlooked the garden.

Drawing a deep breath, Darcy leaned on the balustrade, closing his eyes for a moment to savour the less oppressive air outside, and found when he opened them that his sight was well enough adjusted. He was about to turn to his cousin, to lay before him all that Elizabeth had told him, when his eye was caught by a movement below, and as his cousin gripped his arm, indicating that he too had observed the same, an achingly familiar voice could be heard saying,

"Marry you? Oh – Nicholas!" and before their very eyes, Elizabeth threw her arms about Harington as he swept her into a close embrace.

With a discreet hand on his arm, Colonel Fitzwilliam steered Darcy through the mass of people crowding the hallways and, refusing to stop and acknowledge anyone, he guided him gradually to the staircase. One look at his cousin's ashen face was sufficient to assure him that a swift departure was the only choice.

Giving him a gentle shove, he muttered, "Onward, my friend," and urged him down the stairs. Darcy's first steps appeared hesitant, as if he was unsure of his purpose but then his pace increased, and they were soon at the bottom of the grand staircase where the Colonel signalled a footman, giving orders for the retrieval of their cloaks and hats.

"We – I cannot – we must farewell…"

"You can, and you had best not, Cousin. Trust me on this; you are in no fit state."

Gathering their belongings, the Colonel led Darcy out of the doors and down the steps into the street, narrowing his gaze as he looked left and right at the long line of carriages drawn up to the kerb. Unable to determine their own, he removed his glove and placing two fingers in his mouth let out a piercing whistle.

Within moments, their conveyance had pulled up before them, and Darcy was soon installed inside. The Colonel sighed heavily as he observed the blankness of his cousin's stare and the slump of his shoulders as he huddled into a corner of the carriage.

"Bear with me, Darcy. I will follow on directly," and giving word to the driver to proceed, and then return to wait for Bingley, a grim-faced Colonel retraced his steps and entered the ornate façade of Bellingham House once more as the carriage rattled off along the street.

Chapter Twenty Seven

"HAVE A CARE LIZZY! YOU shall surely ruin my reputation!" Nicholas laughed as he released his hold upon Elizabeth, but he reached out to grasp her hands instead.

The lady smiled widely. "I can scarce believe it, yet I am overjoyed. You have asked Serena to *marry* you? It is all that is wonderful."

"Indeed, I have."

"Oh how delightful!" She squeezed his hands fervently before releasing them, her pleasure on behalf of her two good friends mingled with her utter relief, but as his gaze dropped to the floor, her smile faded. "Nicholas?"

With a heavy sigh, he turned to stare out into the darkness, the air of sadness revealed once more.

"One would think so."

He leant on the balustrade on the lower terrace of Bellingham House, his shoulders drooping, and Elizabeth moved closer to him, touching him lightly on the arm.

"Nicholas? What is it?"

"She will not have me."

A frown creased Elizabeth's brow. "But – but why? I cannot comprehend-"

"And nor do I," Nicholas interrupted. "Dearest Lizzy," he placed her hand upon his arm and turned her about, so that they might walk. "I came to London with the express purpose of seeing you, awaiting the slightest opportunity to unburden myself and share my troubles in the hope that you might be able to give me some direction – I have so longed for your counsel." He glanced over at her, pain writ clearly upon his countenance. "You are her only intimate friend. If anyone can discover what this is about, what she is thinking and feeling, you can. You are my only chance to resolve this."

As words from Serena's letter echoed through Elizabeth's mind, "*hope for your counsel and comfort at the soonest opportunity*", she shivered. Now it was all too clear why Serena wished to consult urgently with her and why she felt she could not express it through a letter.

"You are cold. Let us return inside and attempt to find a place of relative seclusion. Now that I have begun, I must tell you all."

"No, indeed, I am warm enough, Nicholas. Let us remain out here, where we are guaranteed a certain amount of privacy. The opportunity for such will be non-existent within."

With a nod, Nicholas paused in their perambulations and looked about and, upon espying a vacant stone bench, directed their steps towards it.

It was the work of but a few minutes to explain the events that had taken place during Eastertide at Sutton Coker. Within days of Serena's arrival, Nicholas had seized an opportunity to declare himself. Though she had clearly been surprised by his application, to his delight, she had accepted. Barely had the words been spoken, however, when they were disturbed by his brother, James, entering the room.

Serena had quickly excused herself from their company, yet within an hour of their parting, she had sought him out to retract her acceptance, begging him to tell no-one of what had passed. He had tried to persuade her to reconsider, struggled to discover her reasons and finally begged her – in vain – to stand by her earlier decision.

After a poor night's rest, he had resolved to renew his attempts to talk to her in the hope that he could make her see reason. Yet it was not to be. A letter arrived that morning from her mother, alerting her to a bout of ill health which had laid her father low, and though there was no indication that Mr Seavington was in any danger, Serena had made haste to leave the West Country and within a matter of hours was on her way north without further communication between them.

Watching the emotions that played upon his features in the dappled light from the terrace above, Elizabeth studied Nicholas thoughtfully. There was something amiss here that she had yet to lay her finger upon. Serena's affection for him had been steadfast and unwavering – though it had at first caused her a great deal of pain. Her immediate acceptance of the offer of Nicholas' hand was unsurprising, but her retraction of it made no sense. What could have brought about such a transition?

"Lizzy?"

Meeting her companion's troubled gaze, Elizabeth shook her head. "I cannot profess to know her mind, Nicholas, but I am surprised at her reaction."

"I thought... I had begun to think-" he stopped and ran a hand through his hair. "These past months, I had been certain there was some sign of affection from her. Her feelings are not easily repressed, as you know." Nicholas paused, his gaze fixed unseeingly somewhere beyond the confines of the city garden. Then he let out a bitter laugh.

"You will recall as well as any her animosity towards me as a child! She was such a tiny thing, yet one was never in any doubt about how she felt about anything. Yet lately, I had sensed a change in her. Oh, she still berated me at every turn, but there was a difference. Perhaps she is not aware of it, but loving her as I do, I could not fail to pick up on the nuances – she does not dislike me, of that I am certain, yet something prevents her from considering me a suitable partner in life."

The hurt and confusion was all too evident in Nicholas' voice, and observing him swallowing with difficulty before drawing in a long, shaky breath, Elizabeth could sense his pain as a physical presence.

"She will be here soon, Nicholas. She must be on her way to Town by this time, and she wishes to seek my counsel – the only hope I can offer you is that I am likely to gain some insight into what troubles her, but you must understand that if I am constrained to silence by her, there will be little I can share with you. I will promise, though, that I will do everything in my power to help you bring this to resolution."

"Dear Lizzy. You give me great comfort, as I knew you would. If you only knew how I have longed to speak of this with you." he sighed. "But come – we have gambled with our luck long enough; let us return to the dance before we are missed."

As soon as they returned to the warmth and noise of the building, Nicholas was once more waylaid by acquaintances and, taking her leave of him, Elizabeth walked slowly down the hallway, deep in reflection. Her relief that no address had come from Nicholas was countered by her worry over what had beset Serena that she would turn down the hand of the very man who held her affections. Unable to come to any reasonable conclusion, however, she walked over to the door into the ballroom and watched the dance that was currently drawing to a close, her eyes scanning the crowd for any sign of Mr Darcy.

Observing her sister standing nearby, Jane Bennet walked over to join her and was greeted with a warm smile.

"Jane, have you seen Mr Darcy?"

She shook her head, casting a quick glance over the couples now regrouping in preparation for the next dance. "Not for some time. But there is such a crush; he could be in any of the rooms."

Elizabeth nodded, her expression thoughtful, and Jane studied her closely, wondering if her sister realised just how much interest she was displaying in that gentleman of late.

"Miss Elizabeth! There you are!"

Jane turned to the person who had materialised at their side, her smile widening as Bingley engaged her sister for the next dance, and she watched with contentment as the gentleman led Elizabeth across the floor to take up their positions alongside her aunt and uncle.

She was about to look around for a seat, that she might sit and watch them in comfort, when she saw Colonel Fitzwilliam enter the room, dressed in his cloak, his air and countenance sombre as his gaze scanned the crowd intently. As his eye caught hers, however, he broke into a smile and walked over to join her.

"Colonel."

"Miss Bennet." He bowed in greeting. "Do you know where I might find Bingley? I would speak with him urgently."

Jane waved a hand towards the dance that had now commenced, a lively number, and she had to raise her voice over the noise to be heard. "He is dancing at present, with my sister." Conscious that the Colonel had let out a grunt at this, she turned to study him more closely. "Is aught amiss, Sir?"

He shook his head. "Nothing to alarm, I assure you, but as Bingley is otherwise engaged, Miss Bennet, may I charge you with a message?"

"Of course."

"My cousin is indisposed and has had to return home precipitously. I intend to follow him on foot, and the carriage will return to wait upon Bingley's convenience."

Jane frowned. "I am sorry to hear that. Is Mr Darcy unwell?"

"No. His health is not impaired. He has merely received some disturbing news; it has affected his spirits, and I felt it best he went home."

"Then I will detain you no longer, Sir. Please extend our best wishes to your cousin, and I will ensure Mr Bingley is apprised of the situation."

With that, the Colonel took his leave, and Jane turned to face the dance again, her eyes seeking her sister and wondering what on earth Elizabeth would make of it when she told her.

Closing the front door, Colonel Fitzwilliam stood with his back to it for a moment and surveyed the dimly-lit corridor. All was silent apart from the ticking of the long-case clock near the staircase. Narrowing his eyes as he peered into the darkness, however, he discerned what he sought: a flickering light emanating from the gap in the door to Darcy's study.

He walked rapidly along the hall, his boots clicking on the highly polished floor, conscious that it was his intention to forewarn his cousin of his approach. He was not surprised, therefore, when the door was swung open before he reached it, and Darcy stood aside for him to enter before closing the door behind them with a snap.

Looking around the room, the Colonel realised that the flickering light emanated solely from the fire in the grate.

"How are you?" he peered at Darcy in the gloomy light.

Though much in shadow, he still detected the wince that his cousin was unable to suppress before he rubbed a hand across his eyes and then ran it through his somewhat dishevelled hair.

"I am perfectly well." Though Darcy spoke words of reassurance, there was a flatness to his tone that bespoke the contrary, and with a huff of frustration, the Colonel walked over to the fireplace and grabbed a taper, letting it catch in the flames before proceeding to light a couple of lamps.

As the light infiltrated the room, he tossed the taper into the flames of the fire and turned to study his cousin more fully. The shadows that had lingered below Darcy's eyes a week ago had returned and there was a strained look about his features. Despite this, however, the Colonel could well detect that his cousin had his emotions under strict control.

"Are you quite done?" Darcy enquired, stirring restlessly under his cousin's scrutiny. "I assure you – I am well. I have received a blow, it is true, but there is a more pressing matter that consumes me for now, and I must trust to your counsel."

The Colonel nodded, throwing Darcy a questioning glance as he walked over to the side table under the window and poured himself a measure of cognac.

"Here," Darcy collected his own glass from the drum table near the fireplace and allowed his cousin to splash some of the amber liquid into it before they both took an armchair apiece beside the warmly glowing fire.

"Well, Darcy. Enlighten me – it has to do with that scoundrel, I take it?" The Colonel took a mouthful of cognac and swallowed hard, his gaze fixed upon his cousin, who met his look unflinchingly. "Well come on, man! Reveal all!" He settled back in his seat, somewhat relieved that Darcy was not so overcome that all reason had abandoned him.

Chapter Twenty Eight

"HE HAS RETURNED TO HERTFORDSHIRE – to the Bennets' neighbourhood."

"*What*?!" The Colonel sat upright in his chair, staring at Darcy incredulously. "But how on earth did you discover this?"

Darcy put his glass back on the drum table and clasped his hands together. "When I had the pleasure of dancing with Miss Elizabeth Bennet-" he paused and swallowed visibly. "She was quite distressed, having learnt that the man had ingratiated himself into her family's household as firmly as upon his earlier acquaintance – even now, he lodges with her relatives in Meryton – and worse, it seems that one of her sisters is enamoured of him."

At this, the Colonel leapt to his feet. "We must do something! You know as well as I that he would not be tempted into matrimony with a girl of no dowry, be she a gentleman's daughter or no."

Darcy too got to his feet and faced his cousin. "No – no, I know that in principle it would be so. Yet, in his reduced circumstances, having flown from his duty and occupation, and with the alternatives so limited, he may well see the association with the Bennets as desirable."

"A man in dire straits will take drastic measures?" The Colonel let out a frustrated grunt. "Can they be so taken in by him still?"

"Why would they not be? Only Miss Elizabeth has been advised of the truth of Wickham's character; and I, fool that I am, did not give her leave to share that knowledge. She has been unable therefore to put her family on guard, though she did send her father an *Express* earlier, but she suspects he will dismiss her fears, for she was unable to divulge evidence to support her allegations."

Deeply disturbed by his cousin's news, the Colonel sat down again, frowning.

"I struggle to comprehend how his reputation remains yet unsullied there."

Darcy walked over to retrieve the decanter and turned to face his cousin.

"He was in gainful employment for the duration of his stay, and they were not camped there for any substantial time – it may well be that his debts on this occasion were too few to cause public concern when he left; however, any other indiscretions will not reveal themselves for a few months yet, as you well know. Further, it seems Wickham has spun some tale about being sent on a mission of some sort, covert in nature, thus he has no need to reveal any purpose for his return."

With a derisory snort, the Colonel leaned back in his chair as his cousin walked over and topped up his glass. "And these people give credit to such an assertion?"

Darcy nodded before returning the cognac to its silver salver.

"I suspect it to be so. I believe the sister who is taken with him, even from my limited acquaintance with her, would see it as a fine joke. Wickham can be very plausible, as you well know, and he was enduringly popular amongst the local populace, no more so than with the Bennets. As such, he appears to have persuaded the family to keep his presence as quiet as possible." Darcy walked back to the hearth. "Perhaps he feels he is safe for now, and if he can secure a situation before any doubts are cast upon his character, he will consider himself saved. Mr Bennet is the principal landowner in the neighbourhood after all." He met his cousin's eye and shrugged, before grabbing the poker and giving the logs a hefty shove.

His cousin's words had struck a chord, and the Colonel drained his glass and dropped it onto a nearby table. "And therein lies his purpose."

Darcy turned to face him.

"You may have the right of it. Though there appears to be little ready money in the estate, Mr Bennet is land rich and the disposal of a part of his acreage would not be out of the question – certainly if it were a means to an end in safekeeping his daughter's – and thus the family's – reputation."

"Then what is your plan?"

Retaking his seat, Darcy met his cousin's keen gaze. "I intend to be at Longbourn by first light to speak with Mr Bennet. I must lay before him my dealings with Wickham."

"I had best send word to Whitehall before you depart. A band of men can be despatched to Hertfordshire to apprehend the scoundrel, and place him under lock and key and no threat to anyone but himself."

"But the penalty for desertion…"

Fitzwilliam shrugged. "He was not on active duty, but all the same-" He made a slicing motion across his own throat, and Darcy paled and sank back into his chair.

"There is no love in me for the man, and even less respect, but I would not wish death upon another soul."

The Colonel shook his head. "This is beyond your control, Darcy. I forbid you to cough up the necessaries to oil someone's palm and have his sentence commuted to transportation. Surely you would not wish his degenerate nature upon the new colonies?"

Darcy's head dropped into his hands.

"I would wish none of this."

"If you want to be passive and allow him the chance to escape, then so be it. We can merely oust him from his nest and watch him fly. But he will only re-emerge to wreak havoc elsewhere."

Darcy sighed and sat back in his chair. "I know. And thus we protect the Bennets but give him leave to prey upon another innocent family." He eyed his cousin solemnly. "It must be done discreetly, for he will surely flee at the first sign of any detection. I must speak with Mr Bennet before his daughters are abroad, that no further opportunity arises for him to sully the family. Speed is of the essence, if we are not even now too late."

"What would you have me do?"

Darcy got to his feet and the Colonel did likewise.

"I trust it is not too much to ask – but I would have you accompany me to Longbourn."

"I am not acquainted with the family. In what way can I be of assistance?"

"I was not popular in the neighbourhood; I doubt my word alone will suffice. If you are there to vouch for my story, especially in relation to Georgiana as her joint guardian, I think we will carry our point – certainly with Mr Bennet. Mrs Bennet – well, let us hope we do not encounter the woman."

The Colonel let out a short laugh. "I must own I have a growing desire to meet this harridan. Clearly, she puts the fear of God into you, man!"

Darcy merely threw his cousin a look. "Well? Will you do it? Will you accompany me?"

Stepping forward to offer Darcy his hand, the Colonel's expression sobered.

"You have my solemn oath. I shall do all in my power to protect Miss Elizabeth Bennet's family."

With a grim smile, Darcy shook his cousin's hand before walking over to retrieve the decanter. To Hertfordshire they would go.

Once informed of Mr Darcy's abrupt departure and the reason behind it, all enjoyment of the ball was over for Elizabeth. Combined with Nicholas' despair over Serena, her spirits felt completely suppressed, and she longed for nothing more than the solace of her bed, that she might allow herself the oblivion of sleep. Though she continued to dance whenever asked, and smiled and conversed as if everything was most enjoyable, within was utter turmoil.

As the evening drew to a close, it took little persuasion for Elizabeth to accompany her aunt, uncle and sister to the foyer and await their cloaks whilst Nicholas went to see that the carriage be brought about. Looking around her at the milling people, their faces wreathed in smiles that reflected their enjoyment of the ball, Elizabeth smiled ruefully. The evening that had held such promise had failed her; or perhaps she had failed herself. She felt entirely responsible for Mr Darcy's swift departure, her mind shying away from what it signified, even though she knew it was not she making a fool of herself in Meryton.

Rousing herself from her interminable thoughts, she allowed her uncle to assist her into her cloak, and then, conscious that Bingley was approaching, she summoned a warm smile.

"I wish you a safe journey to Hertfordshire, Sir."

Bingley tucked his hat under his arm. "I look forward to renewing my acquaintance with your father, Miss Elizabeth."

"May I offer you a word of advice on that score, Mr Bingley?"

"By all means."

"My father has little patience for the politics of certain etiquettes. If you await his call upon you when you return to the neighbourhood, you may wait in vain. It will not be personal, I assure you. It is an offence that he bestows liberally upon all his neighbours without prejudice."

With a smile, Bingley bowed. "I thank you for the good counsel. I anticipate calling at Longbourn directly. Do you have any messages that I may take for you?"

"You are very kind, Sir, but no. As Jane is to follow but a day later, I shall send any word with her."

"Then I look forward to seeing you in the not too distant future, Miss Elizabeth. Enjoy the remainder of your stay in Town."

As Bingley took his farewell of her sister and her aunt and uncle, Elizabeth drew her cloak more tightly about her body, hugging her arms to herself. Saddened though she was over Mr Darcy's swift departure, and concerned as she now was for her dear friends, she could not help but reflect that if one good thing had come out of her stay in Town, it was that Jane and Mr Bingley seemed well on their way to happiness.

As Darcy refilled their glasses, he indicated to his cousin to take a seat once more before resuming his own. "There is one other thing. I wish to leave Town for a short while. You may recall that it had crossed my mind a few days back. I now think it a fine plan for Georgiana – the summer is approaching, and she will benefit from some less dense air."

The Colonel, well aware that the air had nothing to do with this precipitous departure, nodded and waited. Darcy was staring into the fire, his glass held in both hands in his lap, his mind clearly drifting. After a few moments, however, he raised his head and looked back over at his cousin.

"Forgive me." He took a sip from his glass. "I am only uncertain of an appropriate place. I think the coast would be unwise – it would be all too reminiscent of Ramsgate. What are your thoughts?"

The Colonel studied his cousin for a second and then shrugged his shoulders. "I think there is really only one option. It is too far distant to head north to Pemberley for such a short period; thus, if you seek to avoid the coast, which is east and south of us, you must go in the only remaining direction - to Bath."

"Bath?"

"Yes, it is a city due west, have you not heard of it?"

"Very droll, Cousin. But Bath? Aunt Catherine will –"

"The devil take Aunt Catherine. She may think what she chooses. If you cannot go to Derbyshire, yet you desire to go somewhere, what finer place for respite and distraction?"

"Yes – yes, I must go somewhere…" Darcy's voice petered out as his gaze returned once more to the fire. The flames were beginning to die down somewhat and, with the lateness of the hour, it was pointless stirring them up further. "Then Bath it shall be. I shall despatch Thornton at first light to secure lodgings and will follow him once our duty is performed in Hertfordshire." There was a pause as Darcy appeared lost in thought for a moment; then, he sighed. "I would simply ask that you return to Town and prepare Georgiana to travel, and then accompany her the following day to join me."

The Colonel nodded. "As you wish, Darcy – and what of Bingley?"

Slowly, Darcy's gaze roamed the room, coming to light upon his desk. "I shall pen him a note and leave it for him. He plans to leave before noon as it is."

"And Georgiana?"

Darcy raised his glass and drained the contents, placing it on the table at his side. "She knows what took place this evening."

Colonel Fitzwilliam raised a brow, and his cousin added, "We spoke when I returned. I had to tell her something – I was… I was not quite myself."

The Colonel grunted. "Does she know of your intention to travel?"

"No – no, she does not. Of that I said nothing. I merely advised her of the – of the incident we observed."

"And how did she take the news?"

"No better than I did, Cousin. No better at all."

"Well – let us tarry no longer. If we are to start before daybreak, we shall need a good night's rest."

The Colonel observed the hollow expression in Darcy's eyes, realising that sleep was likely to be evasive for his cousin, but he got to his feet and accompanied him over to the door. Pausing on the threshold, Darcy said over his shoulder.

"Thank you for this, Richard," and the Colonel nodded, his face as serious as his cousin's. There was no need for further words.

To be continued in
Volume III – Desperate Measures

About the Author

Cassandra Grafton has always loved words, so it comes as no surprise that writing is her passion. Having spent many years wishing to be a writer and many more dreaming of it, she finally took the plunge, offering short stories to online communities. After that, it was a natural next step to attempting a full length novel, and thus *A Fair Prospect* was born.

She currently splits her time between North Yorkshire in the UK, where she lives with her husband and two cats, and Regency England, where she lives with her characters.

http://www.cassandragrafton.com

https://www.facebook.com/cassie.grafton

https://twitter.com/CassGrafton

Made in the USA
San Bernardino, CA
27 April 2013